Charlotte Armstrong was born in 1905 in Vulcan, Michigan. She attended the University of Wisconsin, and graduated in 1925 from Barnard College in New York City.

After graduation she held a variety of jobs: a classified advertising operator for *The New York Times,* a fashion reporter for a buyer's guide, and an office worker for a firm of accountants. During this time, she also sold several poems to *The New Yorker.* In 1928 she married Jack Lewi, an advertising executive.

After her marriage, Miss Armstrong's interest turned to writing plays, two of which were produced on Broadway. Neither was successful, but during rehearsals for her second play, her first novel, a mystery entitled *Lay On, MacDuff,* was published. She had found her metier.

Eventually, the Lewis moved to Southern California, which became the setting of much of her later work. In 1956 Charlotte Armstrong won the Mystery Writers of America's best novel award for *A Dram of Poison.* In 1957 her fellow Californian, the great mystery critic Anthony Boucher, wrote in his column in *The New York Times Book Review:* "The festival of Halloween ten days ago was, I trust, celebrated with peculiarly fitting rites in Glendale, Calif.; for there dwells one of the few authentic spellcasting witches of modern times: Charlotte Armstrong."

Miss Armstrong also wrote the screen adaptations of two of her novels. *The Unsuspected* starred Claude Raines. *Don't Bother to Knock,* the film version of *Mischief,* featured Marilyn Monroe in her first starring role along with Richard Widmark and Anne Bancroft.

Until her sadly premature death in 1969, Charlotte Armstrong wrote 27 novels, all in the mystery/suspense genre, many of them classics. Library of Crime Classics editor-in-chief Burke N. Hare has hailed Miss Armstrong as "the finest American novelist of suspense of the twentieth century."

CHARLOTTE ARMSTRONG
available from IPL Library of Crime Classics®

THE BALLOON MAN
A DRAM OF POISON
A LITTLE LESS THAN KIND
LEMON IN THE BASKET
MISCHIEF
THE UNSUSPECTED

CHARLOTTE ARMSTRONG
THE BALLOON MAN

INTERNATIONAL POLYGONICS, LTD.
NEW YORK CITY

THE BALLOON MAN

Library of Congress Card Catalog No. 90-80765
ISBN 1-55882-068-X

Printed and manufactured in the United States of
America.
First IPL printing June 1990.
10 9 8 7 6 5 4 3 2 1

Chapter 1

SHERRY WAS SCOURING the skillet in which she had scrambled her breakfast eggs. Under her apron she was dressed for the day. She intended to dash over to the market as soon as Ward got up, or maybe she'd take Johnny along and go sooner, taking advantage of the energy in the morning coffee. Maybe, later, she would go hunting that salesgirl's job and talk to the day care place, because (let's face it . . . She *had* faced it) what good was Johnny's mother to him when she was practically walking in her sleep all the time?

She couldn't get home to bed from her present job any earlier than midnight, whereas Johnny bounced out of his healthy three-and-a-half-year-old sleep at 6 A.M. The trouble was she had to put him down so early, but the rush hour for cocktail drinkers was *before* their dinners. The tips were good, though. Still the day care camp wouldn't cost much more than the baby-sitter's evenings came to. Her mind was going lazily around a familiar track when she heard a stirring elsewhere in the house.

Ward was getting up now? This early? Johnny was still sitting on his high stool at the dinette table, contentedly munching away on some toast. Sherry had time to decide that she would take the child with her to market as soon as it opened, in case

Ward was feeling low and not up to minding his little son so early in the day.

Then her husband, wearing only his pajama bottoms, came through the door. His mouth was open in a strange way. The jaws were tense, but the lips were somehow sloppy and moist. Out of his throat came a soft roaring sound, just sound, wordless.

"What's the matter?" Sherry cried at once.

His eyes were not right. He saw her, but he didn't see *her*. He didn't seem to know her. There was red around the rims of those strange eyes. There was a lot of black hair on his forearms. He came toward her on his bare feet, and his right arm was raised. "Hey! Hey!" said Sherry. "Just a darned minute!"

Did he think he was going to *hit* her?

She sprang toward him and put both her hands on the raised wrist. "What's the matter?" she cried again, straining and holding.

He growled. It was the only word for the sound he made, as he jerked sideways and shook her off. Now his left arm came swinging up. For all the reckless power of his movements, they seemed slow. Sherry ducked the blow and yelled at him: "Ward, will you please tell me what's wrong with you? Don't *do* that! Listen . . . Listen . . ."

But he caught her by both shoulders and began to shake her. She thought: He's out of his mind this time. Hey, this isn't so funny! Ward was no pygmy. She was only a female. So she screamed as loud as she could. Somebody had better come.

At the noise she made, Ward let her go and stepped back and put his hands to his ears. His jaw was moving as if he were trying to make it go in a circle. She thought he might be tensing to come at her again. But she said, in as calm and authoritative a voice as she could produce, "Sit down, Ward. You just sit down and relax, and you *tell* me."

But now the startled child had come out of a momentary paralysis. The little boy slid off the stool, plop upon his two square little feet. "Mommy!" he shrieked.

"No, honey," cried Sherry. It was too late. The child was running toward the only comfort that he knew. But he didn't quite make the distance to her skirt. His father lurched and swung with a scooping motion, and the child went flying, his small light body like a volleyball. He crashed softly into the corner of the cupboard and floor and was still.

Sherry felt her whole inside burst with light. Brain and heart, she blazed. She whirled and picked up the heavy skillet with both hands. The animal was growling; it was groping for her now. She swung the weapon with all her might and hit the top of his right shoulder a fearful crack. He reeled, stumbled, fell—and lay still.

Sherry didn't stop to think about the wreck of all her life so far. She ran, crouching, to the child and sensed his breathing. She knew she ought not to touch him or shift his limbs, but she also knew that she must. Gently, very gently, she slipped her arms underneath to hold him and lift him. Her back was young and strong. She picked up her child and slid her feet on the vinyl almost in a dance step as she went gliding to the back door. Midway there she found a way to bend and grasp in her left hand the handle of her purse, which had been lying ready on the counter.

She got the door open. She crept outside into the light of morning, into the outer peace of the shabby, respectable neighborhood, where people were going to work, where the world was sane. She stepped slowly, carefully down the three steps to the narrow walk, trying not to shift or twist the little body in her arms. She saw the neighbor woman's head in her window. But there was no gap in the hedge, so Sherry walked down her own driveway. As she did so, the neighbor's car, pacing her, came backing out of the parallel driveway.

"Mr. Ivy, please! Mr. Ivy, please?"

"What's the trouble, Mrs. Reynard?" He stopped the car.

"Will you call a hospital? No, will you *take* me? Johnny's hurt. And will you call the police, too? Something's wrong with Ward."

The woman was on the front stoop now. "What's the trouble?" she called shrilly.

"I don't know," said Sherry. "He's knocked out, now. He might get up—"

"Henry!" the woman cried in rising terror.

Henry Ivy, aged forty-two, got ponderously out of his car. He said decisively, "You drive her, Mildred. I'll call. I don't want you staying here alone. Never mind your bag. Try St. Anthony's. And you *stay* there. That way you'll be safe."

Sherry wiggled herself into the front seat, juggling the little body as if it were a plate of soup that must not tip, no matter what the supporting pedestal that was Sherry's body had to do. Mrs. Ivy came jittering into the driver's seat.

"Oh, what happened? I heard you screaming—"

"I'll tell you when we get there," Sherry said quietly. "I want you to drive. Please?"

"All right." The woman took hold of her forty-year-old nerves and reminded herself that she'd be safe in the hospital.

Mr. Ivy went into his house and called the police. Then he sneaked softly down the side of the neighboring house to the back door. He crept up to look in, saw the naked torso, the long limp legs in the striped cotton, cautiously opened the door, and approached to see the blood on the shoulder, where the rim of the iron skillet had cut the flesh.

But dead the man was not, and Mr. Ivy sighed in relief. Who wants to get mixed up in a murder?

Johnny had a fractured left leg and a crack in his skull. The young men in the hospital emergency room were calm and quick and showed no emotion. Neither did Sherry. When the examination was over, they told her they'd take Johnny up to a bed soon. He'd be fine. Would she sign him in? She'd have to go to the office.

In the midst of answering some questions there, as she fumbled blindly in her purse to find her collection of identifications where she kept her hospital insurance card and number, Sherry began to shake violently.

They were very understanding. Somebody brought her something to take. They insisted that it would help her. They had asked the doctor, they said. So Sherry swallowed it. When all the questions had been answered, they told her that two police officers were waiting for her in the lobby.

The men were in plain clothes. One of them said to her, rather severely, that he understood why she had left the scene, but now would Mrs. Reynard kindly tell them exactly what had happened?

"I don't know." Her voice trembled. Although she was a fair-sized girl, she felt very small, very fragile and tiny. She felt like crying out, "Let me alone, a little minute, please. Let me alone to be *me* a minute. I have to get my own feet under me. Don't you know that?"

But she did not cry out. "My husband just came roaring out of the bedroom and started in to beat me," she said flatly and sat down, hard.

"What was his reason?" one of the men asked mildly, as he seated himself beside her. The severe one remained standing.

"I don't know. There wasn't any reason." Even as her teeth chattered on the words, Sherry wondered if the words were true. It seemed as near the truth as she could get in the moment. (Oh, please, let me alone!)

"What did he say, Mrs. Reynard?" the mild one persisted.

"He didn't say a word. He made . . . noises." Sherry made a gesture that seemed too flip. She sensed that. She was a natural blonde, and her eyes were large and beautiful. She couldn't help it if there was a going image, an assumption that any big-eyed well-shaped blond female was in the world for fun, alone. But *she* shouldn't make flip gestures. She knew that, although she didn't know why not, really.

"You say he started in to beat you?" Severe was severe.

"He sure tried." Now the scratching on her nerves that had made her arm move so abruptly as to seem flip, that sense of being very close to screams and howls, was beginning to recede, under the influence of whatever drug she had just been given. Sherry said calmly, "Look and see." She pulled her dress away from one shoulder and showed them the mark of Ward's cruel fingers.

"And what did you do, Mrs. Reynard?" the severe one asked coldly.

All right, her flesh was fair, but he needn't think she was trying allure. Sherry conquered a sense of injustice.

"First, I tried to make him sit down to talk to me." But she could hardly remember. She didn't want to remember. That kitchen was going into mists, far away. Her eyelids were feeling heavy.

"And then you struck him with the heavy iron frying pan?"

"No, no. Johnny was there, you see," she said. "The whole thing scared him. He's only three and a half. He started to run to me, and that's when Ward threw him . . . just threw him across the room." Her voice was strange in her own ears. How could such things be?

"Is the little boy hurt badly, ma'am?" The mild one was sympathetic.

She repeated what the doctors had said in much the same way the doctors had said it. Their dry detachment wasn't natural in her mouth.

"Then it was after the child had been hurt that you hit the man?" said Severe.

"Of course," she said wonderingly. But she seemed to know that her story needed some element that wasn't there. She couldn't think what. Stronger passions?

Severe asked whether she and her husband had had marital difficulties. Quarreled often, did they?

"No, I wouldn't say so," she answered in a dreamy manner.

"What kind of work does your husband do, Mrs. Reynard?"

"He's a writer. That is, he hopes to be. It takes time to get started."

"Then he doesn't have a job?"

"That is a job," she said patiently. "He's self-employed, I guess you'd say."

"You go to work, do you, ma'am?"

"Yes. Until he begins to sell his stuff, somebody—" She couldn't explain any further. Her tongue wouldn't lift in her mouth. Didn't they understand?

"You resented being the breadwinner, did you?" Severe said with a sudden smile.

"No. Lots of wives send their husbands through graduate school," Sherry said, repeating mechanically what she had so often said. "No, I didn't mind too much. Except sometimes . . . I suppose—" She could have slept where she sat. Who cared?

"You work as a cocktail waitress? At—" Mild named the Club.

"Yes." But Sherry was sensing a shift of the wind, and she lifted her head. Surely, they were not going to assume, as her mother-in-law had always assumed, that to be a cocktail waitress was to be the servant of the Fiend. "I don't have any office skills," she said dully. "I never went to business school. So I do what I can do."

"Night work?" the mild one said gently.

"Well, that's because I wanted to raise my baby myself." Sherry roused. "I thought it was important. But I have clerked. I can clerk in a store. Now, I guess—" She stopped because she didn't know what now.

"I get the impression," said Severe, a touch of human curiosity creeping into his voice, "that your husband's people are, er, well-to-do?"

"Yes."

"But his father doesn't contribute?"

"No. Oh, no."

They spoke no question, but the question was there. "See, Ward took out on his own a long time ago," she said, to answer the question. "Ward's folks didn't like that. And then, of course, they never did like it that he married me."

"Why was that, Mrs. Reynard?"

"I don't know," said Sherry. "I didn't care. We were in love." But her voice was dreary, and there was something wrong with this whole interview—something, for instance, that she had forgotten. She grasped for it. "How *is* Ward?" she asked, much too late—much too late.

"His condition is satisfactory," droned Severe.

To whom? Sherry wondered. It struck her funny. She realized that she might even be smiling. She had an impish smile. It was the way her face folded.

"Where is he?" she asked, but without enough interest. Or else too cheerily. Because it didn't really matter anymore where Ward was, except that he must never again be too near.

"I believe his father had him taken to his home. The parents' home, that is."

"I see," she said numbly. Oh, she saw! These men had been talking to Edward Reynard. Well, she ought to have guessed that. "How did *he* get into the—" She didn't finish her question.

"I believe your neighbor phoned the father," said Mild, having finished her question on his own.

Sherry said nothing.

"Now, you say that your husband came into the kitchen and attacked you without any warning and without any cause." Severe's voice made no judgment.

"I suppose there must have been a cause," she said wearily. "I don't *know* what it was."

"If what you say is true, you may have legal grounds—"

"For divorce?" she said. "I know."

They both reacted with a blinking that told her she hadn't quite taken the meaning.

"Are you bringing charges, Mrs. Reynard?" Severe asked patiently. They might be wanting to know what they were to do with the testimony they were collecting.

But Sherry said, staring beyond them, "I can't let Ward anywhere near Johnny again. How can I?" Couldn't they understand?

"Might you put it this way, Mrs. Reynard?" the mild one asked smoothly. "The child came between you and your husband, as you two were physically fighting. So that his injuries were, in effect, a kind of accident?"

"You could put it that way," she said slowly, knowing who had, "but it wouldn't be right."

"How is that, ma'am?"

"Because how could he throw *Johnny?* How could he do that? Johnny wasn't doing anything he shouldn't. All Johnny wanted was for somebody to comfort him. How could Ward not know that?" There should have been passion in what she had just said. Sherry was glad to feel tears start, and she thought, with a peculiar detachment: And about time, too.

"The child was frightened by the violence?"

"By the noise, I think. You see, *I* screamed. *I* was scared, if you want to know." She wiped her hand across her face. "The only thing I can think of is that Ward was out of his mind. He didn't seem to know me. Or Johnny either. Or even know that Johnny was just a baby. Well, then Ward wasn't in his own mind, that's all." She couldn't go on. It wasn't any use to go on.

"Temporary insanity," Severe said with a faint distaste.

"What does Ward say?" she droned.

"We haven't been able to talk to him as yet," Mild said in an apologetic manner.

"It doesn't matter," she murmured.

After a bit of silent gazing at her, some signal went between them, and they left her.

Now Mrs. Ivy, aflutter, drew closer. She must have listened to a good portion of the interview. She had also already found out how Johnny was. So she sat down and told Sherry chattily that she had just phoned Mr. Ivy at home. The neighborhood was quiet again. The police had come. (But, of course, Sherry knew that.) And there had been an ambulance, but Ward Reynard had not been too badly hurt, or so it was thought. Mr. Reynard's father had come and kind of taken over. Well, see, Mr. Ivy said that when Ward Reynard had come to a little bit, he'd been asking for his mama. But everything was under control now. Mr. Ivy was coming here, and the Ivys would be very glad to drive poor Mrs. Reynard back to her home.

"I can't go," said Sherry. "Oh, I want to thank you both for everything. But I can't leave here. I have to be here when Johnny wakes up and wants me. I have to be here to try to put things back together for him, if I ever can." She bent double. Something's wrong with me, she was thinking.

Mrs. Ivy was nibbling on her lips. She felt nervous. She had already been as much of a heroine as she could bear in one day or perhaps in a lifetime. It wouldn't do to get too deeply involved with these young and, after all, mere neighbors.

"Do you know a lawyer?" Sherry asked. "A divorce lawyer?"

"Oh, now, do you think," said her neighbor, who felt that everything ought to slow down, "you should make drastic decisions when you're so upset and all?"

What decision? Sherry thought.

But she was listening to her own blood, how it was coursing. She thought: No, I'm not upset *enough*. Whatever they gave me has made everything too meaningless. It's changed me. She looked up at her neighbor and thought: She could be right. I shouldn't talk. I shouldn't act. Not until I am thoroughly me . . . what I *am*—whatever that is.

"I wish I could thank you," she mumbled.

"I'm so terribly sorry for your trouble," said Mrs. Ivy. (And my stint is over, isn't it? her tone implied.) "He certainly never seemed to me to be that kind of young man."

And he wasn't, thought Sherry. He isn't. Something put him out of himself, something with the power to change him. That's what I think, but I can't prove it. What does proof matter? I've been afraid it might happen, and it has happened, and who can trust it not to happen again? So there is nothing to decide.

I remember when it was decided. This morning, and I was myself then. Oh, Ward, there it went, down the drain, all of it. And I can't help it. Can't help you. Can't forgive you. Well, I could, probably, but I haven't got the right to take the risk when there's Johnny. So good-bye.

Chapter 2

"Try not to cry anymore, Emily, will you? Please?" The man spoke softly. The big house was still. Edward Reynard and his wife, Emily, were standing in the upstairs hall, where they could see, through the half-opened door of the darkened bedroom, the long body of their grown-up only son lying quietly in his own bed.

"He's all right, you know. Oh, it was a vicious blow, and he's going to be mighty stiff and sore for a while. But he's all right. And he's home." Edward Reynard took some restless steps on the deep blue carpet. "I'll stay till the nurse comes," he said, although he was fuming with energy.

He was a short man, a head shorter than his son, with the very straight back that short men often develop in an effort to stand higher. He was a gray man; he ran to gray clothing. His hair was gray, and his face had little color. His eyes, however, were a bright brown.

His wife, Emily, a woman who was slim at the hips but top-heavy, trailed after him on her tiny feet. "He could have been killed," she wailed.

"Violence." Her husband's lips twisted. "*She* may come of a class where this sort of thing goes on."

"That the baby was hurt!" Emily was crying again.

"His doctor says that John will be all right. This time," he added grimly.

"Oh, Edward, what can we do?"

"Sssh." The man moved farther from the open door. "Plenty," he said. "Plenty. It's time we stepped in and simply did what we ought to have done long ago."

"I can't understand it," Emily wailed. "I can't understand how this could have happened."

"They fought," he said. "They actually physically fought— like animals. Well, there's just so much a man can take. What did *she* care that her child was in the room?"

"Poor little fellow! A helpless child! Such a terrible thing!"

"Oh, you bet it is," said her husband. His bright eyes focused on her. "Ward's had a bad shock. You realize that, don't you?"

"Oh, his heart must just be breaking," sniffled Ward's mother.

"At least it's over," snapped Reynard.

"Ward must agree this time."

"He will, don't worry. She has to be got rid of. Just simply got rid of. I told him, years ago, that he had better cut his losses."

"What about little John?" said Mrs. Reynard. Her eyes were a mild blue, and they were peering at him fearfully now, over her handkerchief.

"We'll take care of John. I'll see to that." He stood in his right-eous resolution, nine feet tall. "I'll go call Murchison." Murchison was a lawyer. The phone was not in the upper hall.

"Edward, will it all have to come out?" she quavered, reaching for him. "It seems so impossibly sordid. I just can't—" She began to weep afresh. "Don't leave me yet."

"Ssssh. Ssssh. All right, Emily." He held her with an arm around her shoulders, and she responded by vigorously wiping away her tears and trying to hold her head up.

So they stood there, in the upper hall of the big silent house, near the open door to the room where their grown-up son was lying quietly, and did not ask themselves, or each other, exactly why the woman did not want to be left standing there alone.

At noon Sherry was drooping in a chair by Johnny's bed. He had come to himself, whimpering pitifully, not quite remembering (she thanked God for that), yet knowing all the same that something very terrible had happened to him. Sherry had pumped up comfort and good cheer. She had told him that Daddy was very sick, and it was too bad; but doctors were taking care of him. Somewhere else. But Mommy was here, and doctors were certainly taking care of Johnny, weren't they? Look at him, tied up in a kind of swing. They wouldn't let him hurt very much. Not now. There were nurses all around, and they wouldn't either. See, the ladies dressed in white? They all were trying not to let anybody hurt and to make children feel better. See all the other children in the other beds?

Johnny had seemed soothed and reassured, but she knew she couldn't have accomplished this deeply enough so quickly. She may have made a start, but there was far to go.

Now that he had dozed off, she felt exhausted. The hospital was tolerant of mothers. Johnny was in a ward, but Sherry had been permitted to stay all morning. Still, she couldn't stay here twenty-four hours a day. She didn't know what to do with herself. In a moment her wits would begin to work, and she would figure out something. Through her exhaustion now came little sharp twinklings of nervousness, although she was not going to scream or howl. That was past. The sedative or tranquilizer was wearing away, but she was able to feel grateful, now, for the duration of the drug's cushioning.

She heard him coming, turned her head, saw who was walking toward her, and felt a reserve of energy suddenly begin to flow. Edward Reynard had no word for her, nor did he make even a sign of greeting. He came near enough to look down at the child's sleeping face. Only then did he nod sharply and make an imperious gesture to summon Sherry out of there.

She left her apron over the back of the chair. With it, she left the past. Very well. All the world was different now. She had better face him. He was her enemy, and he always had been, although she had never understood why. But everything was different now. There was no compulsion to try to please him, in any way to concern herself with trying to get along with him. There was a relief in this so great as to seem almost a joy.

In the corridor he said, "I've talked to John's doctor."

She said nothing. He wasn't after news then.

Edward Reynard was taking strides too long for his height toward a small waiting room down at the end. Sherry followed at her own pace. She would not hurry. Reynard, having been forced to wait, took this for insolence and faced her with fury in his eye.

"I'll have him moved to a private room," he said.

"No, you won't," she said at once. "He needs people around."

"He'll have nurses around the clock," he said contemptuously.

"No, he won't. They're expensive and not necessary. He's better off in there with other children."

"I'm paying the bills."

"No, you're not," she said, following a deep instinct. "I have insurance. I'll take care of my son."

"Ward's son," he said severely. "Although this marriage is over."

"Yes, it is," said Sherry. "As soon as I can see a lawyer—"

"We'll see about lawyers," he said angrily. "If you know no better than to get into a violent fight, in the presence of a small child—"

"Believe me," Sherry said firmly, "Ward will never get near enough again to hurt Johnny. Or attack me."

"You're a liar," he said. "Who attacked Ward? Who hurt *him?*"

"Oh, I did that," she said almost cheerfully. She thought to herself that she hadn't the strength to waste trying to change the notions in this head.

"While I doubt that Ward will want to make public any such behavior on the part of a woman supposedly a loving wife and mother," Reynard said cuttingly, "any more patience with this marriage is impossible."

"That's right." She watched his face with something like pure curiosity. She had never understood him, and now she didn't have to try; but why did he take every word she said as some kind of insolence? Maybe it *is*, she thought, and smiled.

"Since you ask," he snarled, infuriated by the smile, "Ward is at home where he can be properly looked after. I came to warn you that he'll never go back to that house. I intend to notify your landlord that Ward is no longer responsible for the rent."

Sherry laughed. She couldn't help it.

She saw the need his hand had to come up and strike her. She also saw his strength that controlled it. She thought to herself: I shouldn't have laughed. No, I shouldn't have laughed.

She said gravely, "I suppose the lawyers can fix some property settlement. Half the car. Half the furniture." She shook her head sadly, and her mouth went wry.

"You're welcome to all that," he snapped. "You're welcome to a settlement in money, if that's what you want."

"Whatever is legally mine," she said, "I'll certainly take," and saw *this* count for insolence.

"Emily and I will, of course, see to the well-being of our grand-child," he said pompously.

"No, you won't," she said, dragging out the words.

"You don't imagine that *you* can?"

"Why not," she cried, suddenly furious, "when I've supported both a child and a husband for quite a long time now and been, by the way, responsible for the groceries, as well as for the rent?"

"Your choice, wasn't it?" he said coldly. His lip curled. "Will you go on being a cocktail waitress, or do you plan to go back to being a show girl?"

Sherry didn't answer. In the midst of rage, she pitied this man his ignorance. He didn't seem to know that she had only tried show business long enough to find out she couldn't make it. He didn't seem to know that she was not only inexperienced, but too old at twenty-six and, furthermore, a bit out of shape. He didn't even know it wasn't easy to be what he called a show girl. He thought this was a sensual indulgence of some kind. Ha, not of *my* senses, she thought sullenly.

He was saying something about "no life for a child."

"As soon as Johnny is well," she interrupted, the decision making itself in her mind as she spoke, "as soon as possible, I'll take him back East, where my folks came from."

"No, you won't," he said, dragging out his words now. "I doubt very much you'll do that. You have no right. You've done your best to wreck my son. But you won't wreck my son's son."

His face had turned white. He wrenched his body into motion and left her abruptly.

Sherry thought again: No, I guess I shouldn't have laughed.

She went directly down to the main lobby and spoke to people in the office. By no means was Edward Reynard to be allowed to make any changes whatsoever in the conditions or the cost of John Edward Reynard's care here. He hadn't the right, she said.

Then she sat down in a corner to sort out her affairs. She was trying not to feel frightened. She had better call the lawyer whose name Mrs. Ivy had given her.

She wouldn't have asked any of Ward's friends to recommend a lawyer. They were, in the first place, none of them the kind to know a respectable lawyer. In the second place, they were not and never had been friends of *hers*. Ward never had liked any potential friends of hers around. It was just that he was the peacock. He had to be the attraction. Sherry had been too busy, really, to mind that so very much. Or at least she had put up no firm fight in the matter since they had moved West. *Her* friends, around here, consisted of people on the job, whom she had scarcely ever seen anywhere else. Face it. She had no friends of her own in this part of the world.

Well, then. Call, make an appointment, and go see the lawyer, she supposed. But not this afternoon. She was too beat, too exhausted, and she mustn't be too far from Johnny, not today.

Then *she* couldn't go back to stay in that house either. (So the meat would spoil and the milk sour. Those crumpled sheets would mold. She would never lie in that bed again.) All right. (Gates clanged shut.) The fact was, the house was too far away. She didn't have the car. Nor would she have it, because the old vehicle was in a garage for repairs at the moment, and she realized that she did not dare pay away the money it would cost to get it out of hock. She did not, in fact, have very much money, either on hand or in prospect.

She opened her purse. She'd had some cash, and her last night's tips were still in there. Lots of silver, many one-dollar bills. She counted. Sixty-seven dollars and seventy-five cents. Hey, not bad!

She also had the bankbook for their joint savings account. Nine hundred twenty-seven dollars and fifteen cents. But she wasn't sure she could draw on that legally. She'd have to ask the lawyer. She had a hunch she had better not do one slightest thing that wasn't absolutely correct, legally speaking.

Probably she couldn't sell the furniture yet. Half the value of the furniture wasn't going to be a fortune in any event. And how could she keep her job? The Club was even farther away. How could she afford the time to bus all that distance, let alone the strength?

All that distance from where? From here? But she couldn't *live* in the hospital lobby, not for the weeks they'd be keeping Johnny. Well, then, the first thing . . . All right.

She got up and went to the information desk. "Do you know," she asked the woman sitting there, "of any place nearby where I could rent a room? A single room for myself? But not expensive?"

"Well, I really—" The woman looked at her sharply.

"You see," said Sherry, reeling, "I can't go home. I need a place. I've had a kind of bad day. All I want—"

"Yes, well . . . Could you wait a minute? I've just thought—" The woman picked up her phone.

Sherry's senses had begun to whirl. She hung onto the edge of the desk. She didn't want to fall or faint. She hung her head. Okay, things were a little tough. Okay, so they'd get better. They couldn't for sure, she thought, get much worse.

Just as she might have fallen, a young man in a white tunic caught her with one arm. "Hold it. Hold it. Okay, lady? What's all this, Myra?"

"She says she needs a room to rent nearby," said the woman behind the desk. "That's why I thought of you, Doctor."

"Looks to me," said the man, "as if she sure ought to lie down someplace. Right, lady?"

"But I have no place," said Sherry. "So that's the first thing. Anyplace, but not too far. And not expensive."

"Right. Right," the man said amiably. "I see what you mean." Sherry couldn't help leaning against him.

"I know a place," he continued cheerily. "It's just a rooming house, but you don't care, right? I'm pretty sure Mrs. Peabody's got a vacancy."

"Where is it, please?"

"Right across the street."

"Oh, show me! Point me there!"

"You're sure, now? It's a pretty crummy old joint. But convenient, as I should know."

"I hoped you would, Doctor," said the woman at the desk, beaming to think that she had been clever. "I happened to remember—"

"Tell you," said the young man. "Why don't I walk you over there, Miss, uh—"

"Mrs. Reynard," the woman supplied.

"And by the way, I'm Dr. Bianchi, boy-intern. If I live there myself, believe me it's cheap. Also convenient. Right? Come on. See what we can do."

His hard young arm was guiding Sherry toward the exit doors, and she leaned on it.

"Course *I'm* stowed away on the second floor," he went on merrily. "This landlady, she's got old-fashioned ideas. Males upstairs. Females on the ground floor. How unrealistic can you get, right? Come on now. Left foot. Right foot. That's the girl."

He seemed kind—young, breezy, brash, but kind. Sherry, in the moment, loved him.

He took her across the street, keeping between the white lines drawn for pedestrians. Then they turned, to go a few yards to the right and come to an old frame house, gray with discouragement, which stood muffled untidily in ancient shrubbery.

There was a big bay window in the sitting room; it came bowing out of the front of the house. A round table was embraced within its curve inside, and at the table, on three velvet-seated old chairs, there sat three ladies who had been inhabitants of the house for many, many years and were accustomed to watch how the world went, from this, their lookout.

Chapter 3

"DOESN'T HAPPEN OFTEN, you know," said Sam Murchison, lolling and letting his chair swing in a short arc. "Goes against the tide. How old is the child?"

"John is between three and four."

"Then he doesn't get asked his preference. In the case of a child under twelve the normal thing is for the child to go with the mother."

"What have I said to make you think this is the normal thing?" barked his visitor. "What I want to know is this. In the eyes of the law, what constitutes being unfit?"

"Unfit mother, eh? It'll be in the eyes of some individual judge, most probably. Well, it has to be pretty drastic, I can say that. And pretty clearly demonstrated."

"For instance?"

"For instance, insanity. And not just borderline, mind you."

"What else?"

"Criminality, I suppose. Of a crime convicted. Or an addiction. Acute alcoholism? Possbily. Incurable disease, serious physical disability."

"Immorality?" snapped Reynard. "Promiscuousness?"

"Depends. If it's flagrant enough, I guess so. And current, by the way. For much is forgiven." Murchison swiveled gently. "Depends, of course, on the judge's degree of sophistication." The lawyer was calm and slightly amused.

"Vulgarity? Ignorance?" Edward Reynard had set his pale jaw. "Nuh-uh."

"Inability to support the child in any decent comfort?"

"Don't fool with that," the lawyer said promptly. "It may occur to a judge that if Edward Reynard is really concerned that money be spent on this child, why doesn't Edward Reynard simply supply the money? In your son's behalf, of course. As a matter of fact, your son is responsible for the child's support."

"*He* has no money."

"He may find he'll have to hustle—" the lawyer began. Then he read the look on his client's face and said, "I'm no good to you if I don't warn you what you're up against. You want this divorce? You don't want the wife to raise the child? Your son feels the same, does he?"

"Of course he does."

"He didn't, er, come along this afternoon?"

"He happens to be flat on his back in bed, from physical injuries inflicted on him by this woman. Why can't that in itself be used to show she's unfit?"

The lawyer scratched his nose. "Is your son puny? Is she an Amazon? Was there *no* provocation? Any witnesses to swear it could not possibly have been in fear of bodily harm? Is she pretty, by the way? I'm sorry, but I must say this. Such an argument strikes me as setting up a fairly ludicrous scene."

"The child was injured in the melee," Reynard said grimly.

"Oh-oh," said Murchison, "and it takes two to tango." He played with his penholder. "Child beating, wife beating—or husband beating, for that matter—those things are unlawful. Of course, the law's not going to *start* anything." He looked up.

Reynard wasn't paying attention. "Suppose I brought you evidence?" he barked.

"Of what?"

"Of the truth," Reynard said fiercely. "There has to be some justice. She can't ruin the best years of my son's life and then just walk away with his child. I tell you, that boy is a nervous wreck."

Murchison, who was taking note of the voice, the sudden color in the face, the light in the eyes, felt surprise. He had dealt with Reynard for a long time; he had thought the man to be tough-minded, bullheaded, one who rammed through the world with so little understanding of human emotions that he did not even know how ruthlessly he behaved.

But there the lawyer seemed to be recognizing the signs of passion. The eyes were hot; the voice was coming from a throat constricted with feeling. The feeling seemed to be an almost senseless fury.

"I wouldn't make a point of your son's emotional collapse," he said gently.

"You mean to say that everything is weighted on the side of the woman? That I *cannot* win?"

(You, eh? thought Murchison. I thought so. But what did this poor girl ever do to you?)

"I said it doesn't happen often," he told the client. "That is, *if* there is conflict. Now in the event that she really doesn't want the child—can't be bothered, you know, doesn't like the responsibility, or, for instance, is involved with another man and wants to be free to remarry, and is willing to come before a judge and present herself as an unloving mother and whine about the nuisance of it all—well, that might be different."

"She can voluntarily give the child up?"

"No. No. The judge makes the decision. But such an attitude well might influence him, don't you see?"

"I see. Can she take the child out of the state?" Reynard demanded.

(Ho, thought the lawyer. So she does want the child.)

"As soon as she has custody, she can," he said. "Of course, she could simply take off, illegally, at any time. No barbed wire at the border."

"If she does *that*—" Reynard did not go on, but his face threatened ugly reprisal.

"Custody," said the lawyer, "is normally decided at the time of the hearing for the interlocutory. Of course, if there is a custody fight, the fight can go on and on, a long miserable," he cautioned, "and pretty soul-destroying process."

"I see. And when is this hearing?"

"Who can say?" The lawyer shrugged. "Fairly soon."

"You would agree it's just as well if she is prevented from taking the child out of the state before this hearing?"

Murchison said, "Prevented?"

"I don't see how she can drag him around the country," Reynard said bitterly, "until he's over his injuries. She certainly hasn't the money to hire ambulance planes and all that sort of— What about their property?"

"A settlement should be arranged between them," said Murchison, watching him closely.

"I don't want them to meet. She'll have a lawyer. Can't you—"

"Counsel might discuss it. What is your son's position on the property?"

But Reynard asked another question. "Can she take possession of whatever cash there may be?"

"She can, as soon as the settlement is agreed upon."

"Then it won't be agreed upon."

"Just a minute, Mr. Reynard." The lawyer straightened.

"My son is an injured party. Whatever property there is, he will claim it all." Reynard leaned back.

"He won't get it," the lawyer said sharply.

"Take a judge to say so, I presume?"

The lawyer stared at him for a moment. Then he said, "That's your idea of preventing her from taking the child anywhere? Aren't you being unduly suspicious? You risk putting a judge's back up, believe me, under the circumstances. Don't do this, Mr. Reynard. Why are you so afraid she'll try to run away with the little boy?"

"She told me so," snapped Reynard.

"You're sure? You didn't misunderstand?"

"I understand this," said Reynard. "The sooner the whole thing is legally decided and Emily and I can begin to take some decent care of that child, the better. I don't want delay. I don't want any long miserable process. And I don't want to have to send people chasing after her either. I intend to see about this proof—"

Murchison said sternly, "Let me advise you. Don't throw your money around and set dogs on her, Mr. Reynard. Evidence of hostility won't help you one bit. Obviously you are hostile. Hold that down, will you? The judge is obliged to be on the child's side, but you can put him on the mother's side if you don't watch it. There may be evidence already that you and your wife never willingly accepted her. I take it there is evidence that you have not been generous in the last year or two. I strongly advise you to remember that there can be a prejudice *against* money."

"Thank you for your advice," Reynard said coldly.

"Will you look what the cat's dragging in?" said Mrs. Moran. "Here comes Dr. Bianchi, with a babe."

"What's this? What's this?" said Mrs. Kimberly. "He wouldn't dare!"

"What will the Madame say?" said Mrs. Link, and all three rocked and hooted softly.

They were playing their endless game of cards, which they interrupted with the ease of long custom whenever there was anything to be seen in the street, or across the street at the hospital entrance, or especially along the short driveway to the emergency section, into which, from time to time, would screech an ambulance.

Some blithe and literate soul, who had once paused briefly in one of the upstairs rooms, had given them a title that had been passed along. The three ladies were known in the house, and in what part of the street was aware of them, as the Norns.

Dr. Joseph Bianchi (who knew them and their ways) guided Sherry Reynard (who did not) up the walk and between the tall stalks of timber that held a high signboard. It crested above the porch roof and read: *Site of St. Anthony's New $2.5 Million Out-Clinic.* Sherry didn't even notice that there was a sign.

The young man rang the doorbell. "You'll have to talk to the Madame," he said. "Excuse me, I mean Mrs. Peabody, the land-lady. Might as well ring, right?"

But the female who opened the door was too young to be a landlady. She was an odd-looking girl, perhaps fourteen, perhaps fifteen years old, with an outsized head and heavy, but somehow extremely bland, features. She was short and too well developed for her childish blue cotton dress.

"Hi, Elsie," said the young man. "Go get your mama. That's the girl."

The girl gazed at him without expression.

"Go get your mama. That's the girl," the young doctor repeated, and this time the message was received. The girl looked very pleased to have received it. She nodded and went ambling away.

"What you call mentally retarded," Dr. Bianchi said into Sherry's ear. "Nothing to bother anybody."

They had come through the wide old-fashioned house door into an almost square entrance space, paved with worn parquet. At the left was a staircase, six steps to a landing, from which another flight went up at a right angle. There was much varnish. The risers, the treads, the banisters, the rail, all the yellowish brown wood wore a high gloss.

Under the landing there was the usual mirror on the wall, the usual semicircle of tabletop bearing some scattered pieces of mail. The wall to the right was papered in a dizzy geometrical pink and yellow, and there was a pay phone affixed there. Directly ahead of them there was no partition, but the sense of a large dim room beyond that was full of furniture.

Around from some region on the staircase side came a willowy woman in a tan dress.

"Mrs. Peabody," said the young man, "here's somebody who was asking at the hospital about a room."

The landlady tilted her head, on which her dark brown hair was arrayed in such a way that it seemed to have been put on like a hat. Perhaps it was a wig. Her dark eyes did not track perfectly. The right one wandered, although very slightly. Her voice was thin and slightly frosty.

"Oh, yes, Miss, er—"

Sherry had to rouse to explain herself to some degree. "I'm Sherry Reynard. Mrs. Reynard. My little boy is in the hospital over there. I need a place to stay, where I can be near him. Just a room?"

"I see," said Mrs. Peabody. "Well—" She half-turned, rather reluctantly.

Young Dr. Bianchi suddenly abandoned the scene and went leaping up the glittering stairs, three steps at a time.

"Are you a friend of Dr. Bianchi's?" the landlady asked coldly.

"I beg your pardon?"

"Of Dr. Bianchi's?" The landlady used a patient duplication of her original tones that reminded Sherry of the existence of the mentally retarded daughter.

"Oh. Oh, the young man? No, no. The lady at the desk asked him."

"I see." Mrs. Peabody became slightly more cordial.

Sherry followed her into the big room, which had windows on the back of the house, all thoroughly muffled by glass curtains and some faded pink-to-tan draperies. She received the impression of space, clutter, yet a kind of old-fashioned elegance. Carved frames of wood around hard tight upholstery, china ornaments, fringed lampshades. Mrs. Peabody was leading her all the way across the space, but Sherry realized that there were people in this room. The light was stronger on the street side, and now she could see that in a huge bay window, there, three old women were seated at a table. They said nothing. Cards slapped on the tabletop. Even so, Sherry sensed that although they did not turn to stare, they were listening intently to every fall of her foot.

"The room I have," Mrs. Peabody said rather plaintively, "used to be a sun porch, but that makes it very airy, of course."

She went around a carved wooden screen that partially blocked a doorless passage, and opened the first much varnished door on the left.

It was a small room, with glass on two and a half sides. All the glass, including one patch that seemed to descend to the floor and may have once been a door, was covered with shirred white fabric. The light was very cold, but the room was clean. It held a single bed, a narrow tall dresser, one chair, and a tall wardrobe cupboard that stood out from one wall.

"It looks very nice," said Sherry, "if it's not too— How much is it?"

"Twenty-five dollars a week," Mrs. Peabody said quickly and hostilely. "Of course, that does include a Continental breakfast."

"Oh, that sounds very—"

"I can't have cooking in the rooms," said Mrs. Peabody, interrupting. "But people *will* try to make breakfast. So I provide it, and that saves trouble. I don't serve luncheons or dinners."

"I see."

"Now the bath's not private," said Mrs. Peabody, seeming to need to go into a conscientiously soft sell, "but it is quite convenient. Very large. Just at the end of the hall."

Sherry, who really wanted to cast herself down on the bed no later than right now, nevertheless followed to inspect the very large bath. It was ancient. The faucets leaked. But it seemed clean. It would do.

"How long would you want the room?" said Mrs. Peabody, and now her slightly crooked gaze was running rapidly up and down Sherry's person.

"I can't say. I don't know." Sherry was almost too weary to speak. "It depends on how my little boy gets along. Could I pay you for a week and take the room? I'd like to rest, and then I'll have to go get my things. It was an emergency when we brought him to the hospital this morning." (Oh, please, hurry, let me pay you, and let me alone.)

Rooms, however, are not rented as fast as this. Cautious ceremonies are necessary. Mrs. Peabody must inquire about the nature of the emergency, the age of the child, the prognosis in his case, and the whereabouts of his father.

Sherry told her what Johnny's injuries were. She said that she was separated from her husband.

"The room is single," Mrs. Peabody said sharply. "I don't allow gentlemen on this floor of the house . . . As I do not allow ladies upstairs."

"Yes, I understand," said Sherry. She had opened her purse. Now she held out the money mutely.

"There is a bolt on the inside," Mrs. Peabody said in her frosty way, "but no key, because of the cleaning. Although my people are honest, you ought not to leave valuables around."

"I'll be sure not to do that," Sherry said solemnly. "Thank you." Then mercifully, at last, she could close the door of the strange little room and slide the inside bolt and be alone.

She put her bag on the dresser. She sat down on the edge of the narrow bed. Her toes nudged off her shoes. Very slowly she let herself down to lie full length in the glaring light of this stark place. She thought: This is all right. It will do.

Mrs. Peabody told the Norns everything that Sherry had said, most of which they had already heard, but they listened avidly just the same. When the landlady left them, Mrs. Moran said, "I'm surprised at the Madame, letting in a female under the age of ninety." Her pale dry lips quirked under her white mustache. Mrs. Moran was sixty-eight.

"The doctor may linger longer at breakfast," said Mrs. Link, pushing archly at the pile of pale straw the rinses had made of her hair. Mrs. Link was seventy-three.

"She won't be here long," said Mrs. Kimberly, who had a squirrel face, pouch cheeks, and a tiny sharp chin. "The husband will come arunning. Or the boyfriend. Or both." She giggled. Mrs. Kimberly was sixty-five, the baby of them all.

"Ah."

An ambulance pulled in across the way.

"Nothing serious," said Mrs. Moran. "No siren."

They watched a stretcher being lifted from the vehicle.

"There she goes," said Mrs. Link. "Late again. Look at her run." They watched the nurse scurrying on the sidewalk.

"New baby," said Mrs. Kimberly. "Look at mama in the wheel-chair. Last time she'll put her feet up for a while."

"Look at papa. Don't he feel clever?" said Mrs. Link.

"Oh-oh," said Mrs. Moran. "Here comes the Great Profile."

The cards slapped. They listened to the house door open and the sound of Lawton Archer's feet going up the stairs.

"He didn't get the part," said Mrs. Moran.

"He never gets the part," said Mrs. Kimberly. "All right, girls, which one of you is giving me the queen of spades?"

The name of the game they played was Hearts.

Out in the huge old-fashioned kitchen the landlady said, "Well, I've rented the sun porch."

"That's good," Mr. Peabody said vaguely. He was sitting in an old wicker armchair, which he had adopted as his own nest, in the kitchen corner, reading the papers and sipping beer.

His wife sat down rather suddenly in a hard chair. "I have to take in anybody," she said bleakly, "while I still can. I don't know what we're going to do, Harold."

"Don't worry," he said. "Don't worry. They can't tear the house down till September." He eyed the money in her hand. "Want anything at the supermarket?" he asked hopefully.

She gave him a hard glare and folded the money into a tight wad. The supermarket had a liquor store.

By the time Sherry, having rested an hour, gone back to see Johnny briefly, and taken a bus, rang Mrs. Ivy's bell (duty bound to thank her once again), it was 4 P.M. Mrs. Ivy did not answer. Sherry walked up her old front walk, put her key into the door of the house she used to live in—that morning.

She braced herself against the inner air that was already some-how dead and went briskly through to the bedroom, took down two suitcases from the closet shelf, and packed them as fast as she could, one for herself and the other with Johnny's things. She was nervous. Time pressed. She didn't want to be long away from Johnny. She wanted to get away from here.

She rooted around in her jewel case, in which there was no single precious stone, but only junk, and she found the twenty-dollar bill she'd hidden there long ago. Should she drag the suitcases on a bus or call a cab? She couldn't think.

She did not want to go into the kitchen at all, but while she was trying to think, she did go, long enough to take the most perishable foods out of the refrigerator and throw them away. She tasted nothing. She ought to have been hungry. She'd had no lunch. But she couldn't put this food into her mouth. Then her mind seemed to make itself up, and she used the phone (Who would pay that bill?) to call a cab.

While she waited for it, she called her boss, Mr. Dodd, at the Club, who made exclamations of regret and sympathy and promised to mail what pay she had coming, which was very little. After all, on that job it was tips that counted, not the salary. Sherry gave him the address of Mrs. Peabody's rooming house.

This made her think of the mail. She looked into the tray under the door slot. There was nothing but the gas bill. Who would pay it? She thrust it back. Couldn't afford to think about it. She wondered whether to give the post office a change of address. No, at least not now.

She rather enjoyed thinking that nobody knew where she had gone to earth. Tomorrow the lawyer would have to know. She had an appointment.

She lugged the suitcases out, and having locked the door behind her and not doubting for a moment that some neighbor's eyes were on her, she stood alone at the curb, beside all the possessions she could afford to carry. Now she had no home, no husband, no job, very little cash on hand. She had a child. And I've got my health, Sherry told herself grimly.

But she also had a habit of mind that kept putting good hope into the balance. All right, the fact was, she did have good health. And the fact was, she did have friends—good friends of her own.

Oh, not here, but old friends back East, people who had known her people. And her best girl friend and ex-roommate, who was married now.

She must get her stuff to her new place and then go over to the hospital, where she could eat a meal of some sort in the coffee-shop and see Johnny tucked in for the night. Then get hold of paper and envelopes. She could have taken some from the house. No, she wouldn't go back in again, never. Then she'd write to her own friends, old friends. They would help her.

She didn't know how long it was going to take to find out what she had in this world except what was on her person now. She had better not be reckless. She couldn't be sure how much of the nine hundred twenty-seven dollars she could keep either. And there were a lot of expenses coming up. Yes, she must, in all sensible caution, write to her friends and ask them to help her with money.

She was able to ride away and not look back, because she was busy with arithmetic. Let's see. Sixty-seven dollars and seventy-five cents plus the twenty dollars made eighty-seven seventy-five. Minus twenty-five dollars to Mrs. Peabody. Minus the bus fare, forty cents, and soon minus whatever this cab would cost, and then, of course, her dinner. And paper and envelopes. And stamps.

Only when she had paid the driver and was lugging her suitcases into the rooming house did she remember that she had not been in touch with the baby-sitter, Miss Erskine. Well, Mrs. Ivy would tell her what had happened, surely, and soon enough. Sherry walked by the pay phone on the wall, thinking of what she could or could not afford. In the purse under her arm there was sixty-two dollars and thirty-five cents. She owed the baby-sitter nine dollars. It seemed a lot.

Chapter 4

ON THE EVENING of this day a young man named Clifford Storm was studying his host and wondering what the old coot wanted. Cliff sat on the leather couch, sipped his drink, and answered the pseudofatherly questions about how he had been, but he was pretty sure that Edward Reynard hadn't asked him to this house to find out how he'd been.

"I've been thinking," said his host, leaning back in the leather chair, "I've been wondering, Cliff, whether your father's company still interests you at all."

Cliff thought this gray head against the colorful bookbindings made a nice shot. "You mean," he said, "the company that used to belong to my father? Before he lost it?"

"Now, now," said Reynard, "I bought. He sold. Nothing to feel bitter about. Especially since you, as I remember, walked away under your own steam."

"So I did," said Cliff. "Young, wasn't I? Didn't fancy going to bed the heir and waking up the hired hand. Now you want to know whether it still interests me? Well, there's my name on it." Storm and Savage Productions. He did admire the name. "Old Mr. Storm's little boy can't help keeping an eye on, even from the outside."

Cliff settled back, smiling. Bitterness *was* stupid. His father was dead now, along with long-dead Billy Savage. Cliff was no righter of ancient wrongs, on any color horse. He bent his wits to discover what Reynard wanted in order to see how Cliff Storm could profit from whatever that desire might be.

Storm and Savage Productions was a small film-producing company that made shorts—educational and training films for the most part, but now and again, even in this market, a short subject for consumption in a theater.

"Still active, are you?" said Reynard. "Producing? Directing? Cinematography?"

"More or less. More or less," Cliff said genially. If it was rather less than more at the moment, Reynard didn't have to know. The trouble with the industry was the unpredictable movement of mysterious tides. Sometimes you were hot. Then again, for no reason you could pinpoint, you were not.

"I want to make you a proposition," said Reynard. "Something I want you to do for me. Now, I was thinking about what I could offer as compensation. It's not the kind of thing that can be paid for by the hour or, for that matter, in cash really. It's a little difficult, a little delicate. I think you could help me. So I am wondering whether you might not like to go back into the company."

"Back?" said Cliff. "In what way, back?"

"Be in charge," said Reynard. "Manage it."

"Well, well," said Cliff. "Does sound attractive. What do you want me to do? Kill somebody? Why not? That's if it's an authentic bad guy you're gunning for. After all, we do have our principles." He drank deep.

He thought: Wait a minute. Maybe it's stupid, to be making cheap cracks here. On the other hand, posture of hard-to-get rarely does any harm.

Reynard's face had frozen. Then he spoke crisply, reproving nonsense. "I want an investigation made. I need some proof, and I need it collected rather quietly by someone not in the profession, someone who might plausibly have a personal reason to take an interest in the matter."

"You want a detective who won't show up on record as such," Cliff said quickly.

"You're intelligent," Reynard said sourly. "And I have reason to believe that you know your way around some of the seamier sides." His bright eyes flashed.

Cliff, in whose opinion Edward Reynard was just as crooked as anybody else in business, and also just as hypocritical, felt both amused and violently curious. What did Reynard need of somebody who had "been around"?

"Are you interested in some such proposition?" his host asked.

"I'm interested in the hitch," Cliff said cheerfully. "Tell me, is it illegal, immoral, or just fattening?" He was beginning to enjoy himself. The old coot wanted something all right. Cliff was the boy to sell, if he had a buyer. And push the price as high as it could go.

"Not at all," Reynard said stiffly. "I want to get hold of proof of what I know to be true. But I can't go after it, all out, openly, hammer and tongs, because (as I said) the thing is delicate. There are certain traditions to overcome, prejudices, that sort of thing. I don't dare."

"Dassn't tarnish your image, eh?" Cliff said impudently. "And all you want is proof? I'm not supposed to rig anything?"

"Certainly not." Reynard's neck hardened.

"Not even put a little pressure on, here and there? Maneuver contracts, time deadlines to coincide awkwardly, and fix to catch some poor chap in a financial trap so that you can take *his* company away from him?"

Reynard let out a forceful gust of air in a disgusted sigh. "Never mind," he said. "Tell me, are you married, Cliff?"

"No," said Cliff. "I was. I'm not."

"Any interesting credits lately? I haven't followed—"

Ohhh, yes, you have, thought Cliff. He knew he had made a mistake. He had lost ground. The man knew Cliff was in the trough of the wave. Power was shifting. Reynard was an employer and knew that Cliff needed a job.

"Storm and Savage keeps up the good work," said Reynard. "Very steady."

"It's in a decline," Cliff said promptly. "It's not what it was in my father's day. It's a workhorse. Picking up routine assignments. The creative imagination's gone out of it."

"Put *your* imagination in it, then," Reynard said carelessly.

Cliff's imagination took a leap. What do I want? he asked himself. I know what I want. I want the company. I'm over thirty. I'm getting old and tired. I've "been around," I have. I want my company for myself.

"Losing money, is it?" he said carelessly.

"No, no. It's comfortable."

Cliff did not believe him. "Maybe you'd better tell me what you want," he said.

"I want my grandson," said Reynard, and Cliff felt shocked. Reynard leaned forward now. His normal austerity was falling away. "You and Ward were schoolboys together," he said. "You are an old friend of his. You may even have met this Sherry he got himself married to."

"I, er, believe I did meet her once. Some party. I never knew her."

Cliff didn't add that he had long ago dropped Ward Reynard off his list of friends, old or otherwise, because the fellow had begun to bore the hell out of him, rich man's son or no. But he was now scenting *emotion*. Cliff fancied himself as one who understood human motivations. If old man Reynard cared, really *cared*, for something, then Cliff might have a lever here.

"Even so," Reynard was continuing, "it's understandable if you were to take enough interest to ask some questions about her."

"What is it that you want?" said Cliff. (And how bad do you want it, old man? he thought to himself.)

"There's going to be a divorce. I want evidence to convince some judge that she isn't fit to raise that child."

"Proof, you said? Of what you know is true?" Cliff's shocked wits were racing.

"That's right. I'm told that it has to be something drastic and also clearly demonstrated. But it can be found. Let me go into this a little bit. Ward went off on a kind of sabbatical, tired of the books, you know. And he got involved with this cheap little— Some rustic background. Loose by herself on the town. First thing you know, she'd got him to marry her, although I'm sure he needn't have. Emily and I went to New York with the kindest intentions and found them in a positive slum. Well, of course, we wanted to get them out of there, better their conditions, but no . . . Not until she got herself pregnant. *Then* they came whining to us, and we opened our home. We took care of everything. Doctors, nurses . . . But that girl is impossible. No breeding. No education. No values. No conception—"

Cliff, listening, thought: Yeah, yeah. The old man is hipped on this. He really is. Well, well!

"She wanted out," the man was saying bitterly. "And she took the baby, and she took our son. All I want is a way to show her up for what she really is."

"Shouldn't be too difficult," Cliff said soothingly. "Maybe I see what you mean about, er, knowing where to look. Will you *sell* me the company?"

"Sell!" Reynard leaned back, blinking.

"For a dollar and other? The usual? Amortize your investment out at some pace that I can handle?"

"Why should I do that? In effect, give it to you?" Reynard's eyes glittered.

"To pay me," said Cliff, "for what you want. And not seem to have paid one penny. Let's pretend I'm talking you into this." He began to talk fast. Let there be an agreement drawn. Reynard need not even seem to be taking a tax loss for himself. In fact, he would get his costs, or near enough. The transaction would be set up to look as if a man, who had many other businesses, had lost interest in this one small weakening outpost of his far-flung empire and didn't mind getting rid of it. Especially if Cliff, a young tiger, had come roaring back into the arena, passionate to rehabilitate, reinvigorate, rescue, and expand the company which his own father had built and which bore his name. Most natural thing in the world!

"Furthermore," said Cliff, "I came here tonight to talk you into this, and you told me about Ward's troubles, and how can I help feeling sorry for my old buddy? And looking around a little?"

Reynard said, "Can you get me what I want?"

If Cliff had been a cat, his whiskers would have quivered at the brush of something unseen and unheard, but nevertheless solidly here. What did the old man want?

Cliff said smoothly, "Tell me this first. Suppose this is a deal. How will you and I agree that you have got what you want? Who will be the judge?"

"I have no idea what the judge's name will be," said Reynard. "Whatever judge it is who gives Ward custody of his son."

Cliff settled back in some dismay. "And then," he said, "I get the company?"

"And then," said Reynard, "you get the company."

"Not good," Cliff said in a moment.

The other man raised his chin haughtily and stared.

"Let me put it this way," said Cliff. "You're going to war. I'm hired to provide the ammunition. But you don't intend to pay me until you win the war. Or I might say that a bet on some unknown judge is too chancy a proposition. Meantime, I'll have done the work."

"And I'm taking the chance that you can do the work," snapped Reynard. "Somebody else might do it better."

"Supposing," said Cliff, "I root around, dig up all there is to dig, and there's nothing? There again, I do the work."

"There's something," snapped Reynard. "All I want to know is exactly what it is and how to demonstrate it *clearly*. That is what I want."

Yep, thought Cliff, that's what you want. And that's what you're going to get. And somebody is going to get it for you. The proof, eh? You bet. And if there isn't any, then you want her framed. Oh, you'll never admit it, will you, old man? You wouldn't commission that. You won't even believe that it is a frame when

it happens. But what you want, you'll get. So I may as well be the
boy who gets it for you.

Cliff decided not to press for better odds at the moment. After
all, the prize was enormous if he won. And if he lost, he lost
nothing.

"For Storm and Savage," he said aloud, speaking deliberately,
"I could, and would, do almost anything."

Reynard did not wince. He let the implication bounce off his
mind. He did not entertain it. But he must have known what it
was; he did not indignantly reject it this time.

"Very well," Edward Reynard said cordially. "I'll give you all
the help I can, of course."

"What about expenses?" Cliff said rather impudently. He
couldn't help a certain jubilance.

"I can see that there may be some expenses," Reynard said with
a thin smile.

(For bribes? thought Cliff. But did not say so.)

After a while Cliff, loaded with names, addresses, dates, and
some cash, followed his host up the fine staircase. It seemed wise
for him to pay a sick call on his suddenly reconstructed old boy-
hood chum.

Cliff was curious anyway. How the devil could a woman put a
two-hundred-pound man out on the floor?

Ward's room was, as Cliff was amused to note, still a boy's
room. It did not actually have banners on the walls, but there
were trophies. Mrs. Reynard was sitting under a lamp with a book
in her lap. Ward, in the boyish bed, was resting against high
pillows. Somewhere in the room there was a man in attendance.
A nurse? Male? Odd, Cliff thought briefly and discarded the
thought. Not necessarily odd. Maybe a touch prudish.

"Oh, hi! Say, Cliff!" Ward said in the old way.

Cliff thought he looked terrible. No single blow could have put
that drawn look and that pallor on Ward's formerly rosy, squarish
face, or coarsened those pores, or thinned and dried that formerly
glossy brown hair.

"How nice to see you, Clifford!" Mrs. Reynard was saying in the old way, as if Cliff had stopped by after football practice.

"Mother was reading to me," said Ward.

"It's still hard for him to focus, you know," said Emily Reynard, "and I don't mind. In fact, I've always enjoyed reading aloud."

It occurred to Cliff that her mind could qualify as a museum wherein were stored all the clichés of the last forty years. Well, no, not the last forty. Skip a decade or two. She hadn't acquired a new idea in the fifteen years he remembered. He didn't ask what she was reading aloud. He shuddered to imagine. He looked at Ward.

"Hey, you got yourself a wild-looking shoulder, guy," said Cliff. Through the thin cotton the black line of a healing cut was visible, imbedded in swollen multicolored flesh.

"It's terribly painful, still," cooed Mrs. Reynard. "He can't even turn easily without help. But we keep him as comfortable as we possibly can."

"I'm sure you do," Cliff said politely, abandoning a half-formed resolution to try to talk to Ward alone.

So very shortly Cliff went downstairs on Edward Reynard's heels, not having taken what he had recognized to be the risk of being called off his quest by the child's own father. Ward Reynard, tranquilized to the gills no doubt, was not agonizing over a broken marriage or the loss of his child. He had mentioned neither. In fact, Cliff judged that Ward *was* the child—at least just now.

Well, poor fool, he'd never had much of a chance to become anything else. Or if he had tried, the effort must have been too much for him. Back in the nest was the fledgling—the thirty-one-year-old baby bird. Cliff Storm, at the same age, considered himself well seasoned by adversity and other things. He had no childish illusions about what he had done, was doing, or would do. He had worked this deal up into a gamble that was really worth his while. He thought he could win it. After all, he was not only a realist who accepted what Reynard had called the seamy side, but also an illusionist, by trade. He felt himself really very much interested in this problem. It presented what people call a challenge. It certainly did.

"You can see," his host said pathetically at the door, "what she has done to my boy."

And Cliff felt shocked again. What kind of pious sentimental bleat was this to be coming out of Edward Reynard's mouth? He could scarcely believe his ears.

"You buy. I sell," he said amiably. "I'll get busy."

"By the way, Cliff," said Reynard, suddenly crisp again, "see to it, will you, that she doesn't run off with the boy? She may try to take him out of the state. I don't want that. Mess and delay. I think, however, she may be low in funds. Now I can't imagine she'd have much of a credit rating."

"No, I can't really imagine that she has," said Cliff, letting his teeth show.

"Or wealthy friends," Reynard said musingly, "who would trust *her* to pay back any considerable sum. After all—"

"I doubt that, too," Cliff said soothingly. "That is, if she's the kind you say."

"Oh, you'll have no trouble," Reynard said with a flash.

So? thought Cliff. Those implied instructions seemed more clearly instructions to Cliff than to the man who gave them?

Well, what did Cliff care? What a prize he was after!

What luck, after all!

Chapter 5

IN THE MORNING Sherry discovered what made Mrs. Peabody's breakfast Continental. After the orange juice (the only American concession) all you got was coffee and toast.

It was served from seven to eight thirty in the large dining room, where Mrs. Peabody, in person, starched and crisp for the day, presided over the coffeepot at one end of the table in such a way as to make one ashamed to ask for more than a second cup.

Dr. Bianchi was evidently an early bird. He was already breezing off when Sherry appeared. The three elderly ladies from the first floor came in together and settled down to suck the utmost value out of every bite and sip. Sherry was soon introduced to another tenant, a man named Lawton Archer. He seemed to be, in a young sort of way, detached, yet not as young as he wished to seem. He had long dark locks, sad eyes, and too bulbous a nose. He was very slight in the body, but his voice was deep and rich and much too big for him. His clothing puzzled her. Either it was very modern indeed, or it was just plain old-fashioned. He was an actor; he was always "on." He hardly glanced at her but ate quickly in a picky fashion, terribly conscious of himself and watching out, Sherry soon discovered, for the landlady's daughter, who had a crush on him. This was pathetic.

Sherry took the trouble to divert the poor half-witted creature's attention, as best she could, by thanking her profusely for the pouring and serving of the orange juice. This seemed to be Elsie's morning duty. Everyone else accepted it as such, although Elsie acted as if she were performing, for the first time in her life, a prodigious task.

Mr. Peabody came in briefly, evidently for the sole purpose of being introduced to the new tenant. He had a soft face, and his small eyes, imbedded in and peering cautiously forth from the flesh, had no life in them. He breathed on Sherry with a beery blast and took Elsie off with him. He and his daughter evidently breakfasted in the kitchen, perhaps more heartily. In the dining room Mrs. Peabody contrived to make the toast limp by making it before it was in demand and keeping it under a close cover. The coffee was weak. The company of strangers made Sherry feel as if she were up for examination, although she had no idea what it would take to pass or fail. She'd had a bad night. Never mind. All this must do.

At the hospital she found Johnny wan and fretful, and it worried her.

"Wow," said Sherry to the lawyer that afternoon, "it sure shocks you to have to stop and add up what you thought you had. Everything kind of seems to vanish."

Allen Jordan, the lawyer, was neither young nor old. He wore rimless glasses and seemed very quiet and attentive. They had been discussing property. Sherry's clothing, personal things? Yes, Sherry had taken all that she could carry or was worth carrying. As for the house, it was only rented. The car was best left where it was. It wasn't worth the repair bill, really, in resale value. The furniture would be sold one day and might have to be offered soon, *in toto*, to some secondhand dealer, because it wasn't worth storage charges. Was there anything Sherry wanted to keep, such as wedding presents? Sherry told him they hadn't had that kind of wedding. And she wasn't going to drag sheets and towels or pots and pans all the way to New York.

About the money in the bank, Mr. Jordan said there must be an agreed-upon property settlement before it could be touched. He would approach the other side. He would ask for her, and he felt quite sure that she would be given all that money. This would be normal.

Sherry's brow cleared. "Now, I know, for instance, where your fee is coming from."

Mr. Jordan smiled and said it all would work out. Would she ask for alimony?

Sherry said she didn't see how Ward could pay any. And even if he were liable for child support, how *could* he pay?

"That's his problem," said the lawyer.

"What do you want to bet it's mine?" she said with her impish smile. She was feeling better. She was doing something. She was beginning to get life sorted out. Her biggest problem, she could plainly see, was going to be financial.

She said, "I have enough to live on for a while. But I don't know how long they'll keep Johnny. Three weeks at the very least. And the hospital bills won't all be covered by the insurance. I just don't know what they'll be. Then, if I can't take Johnny traveling right away, I'll have to find a place where he and I can stay. And when I do take him back East, there's the plane fare. I wish I knew what I could count on. How soon is everything going to get unscrambled?"

"We can settle the property immediately," he told her. "But some things take time. We will ask for a hearing as quickly as it can be had, and give good reasons for speed. Once we get the interlocutory and settle the custody—"

"There can't be any trouble about that, can there?" Sherry fixed her gaze on his face, seeking his wisdom.

"Why do you ask?" he said.

So she told him that she had been threatened. No other word for it. "See, Ward's father has always been my enemy," she said.

"I'd be a little careful, Mrs. Reynard."

"I know," she said. "Oh, I know. Nobody is ever *really* persecuted. It's always just a delusion."

"That's the superstition," he said, and she thanked him with a look. It was marvelous to be able to sit here and say what she wanted to say to an intelligent and attentive man.

"I never could quite figure it out either," she told him. "Ward ran out on his parents before I ever met him. By that I mean he dropped out of graduate school. And went to New York by himself, on his own. Well, he wanted out from the pressure or something. But they were mad as hornets. His father, of course, *he* thought that if he cut off the money, Ward would have to come running back. But Ward didn't. At least, he didn't then. He was just scrounging, living in a messy old dump with a couple of pretty far-out characters, when I first met him. See, I was rattling around New York by myself, too. Oh, I had a job. I never had any particular training, though. I only had a year and a half of college. It was local—just a small college in my home town. Ward says it's a glorified high school." She sighed. "But my folks died. Well, my mother had been sick for a long, long time, and when she finally did die, my dad . . . I guess he suddenly felt how worn-out he was. Because he got sick right away." The old sorrow waxed and waned.

"So I took off for the bright lights and the big city," she went on. "I was waiting on table when I met Ward at this . . . I guess you could call it a party. Anyhow, it was at my girl friend's girl friend's place. And we—"

No, not even to this intelligent kindness would Sherry go into details, about how they had courted each other, backward, in the modern way. First you go to bed. Then you begin to get interested.

So she said, "After about three months we just got married. At City Hall. And at that, his folks just about had a fit."

She didn't say aloud that the Reynards had always acted as if it had been a shotgun wedding, although anybody who could count as far as nine must have known for sure that it wasn't.

"Pretty soon both of them came steaming to town," she went on. "What wicked woman had got hold of their precious?" Sherry sniffled and took out her handkerchief. She was not crying. She didn't feel like crying. She was upset all the same. "Well, Ward had moved into my place. It was awfully small, I'll give you that, and the neighborhood wasn't Park Avenue. But it was okay. I don't think his folks even know how real people live. They seem to think that if you're not rich, you've got to be stupid or else something *low*, you know? My father made good money, but my mother's illness— Well, he was glad he could pay. And I— Excuse me." She used the handkerchief and got control. "But Ward had a card table and his typewriter, and he used to work all day in the room while I was on the job. We didn't think it was so terrible.

"*They* did, though. We had a chair with a tear in the arm. Wow, Mrs. Reynard seemed to think rats were going to come out of that torn place. It wasn't dirty. I should have sewed it up, sure, but you get used to a thing like that. So she wanted to buy chairs. Well, I was all for it. Why not? But I could tell Ward just hated the idea. So he wouldn't let her. And we wouldn't move either.

"And one *bad* thing: By the time they came, it was just about that time somebody had talked me into trying to get into this nightclub act that had a chorus. I can dance some. I've always loved to dance. This friend of mine conned me into thinking it was easy to bluff your way in. Hah! If I could have, the money would have been great, you see?

"But that really did it, as far as the Reynards were concerned. Right away I was no good. Absolutely no good. Why is that, Mr. Jordan? They don't know *one thing* about that kind of work."

"Prejudice," he said lightly.

"They sure hung a lot on that," Sherry said soberly. "Although I'd bet they didn't want Ward married *at all*. But if I was a show girl, then naturally I had this evil power. I was a big old seductress, and it was all my fault. Can I have a cigarette, Mr. Jordan?"

"Of course. I'm sorry."

"I don't smoke much. I can't afford it. But this . . . is making me nervous."

"Yes, it does that," he said, "to many people." He lit her cigarette. Sherry liked him very much.

"Well, they must have had some tough kind of talk with Ward. He didn't tell me; but I'm pretty sure they wanted him to ditch me, and he wouldn't. Anyhow, his folks gave up and left. Of course, he wasn't going to get a nickel out of them. The naughty boy doesn't get the candy.

"Well, that didn't bother me. When I couldn't get anywhere, trying to be a show girl, I just went back to waiting on table. We got along—till I got pregnant.

"Oh, Ward was really, you know, all *for* that. He even gave up trying to write to take care of me. He really did. He got a job clerking in a men's clothing store. I started to show too much pretty quickly, so I stayed home, and we got along for a while. Until Ward got sick. And that was really bad."

"What was his illness?" the lawyer said in a gentle tone.

"I see what you're wondering," she said. "It was the pressure? Sure. I guess so. And a lot of his friends kept telling him how it was too corny for words to be having a baby anyhow.

"Well, he wrote his folks because he had to. He was too sick to work, and I was going to pop any minute. So they wrote back stuffy kinds of letters, but they sent tickets. And that's when we came out here to Los Angeles. And we moved into their big fancy house, and everything was supposed to be lovely. Ward had three doctors. That's right, I counted. He had the whole world, on a tray. Me—I crept around the corners and tried not to make my big belly too disgusting or embarrass their friends by saying anything except, 'Yes, isn't it nice?' and, 'Yes, we are *so* happy.'

"So Johnny was born, and then *I* had everything. Or no, I guess you could put it this way. Johnny had everything. The first thing I knew, there I was, home from the hospital, feeling fine, and it took me quite a few days to notice that I wasn't getting to take care of my own baby. They hired a nurse. Very special. *She* knew everything: how to feed him, how to burp him, and change him, and all those things. When I'd want to do it, they'd say, 'Poor little precious, now you're just upsetting him.'

"You might think," she went on, "that I'd have relaxed and let the nurse do the dirty work, and all I'd have to do was eat and drink and lie around and do my nails." Sherry's head bent forward.

"You weren't the type, I imagine," Jordan said sympathetically.

"No. But the real point was Ward. By now, his mama finds out he's going to be a great writer. So she fixes him a study, all his own. Nobody can go in. *She* could, of course. But nobody else. Not me, for instance. His mama buys him an electric typewriter and a fancy lamp. And she makes everybody tiptoe past his door.

"And I could see what was beginning to happen to Ward. He took to going out, leaving the house, staying out all hours. He said he was observing, doing research. Maybe his mama believed it. But once in a while, when I'd get to go with him, I could see he was just going back with the far-out characters. He wasn't doing one single thing in the way of work.

"Well, I guess you read about it all the time. You're supposed to find yourself, they say. So I'm too dumb to understand. But it seems to me that I'm right *with* myself all the time, wherever *I* go." She looked at him fearfully.

The lawyer smiled at her.

"But you know," she said soberly, "the Reynards have a trap there. It's like blackmail. You can have everything you could possibly need and all the best, BUT— You've got to do as they do, act the way they think you ought to act.

"See, Ward's supposed to sit in his gorgeous private study and write great literature. And if he can't do it that way, his mama can't see why not. What can be the matter? The conditions are ideal! *Nothing* could ever get it through to her that she might not know how this stuff gets done. So, poor Ward.

"I thought: All right, we've got to get out of here. And we've got to get Johnny out, too. Because why should Johnny grow up inside a trap like that?

"Well, I finally— Oh, I had to fight! But I finally got Ward to agree. And wow, were there ever ructions then!

"Why in the world did we want to leave the good, right kind of life? It had to be *my* fault. *I* must want lowlife. *I* couldn't stand polite society. *I* didn't know how to behave in it. I wanted to *carouse.* (What's that, Mr. Jordan? That's what they said.) Oh, and I was a slob, too. Cleanliness and order made me unhappy, they said. I had corrupted Ward, too. *I* liked everything higgledy-piggledy (What's that, Mr. Jordan?) in some slum. Because, they said (get this), *I* didn't like discipline and responsibility.

"Well, the more they said, the worse it got, because they were driving Ward out of his mind. He had to stick up for me. Still and all, it scared him, I guess, that they said all that stuff about me. Oh, they weren't faking. They *believed* it.

"So one day I just took Johnny under my arm and walked out. And Ward, of course, came after me. He cried." Sherry stared at a paperweight. "But he came," she said, "so *I* was the villain. Because there I went again with my evil power."

She smiled wanly. "Well, I figured out how to earn the rent and still take care of the baby, most of the time. Ward went back to trying to write. We said to ourselves it was going to be just like it was before. But it wasn't.

"He didn't have even his high hopes anymore. I suppose it was in his head that he'd goofed, under 'ideal conditions.' And what they thought of me, how could he wipe out every bit of it? They were his mama and daddy. *Some* of what they said—he had to wonder whether there was *anything* in it, didn't he? So there he was in a trap and a kind of double trap, too.

"And the worst was, I couldn't seem to help him anymore. If I'd even try to talk about his writing, it always came up that I had no education. I came from the country. I was no intellectual. Well, that's true. I don't guess I'm the brightest brain in the world either. The only thing that I could do was try to keep my own feet under me." She fell back in the chair. "I should have stopped kidding myself long ago. I was saving the money. I thought we'd make it if we could only get ourselves back East. But you see—and I'd better tell you—I'm pretty sure, Mr. Jordan"—she swallowed—"Ward got to fooling around with some of those drugs they all think are so great."

"I see."

"I'm just about positive that's what was wrong with him yesterday morning. I'd seen something like that before. He'd go way off. What they call a bad trip? And wow, it must be bad! And there was a girl; she used to hang around with his friends. She went so far off they had to put her away. You see, he wouldn't have hurt Johnny. He's not a bad, evil brute. He loves Johnny. I know that. He loves me for that matter. But he couldn't *see* us. He was seeing snakes or something.

"So that's why it has to be over now. I could take my chances, but I can't take them for the baby. Now that's just a hard thing. Listen, I can be as soft and stupid as anybody in the world, but not about this. And you see why I can't possibly let Ward have Johnny? You see that?"

"I don't think there's much danger," the lawyer said, "that you won't get custody. It's the usual thing, Mrs. Reynard."

"Even when they have so much money?"

"You mustn't worry so much about money," he chided. Then he said that he had his car; he was leaving the office; could he run her back to her room? She looked very tired.

"Oh, gosh, that would be wonderful." Sherry sighed. "I will admit I've seen better days than these last two." She was turning her ring on her finger. Of course! If the worse came to the worst, as people say, she could always sell her diamond.

"Here comes the boyfriend," said Mrs. Kimberly.

"Oh-oh," said Mrs. Link. "And the Madame's seen them from the pantry."

"He's too old," said Mrs. Moran. "It may be the husband."

By the time Sherry, with cordial instincts, was asking Allen Jordan to come in a minute to see where she was staying, Mrs. Peabody had materialized and was standing with her right hand, palm up, in her left palm, her head tilted, and her odd eyes watching them intently.

Sherry was all smiles. She felt happy and comfortable with this man. He had listened to her; he had understood; he was on her side. In the moment Sherry loved him. But Allen Jordan had a well-trained sensitivity to atmosphere.

"How do you do," he said to Mrs. Peabody. "I am Allen Jordan, Mrs. Reynard's attorney."

The landlady's face changed slightly.

"Now, Mrs. Reynard," the lawyer said stiffly and formally, "if there is anything that I or my staff can do for you, please call. And oh, yes—I mustn't forget. I wanted the phone number here. Yes, I see where it is."

Briskly he wrote down the number from the pay phone on the wall of the entrance area, and then he went away briskly.

In his car Jordan wondered if he ought to call her back right away and say that in his opinion she had landed herself in a darned peculiar atmosphere. But then he thought: Nuh-uh. Mysterious phone call from male. That's only lighting the fuse, that is.

He'd have to trust Sherry to get the pitch.

Sherry was in her room and had picked up her hairbrush when the sense of it hit her. Funny. Yesterday Dr. Bianchi darting away up the stairs as abruptly as he had. This morning, when the actor fellow had not dared to look at her. And just now Mr. Jordan turning off the easy flow between them and pretending he'd come in only for the phone number, all business.

Well! How kind men were! She knew now that she had been protected. (Sherry, on the whole, got along very well with men, one reason she preferred the cocktail lounge to a tearoom.) Now she pondered Mrs. Peabody's rules and obvious fears. She remembered how the young doctor had told her, in the first place, that the landlady had old-fashioned ideas.

Well, well, so Sex was the Devil, and the Devil Almighty at that, and for the landlady with the one walleye, the Fear of the Devil was the Only Way? Why else, for instance, was she nicknamed the Madame?

Sherry grinned to herself and had the pitch. Okay, she thought, her natural optimism rising, so I'll be well chaperoned, and that's not bad, is it, right now?

Just the same, in a little while, she found herself in the sitting room approaching the ladies at their card table.

"Is it all right," she inquired, "if I sit out here sometimes?" Before they could answer, she said, "Oh, what a marvelous view you get of everything, don't you? My little boy is on the fourth floor. I wonder which windows are his?"

"How is he getting along?" Mrs. Link said in a friendly way.

"Oh, all right, but it isn't much fun."

"Has his daddy been to see him?" said Mrs. Kimberly.

"His father is not very well," said Sherry.

"In the hospital, too, is he?" said the third one, who seemed to Sherry to be the sharpest of the lot, although they all were pretty sharp, she had to admit, so maybe she had better say something more.

"No, Mrs. Moran," she said, "he's with his parents. I am suing him for divorce. What is the game you ladies play? Oh, I see."

"Do you play, Mrs. Reynard?" Mrs. Moran asked benignly. Sherry was glad to see that she had remembered the right name for this one.

"I'm afraid I don't know enough about it," said Sherry. "And it's kind of a foxy game, isn't it, really?"

"It passes the time," Mrs. Link said airily.

"Oh, there's luck in the cards," said Mrs. Kimberly.

"It's perfectly all right for you to sit out here, dear," said Mrs. Moran. "One very small room can be lonely."

"Yes, it can," Sherry said gratefully.

"Then you don't know our Dr. Bianchi?" said Mrs. Kimberly, as if she were continuing a topic.

Sherry explained about him. She couldn't help being a little curious herself about that young man. *He* didn't seem the type to be living here.

Mrs. Link answered her unspoken questions. "I believe," she said in her languid voice, "that Dr. Bianchi is the son of an old friend of Mr. Peabody's, which is how he got here in the first place. And Mr. Archer, of course, is a remittance man. That's an old-fashioned expression."

"I've heard of it," said Sherry. "I was *wondering* whether he was old-fashioned."

Mrs. Link's pale brows moved. "I would say that he is rather old-fashioned," she drawled. "Wouldn't you, girls?"

Sherry was working out the expression "remittance man." Didn't it mean that the man's family paid him for staying away? Oh! She let her illumination show and smiled at Mrs. Link.

"The Madame—oh, excuse me—Mrs. Peabody," said Mrs. Kimberly, "thinks that he has such a beautiful voice."

"He does, doesn't he?" Sherry said seriously.

Mrs. Moran nodded sharply, three times. Sherry had a funny feeling that she had just passed the examination. She said a little shyly, "I mustn't bother you," drifted elsewhere, and sat down.

The Norns began to play in a lively fashion, dramatizing the slap of the cards and adding little cries.

Sherry wondered whether she had thought she ought to make up to them, get them on her side. The fact was, what she really ought to be doing right now was writing her letters. But she seemed to have put herself in the position of having to sit here until it was time to go over to the hospital, call on Johnny for the last time today, and have her supper. Why should she have wanted to make friends? Well, why not, for gosh sakes? Her little room, so cold with all the white light, sure was lonely—very bleak and lonely. It was clear to her now that she had worked and worried too long, too close to her problems. She ought to have been finding, in this huge city, some staunch friends of her own, long ago.

She sighed and leaned her cheek on one hand and began to decide how much money she would ask for. What was the least sum she would need, and what was the largest sum she dared ask her Eastern oldtime friends to lend her, and where did the two coincide?

So, with her fair head bent, she sat in the faded blue chair for some twenty minutes. When she sighed and rose, the ladies said they surely hoped she would find her little boy feeling much better. Sherry thanked them.

They watched her cross the street and walk to the hospital entrance. "She's young," Mrs. Moran said in such a way as to indicate that she forgave this.

"Seems so lost," said Mrs. Link.

"She'll marry again," Mrs. Kimberly said briskly. "Whose deal is it?"

Chapter 6

CLIFF STORM returned to his apartment that evening at about seven o'clock and sat down, preparing to tie one on and the hell with dinner.

He was damned tired. He'd had a long day. And nothing to show for it but a lot of nebulous churnings in his mind. He was wondering whether Edward Reynard would give him A for effort but decided, in cold realism, not. He realized that he, Cliff Storm, had been suckered into believing that Reynard had known what he was talking about. Or Cliff had at least given this idea a high degree of probability. He wasn't so sure now.

He had started, in the morning, down his list, beginning in the neighborhood where the young Reynards had been renting an undistinguished small bungalow. There he hadn't found much that seemed useful. Most of the neighbors had simply stared, didn't know, didn't care, hadn't bothered, didn't want to get involved now either.

Mrs. Ivy, next door, had been willing to recount, to an old friend of Ward's, the events of yesterday morning insofar as she knew them. She didn't mind accepting praise for her own Good Samaritanism. But when Cliff began to ask further questions, such as had she heard screams and violent quarreling on other occasions, Mrs. Ivy began to close up. No. None. Not that she recalled. She didn't really know the people. She had set foot in their house only once or twice. No, they were just quiet neighbors.

"There is going to be a divorce, you know," Cliff told her. "Ward is pretty unhappy—very unhappy. I'm only wondering— There's not much a third party can do to help, I suppose. You are a woman of the world, I'm sure." (Cliff felt sure that no woman in the world would deny this. That was as unthinkable as any living person's denying that he had a sense of humor.) "Is there another man, do you think?" he asked her.

Mrs. Ivy had stiffened. She said, "I really wouldn't know."

"Or wouldn't tell?" he said with his version of a warm, admiring smile. "I understand. Mrs. Reynard worked nights. Home late, I suppose?"

Mrs. Ivy said that Mrs. Reynard went in and out like clockwork. *Mr.* Reynard might have kept more regular hours. At the very least he might have sat with the baby more often and saved the cost of a sitter. "Not that it's any of my business," she wound up righteously. He could sense the dawn of wonder. Why was it his?

"So," he said, "Mrs. Reynard did leave the baby with strangers?"

But Mrs. Ivy said that the regular sitter was a very nice older woman, a retired schoolteacher, who lived down at the far end of the block, a responsible person. That is, as far as Mrs. Ivy knew. She was definitely withdrawing, putting a brake on her tongue now.

Cliff studied her as a character. For what kind of part would he cast her? A skittish forty-odd, crept into her burrow, timid, one who would speak no evil, as a matter of playing it safe, if not for principle. Still, later on, when he had got his story line, he felt that this woman's very determination to remain aloof could be tinged with some hint that she might know horrors too vile to cross her pious lips.

So he said that he was glad to hear all this, because there had been rumors. But no wild parties here? No hard drinking? No mysterious males hanging around?

"Not that *I* know," she said, and he saw those lips sew themselves shut and how those eyes turned.

He rose to leave, saying that a good neighbor was a wonderful thing and that if the rumors were false, Sherry Reynard would surely need such a one as Mrs. Ivy fighting at her side.

He could see how the good woman began to panic. Didn't really, she protested, know a *thing* about them, really.

So Cliff walked on down the block to find the baby-sitter, pluming himself on his skill. Mrs. Ivy might be of no use to Reynard's side, but Cliff didn't think she would be much use to Sherry.

Miss Norene Erskine was in her sixties, a sparrowlike creature. Oh, yes, of course, poor Sherry Reynard. Miss Erskine had been so shocked to hear about the dear little boy. Did Mr. Storm know how he was getting along? Miss Erskine did intend to go to see him, but she had thought it not quite wise yet.

Cliff took his pose as the third party, amiably disposed toward both sides, probing in the faint hope of effecting some reconciliation here.

Miss Erskine did not approve of divorce either. Oh, she had seen children from broken homes. She chattered on, and Cliff was given the picture of a working mother who came home on the dot, breathless, to be sure her baby was safe and well. And the picture of an erratic father, who might or might not stay home in the evenings and, if he went out, might or might not return before midnight.

Sometimes, Miss Erskine said, she was called to the house as many as four nights in one week. Of course, more often it was only two or three evenings. Oh, she could understand that for the father to have been confined to the house every night of every week would not have been at all good for his work. She did admire artists and writers. She was, however, much impressed by Mrs. Reynard's determination to be with her child during the child's waking and learning hours. So many women worked these days and left their children to be taught heaven-knew-what by persons almost sure to be . . . well . . . not awfully high on the cultural ladder. Miss Erskine couldn't help regretting the loss of her job, naturally, but she did hope that dear Mrs. Reynard could find happiness again.

A soggy little creature, thought Cliff. God, what lives some people led! How could he use her? A tremor crossed his mind but went away unidentified.

"By the way," he said, "did Mrs. Reynard owe you any money?"

"Why, only nine dollars," said Miss Erskine. "The poor girl hasn't had time to think of me. And it really doesn't matter."

"You mustn't worry," said Cliff. "You do know, don't you, that the Reynards are on the wealthy side? If Sherry doesn't pay her debts, they will."

"Really?" said Miss Erskine, and her head moved in a birdlike jerk. Her large eyes, magnified by glasses, looked hostile.

So he began some undermining tactics.

"They are most concerned, really terribly concerned for that little boy," he told her. "But Sherry is being . . . well . . . stubborn. She seems determined not to take one penny from them. Even for the sake of the child. A poor kind of revenge, don't you think?"

"He is a dear little fellow, such a dear little fellow."

"I hope," said Cliff, "that you won't be embarrassed in the event she asks you for some money to go on with?"

"Oh, dear me," Miss Erskine said with a nervous giggle. "I count it a good week when I make ends overlap by fifty cents."

"Well," he said, "there is bitterness. Don't you find that people, in their bitterness, will ask for outrageous favors?"

"I suppose—" Miss Erskine said with moist eyes. "So often one wishes one could be just recklessly generous."

"I know you must be very fond of her," he sympathized. "But after all, when the Reynards are both wealthy and willing, it doesn't seem fair to ask other help. She can have all the money she'd ever need. Except for that . . . whatever it is . . . pride?"

"Pride can be rather expensive," Miss Erskine said grimly. "I haven't been able to afford much of it."

Cliff took the telephone number of the place where Sherry had worked, which Miss Erskine always kept, of course, in case the child were to become ill or anything like that.

"She's devoted to Johnny, you know," Miss Erskine said in a tearful way. "He is a beautiful child. She had a talented husband. They seemed so devoted. I can't understand—"

"Why it didn't seem to be enough?" Cliff said in a crafty sadness. "All that? People can be greedy in some strange ways, I suppose."

As he left, Cliff didn't think Miss Erskine would visit the hospital. But he had to admit that she hadn't helped his cause very much.

At the Club he spoke to a man named Herman Dodd. "Sure was sorry to lose our Sherry," the man said. "She's a darned good kid. No monkeyshines. No goofing off. Did her job. Cheerful, good-looking, too. I'm hoping she'll be back when the boy gets better."

Cliff said gravely that he feared not. He asked about Sherry's hours and whether she had ever . . . well . . . lingered on after work.

"Listen," Dodd said, "by the time they get off, these girls have had it. They're tired. They're most of them married, see, and they want to get on home, believe me."

"No, er, assignations then?"

Dodd bristled. What kind of place did Cliff think he ran here? Who was Cliff anyhow? The Watch and Ward Society?

So Cliff said quietly, "I work for the government."

This caused Dodd to shut his mouth and stare.

"I'd like to know," Cliff went on, "whether you've noticed any regular customer, for instance, who always sits at a certain table."

"Listen," said Dodd, "naturally I got regulars. I never noticed anything like that."

"Never saw," said Cliff, trying to be gimlet-eyed, "anything passed? I mean to say, given from hand to hand?"

"Nope," Dodd said. And added, "I'm sorry."

"I appreciate your cooperation," said Cliff, knowing very well what the word meant these days. Do what I say, it meant. Agree with me. There wasn't a lot of "co" in it anymore. "Do you happen to know where Sherry is now?" he asked.

Dodd was indeed anxious to "cooperate." He gave Cliff the address and hoped very much that *he* wouldn't have to talk any longer.

Cliff went off, musing the strange ways of a people who "govern themselves" and go in terror of their government.

Still, what did he have so far? Nothing.

So he tracked down Ward's friends, the two names that Ward's father had known and given him.

There turned out to be a nest of them. He found both named men and a third one, living in a tumbledown building on the shabbiest part of the beach. Next door lived two women who were wound tightly into the group. Cliff had a hunch that the living quarters were only theoretically segregated by the sexes and that these animals did not necessarily go in settled pairs either.

The lot of them were definitely dropouts. They were too old to be hippies, but although they had been born a decade too soon, they were a reasonable facsimile. Their kick was art as self-expression, with a tinge of health cultism on the side. Every one of them professed to be some kind of artist, and all vehemently despised the marketplace.

They knew Ward well. Potentially brilliant, they said. A seeker at least. Sorry to hear that he was ill. But had he been, as he ought, tuned in to the proper life currents, he wouldn't be ill. *They* were never ill. Ward sometimes tended to backslide. That was the disadvantage of having too much wealth in his background. He was not as wise as they, not quite.

As for his wife, yes, they knew her. Had met her. Seen her infrequently. Kind of peasant, wasn't she? They never had seen much of her, because she raced with the rats. Couldn't come around nights because she worked nights. Couldn't come around by day; she took care of the brat by day. What a waste, eh? They pitied her. Of course, if she wasn't such a dull clod and basically a coward, she, too, might have joined them in the only good life, although, as far as they knew, she had no creativity whatsoever.

Cliff listened and finally left them, having said little. He felt a slight nausea from the odor of their dwellings, and his mood was also tinged with alarm.

He fled to a bar he frequented, for solace, and fell in with a lawyer he knew. Having pumped him during the ritual of the cocktail hour, Cliff now knew more about the proportions of his task than he had before.

So, in his own chair, he brooded and felt dismay. What had his diligence turned up, so far, but a paragon of all middle-class virtues? A monster, this Sherry, to whom Cliff had already taken a solid personal dislike. She must be impossible! But why the devil hadn't Emily Reynard fallen on her neck? The girl must be just like Emily. But never mind that. Everything he had found out about her so far seemed just the sort of thing some elderly judge would think very noble and fine.

She evidently didn't openly brawl, drink to excess, sleep around, or—worse luck—neglect her child. Well, well. Possibly she had dark and devious tastes and appetites that could be discovered only by a personal watch on her every moment. Edward Reynard may have sensed a viciousness underground.

But if *he* had, then why had nobody else? Cliff could not (although he tried) remember any wisp that had come to him from any of those to whom he had talked today that hinted at such things.

And he was the lad to have caught such a hint. Cliff had antennae for any such currents. He ought to have. Sometimes there was money in them.

He thought, restlessly, that he surely did not want this business dragged out. No, no. Let the gamble be won at the soonest opportunity. If it could be won at all, that is.

Well, it could be won; if not this way, then that way. It seemed fairly plain that the surest and quickest way was to set up some kind of frame on the female. What would Cliff care if the fight were to be resumed in years to come? Or even the frame suspected? He would have won the prize, and he'd have it sewed up, with many signed papers and all that sort of thing, so that nobody could take it back.

He couldn't, offhand, think of any way to frame something on this monster of virtue. It appealed to his sense of fitness to try to use her stuffiness as a part of the plot. Nice little problem.

There was another thing to think about. He wasn't supposed to let her take off with the kid. But how could he stop her without having his eye on her? All right. He was going to have to move in close. He shrugged off the stray notion that he might attempt to put her into some kind of scandalous situation with himself as the party of the second part. In the first place, he had no faith in the efficacy of this kind of scandal in these latter days. In the second place, he was now officially old friend to Ward Reynard and about to become beholden to his father. The scent of conspiracy was there to be sniffed out by some smart fellow, especially if Edward Reynard did not learn better how to conceal his fanatical hostility.

What was that, anyhow? Cliff brooded. It was too strong to be simple snobbery. Surely Reynard, the elder, would never feel Cliff's present personal disgust for cloddish virtue.

What a born sucker this Sherry must be, to slave away so that she could pay Ward Reynard's bills!

But to a conclusion. All right. The upshot was, Cliff had better move in, establish acquaintance by pretending to renew it. He had to appear as himself since, for all he knew, she might recognize him. So do this in the clear, and trust to his luck and his talent. Cliff Storm had two convictions. One: All people could be manipulated. Two: Cliff Storm understood how to motivate them and produce any effect he liked. The question was, of course: What effect?

"I don't think," the male nurse said to Emily through the crack of the door, "you'd better come in right now, Mrs. Reynard."

"Oh, is he sleeping? But it's so early!"

"Well, no, ma'am, but I think . . . better he doesn't get, er, too stimulated right now."

"I see," she said, tipping her plump face with its tiny parrot beak of a nose. "I know he does need peace, most of all. Peace and rest, yes. I wouldn't bother him for the world! He does know, doesn't he, that I am always ready to chat or just sit?"

"Yes, ma'am," said the nurse. "But I think . . . right now— The doctor may come by. A little later."

"Well"—Emily sighed—"the doctor doesn't need me, does he? Perhaps then I *will* run over to my neighbors and play a few hands of bridge, just for an hour or so. It's not far."

"You go right ahead, ma'am. I'm here, don't forget."

"Such a comfort," she crooned. "Of course, you do know best." She turned away.

She tottered along on her high heels and tiny feet, going to her room to fix her face. Bridge would do her good, a little distraction. Ward was well taken care of; she need feel no guilt. His poor broken heart, she told herself, must mend in peace. But she felt a slight impatience, just the same. After all, that girl was a regrettable, unfortunate, but mere incident in Ward's life. She ought to be forgotten as quickly as possible. It must be the child, of course, that was bothering him. Once they had the child safe, then Ward would bounce back. Of course, he would! Emily felt she understood everything.

The nurse closed the bedroom door and looked behind him.

Ward Reynard was coiled against the head of the bed, his knees drawn to his chest, his palms pressed to his ears, his elbows angled sharply outward, his neck muscles taut. His eyes were unfocused, but wild. (Hallucinating, the nurse thought.) From his throat came a not very loud, but rapid, muttering, a stream of wordless terror. Any minute now, it might swell up into that funny kind of husky roaring he'd done a couple of times before.

The nurse had told the doctor about these spells, but he wasn't going to tell the mother. In the nurse's opinion, the old lady was one of those idiots who'd go barging right in where she didn't understand.

The nurse didn't feel that he had told a falsehood just now, because he certainly hoped that his charge wouldn't be "stimulated" or, in other words, "set off." Poor guy was suffering, something awful, and at any minute he might go higher than a kite without any outside stimulation at all.

It was true he hadn't, quite, those other times. He had just finally very slowly come out of it and gone limp at last. The nurse surmised that the fits might be psycho-induced. But still, they were funny. Well, it wasn't his business to decide what they were, but he had better watch himself, because you couldn't always sometimes tell.

He crept warily to a chair, hoping the doctor would get here and see-what-the-nurse-meant before *this* fit was over. Chees, he thought to himself, if the old man's right and it was this lousy dame he married who put him in this kind of shape, then shooting's too good for her! Because *this* shouldn't be happening to a dog!

Chapter 7

ON WEDNESDAY MORNING Johnny was feeling better. He had begun to trust those who were taking care of him, and he had even
struck up a swapping of boasts with the little boy in the next
bed over. So Sherry was able to let herself feel somewhat worse.
She sat beside him and spent another hour on her letters, rewrit-
ing all three. They were not easy to compose. Nothing was easy.

In an effort to raise her spirits, she phoned Allen Jordan, and
he, in a state of tightly controlled indignation, told her that the
other side was contesting for the property. This was, in his opinion, pure harassment, and it was going to guarantee that Sherry
would get it all, every penny, once they came before a judge. Of
course, she could touch nothing until then, except what might be
indisputably her personal possession. He promised that he would
put up a hard fight for an early hearing and felt sure that this
could be had. Sherry thanked him, trying not to sound dismayed.

But she was. The sense of having an enemy was very strong.
She went down in the elevator at noon, feeling blue and knowing that she had to eat even if she didn't feel hungry. She couldn't
afford to feel hungrier later on. As she went toward the coffeeshop, there was a man with a suitcase at his feet who seemed to
be leaning, lost in thought, against a pillar. When she saw her, he

straightened, frowned; then his face seemed to light. "I beg your pardon," he said. "Aren't you Ward Reynard's wife?"

"Yes, I am," Sherry said politely. He had a broad face, a big mouth, and an inconsistently fine-boned nose. She didn't remember that face, not quite. Or maybe . . .

"Look here," he said argumentatively, "I'm Cliff Storm. I've met you. It was a New Year's Eve party . . . mm . . . what year? What year? It was in New York."

"Maybe so," said Sherry, "New Year's Eve being what it is. But I'm sorry, I don't—"

"Look, Ward and I used to play cowboys and Indians in his backyard," said Cliff, who was affecting a joyous relief at the sight of somebody familiar. "I've known him since I can remember. How *is* Ward? And how are you?" When she didn't answer at once, he said, "Were you going in here? Let me sit down, have at least a cup of coffee? I happen to need company in the worst way. Will you, please?"

So Sherry went with him into the coffeeshop and settled at a table beside him, thinking to herself in guilty hope that if he offered to buy her lunch and she let him, it would save money. And didn't most girls think of that?

He stared at the menu; then he said, "Excuse me. I'm sure in a bad state. I should have asked what brings you here."

"My little boy is in here."

"I'm sorry."

"Oh, he's much better today," she said and gave her order to the waitress. Cliff ordered coffee and then seemed to change his mind and ordered a sandwich, too.

"You really don't remember me at all, do you, Sherry? I'm right? It *is* Sherry?"

"I do remember your name, I think," she said.

"Of course, I haven't seen Ward— How is he? Did you say?"

"Ward is with his folks. I guess I'd better say that we are getting a divorce."

"Oh, Lord, I didn't know that. I'm sorry." He seemed dashed down. "Still," he said, "that's the way it sometimes goes." Then he managed to contort his mouth and press his palm to his chest. He bent his head quickly.

"Is something the matter?" Sherry said in a moment.

"No, no." He lifted his head and smiled. "Well, it seems they carved me a little, a few weeks ago, upstairs here. They just now let me out. On a leash, that is."

"But shouldn't you go straight home?" she said with concern.

"Well, I'll tell you." He fiddled with the tableware. "Maybe I need to tell this to somebody. They said, you know, they got it all. That's what they said. But it seems, just to make sure, I'd better have some kind of fancy treatments. Every other day. Does that ring with a hopeful sound of joy to you?"

Sherry thought: Other people have troubles. Maybe I don't know what trouble is. She said, "But what you have to do is just do what they say." She smiled at him. "Who knows? *You* don't, really."

"I guess not," he said. "But it's like being in a kind of limbo. I sure don't feel like throwing myself back into my work, I'll tell you that."

The food came.

"What is your work, Mr. Storm?"

"You called me Cliff," he said coldly, "either four or five years ago. Oh, I'm in motion pictures. No, no, I don't act. Behind the scenes."

"And you like it?"

"Fine," he said listlessly. He was noticing her voice, a little husky, not the most cultivated voice in the world, but pleasant. Her table manners were dainty enough.

"Where are you living?" he said, changing the subject abruptly, as if he felt that he ought to force an outgoing interest.

"Nowhere," she said. "Well, I mean I am, temporarily, right across the street. It's just a rooming house."

"It is?" he said slowly. "Do they take men? Dying men?" he added. "I'd promise not to die on the premises."

Sherry put her fork down.

"Oh, Lord," he said quickly, "I'm sorry. I am a mess. Crawling with pity for me-me-me. I shouldn't be dumping this on you. Forget it, Sherry. Let's go back. I really had a practical thought there. If I do have to show up in this hospital every other day—"

"Oh, you do have to," she said earnestly. "I don't know whether there are any rooms for men or not. You could ask. It's a kind of weird old place, but it's not expensive."

"May not be a lot of point in my saving money. There I go again. Look, I'd go home, if I had one. 'Home is where, when you have to go there, they have to take you in,'" he quoted, while he assessed his progress. He thought she was feeling pretty sorry for him.

"You're not married?" she asked.

"I was," he said, "but not anymore. Or ever." He pretended to choke himself off and notice, for the first time, the three letters she had put down beside her plate. "Aha, you need some stamps," he said cheerfully. "Here, let me stamp those for you."

He picked up the letters and reached into his pocket for his book of stamps. "Airmail?" he asked.

"Oh! Well, thank you. Airmail, yes, please." Sherry was thinking of the twenty-four cents. She couldn't help it.

He licked and placed the stamps deliberately, taking care to fix each name and address very firmly in his memory while he was about it. All the letters were going East. Two to New York City and one to an unfamiliar town that must be upstate. "Shall I mail them for you?" he inquired.

"No, no. I'll do that. Thank you very much."

"Okay. You can pay me back by going out to dinner with me, like tonight," he said.

But her face changed. "I don't think so," she said. "I just don't think I ought to. Thank you just the same . . . Cliff. I'm sorry."

"Another time," Cliff said lightly. "What are your plans, Sherry? I'm guessing this divorce is in progress. Is it? Do you want to talk about it?"

"No, if you don't mind, I'd rather not talk about it. I'm just waiting for Johnny to get well. I guess I'm in a kind of limbo, too."

But her eyes offered no promise of company in a common misery.

So Cliff played it smart. He pushed away from the table. He picked up the check.

"No, no," she said.

"I am very, very sorry," he said firmly. "I would rather have bought you a big fat gourmet dinner tonight. But if I can't, then this will have to do. Please? I think you're good luck for me. There I was, not knowing, really, not knowing where to turn. So what's two dollars and seventy-five cents?"

"It's a lot to me," Sherry said frankly. "So I'll just say, 'Thank you very much.'" She watched him leave a tip, and it was a good one. Sherry approved. She ought to know about tips.

"Will you tell me the number of this rooming house?" he was saying.

Faintly troubled, she nevertheless promptly and generously told him. "There's a big signboard on it," she added. "It's going to be torn down pretty soon."

"I imagine it will stand as long as I need it," he said, rising, and doing so unsteadily, keeping firmly to his role. "See you," he said. "I wish I could be good luck for you somehow." He left the shop thinking: Corny, but not *too* corny for a man in my condition.

Sherry wasn't thinking of him as corny. If the man was frightened and in for long anxiety, she didn't blame him for dramatizing a little bit. She was trying to figure out why it made her uneasy that a friend of Ward's had appeared just out of the blue. She told herself that at least he was an *old* friend, not one of those idiots from the beach. He hadn't seen Ward for a long time, he said. He didn't have to know how Ward was now. Or how she feared he was. And what if she was wrong? Oh, then in miracle would Ward come tell her so?

Cliff was thinking that it had been odd how readily he had known who she was. He couldn't remember having observed her, those years ago, with enough interest to account for this immediate recognition. What was so distinctive? he wondered. She was a well-shaped female. Neither fat nor thin, tall nor short. He'd give her figure a high average. Her blond hair was clean and shining, but he had seen more stunning blond heads in his day. Her face was rather broadened at the eye level, with broad bones there, almost a Slavic look. Peasant, he thought. She was pretty enough. Good skin, the fine-grained kind that always looks clean.

He'd cast her as what? Well, in a feature picture she could be the pal, the good guy who did all the sympathetic worrying for the more interesting heroine. The girl who never got the man. No.

Odd that she simply did not give him the impression of being a dull collection of average physical traits. Nor did she seem the clod he had imagined, a bundle of middle-class moralities.

Why not? All right, it was the eyes. They were blue, and a surprisingly dark blue, in her fair face under the fair hair. It was the eyes that put the spark in, made the impact. The person was in the eyes.

Cliff found himself annoyed. For one thing, he had not expected to have his invitation to dinner refused. What had he done wrong? Not a thing. Unless he had jumped too fast. He had played on her pity, guessing she might be a sucker for weakness. He felt he had been right about that.

Well, then she must be on guard. Watching her step, eh? Figuring to walk the very straight and narrow. How straight and narrow could you get? Going out to dinner was scarcely a liaison. Hm, such caution was suspicious in itself, wasn't it?

He stopped in the hospital lobby to write down those names and addresses in his notebook. He wished he could have steamed open her letters, because they might have given him some clue. One of them was going to a man. The other two were for women. Well, the names might be useful. Wait, couldn't he be pretty sure these people must be old friends of hers from other days?

Yes, and it did seem that she might well be low financially. Take her crack about the two seventy-five. He knew she had left her job. He felt sure she had no other income. Whatever she and Ward had had together would be tied up. He knew that.

Hm, and she was stuck by herself in this decrepit rooming house. In a kind of limbo, eh? Hm, let her begin to be pressured, confined, restricted, lonely. Let her begin to crave whatever it was she had an appetite for and crave it pretty bad. One of these days she's going to talk to me about it, Cliff told himself, because wasn't I damned smart to make myself the safest confidant in the world, a dying man?

He grinned, pushed through the door, and remembered to cross the street at a snail's pace toward the old house he had already spotted. He thought: What a set for a Gothic, American style!

"Company?" said Mrs. Link. "Anybody know this fellow, girls?"

"If he's company," said Mrs. Kimberly, "it's got to be for Blondie."

"Suitcase," said Mrs. Moran. "He's company for the Madame."

They rocked and slapped the cards.

Cliff, pretending to inspect the front room upstairs, continued to study Mrs. Peabody. Even before he had heard her speech about the separation of the sexes, he had trotted out his tale of being a dying man. He had guessed that otherwise he might not get into the house at all. He would have cast her as a spinster, a small-town *Miss* Grundy, one who could be horrified by the slightest rumor that anybody had gone to bed with anybody at all. Well, she was too rigid for his purposes. Too easy to shock her, he thought. She's out of it.

He said, in the somewhat courtly manner he had assumed for her benefit, "If you will allow me, ma'am, I'd like very much to take this room." He gestured toward one of the windows which was half obstructed by the sign outside. "I don't mean to pry," he added, "but does that sign mean that this house hasn't long to stand?"

"It has until September," she said frostily.

"What a shame," he murmured, "that these fine old mansions don't seem able to survive! There is a need for rooming houses in this world, I'd say. Especially for lonely people."

"I don't know what my ladies will do," Mrs. Peabody said with a lift of both hands that added the old-fashioned "la."

(She's a relic, thought Cliff, a genuine antique!) "Excuse me, excuse me!" He feigned excitement. "I've thought of something. You have a Mrs. Sherry Reynard here? I know you do. You see, I ran into her at the hospital. It was she who sent me here."

The landlady's face was tightening.

"I'm a very old friend of her husband's family," Cliff said quickly, "and the point I want to come to— Edward Reynard (that's her father-in-law) happens to be a very wealthy man, with a good deal of property here and there. And I know, for instance, that he owns just such a house as this one. I should say it is about the same architecturally. At least as large. And it looks to be in excellent repair. Now Mr. Reynard doesn't want to sell the land it's on, not yet. He wants to hold it for several years. But, in the meantime, why shouldn't that house be occupied? He might be very glad to know of a person like yourself, who understands such a place and who is experienced at managing a rooming house. And, if you pardon me, Mrs. Peabody, would do so in a thoroughly refined and respectable way. I should think," he went on, watching the astonished hope blooming on her long plain face, "that he might be very willing to turn it over to such an experienced and reliable person at some low, perhaps only token, rental. Enough to cover, say, a part of the taxes. It would surely be worth something to him if the house were occupied. An empty house just goes to pieces. We all know that."

"Where is this house?" she asked breathlessly.

"I can't give you the exact address," said Cliff, "but I'll tell you what I'll do. I'll find out all about it tomorrow."

"Well, I . . . yes . . ." She was all afluster. "I wish you would, Mr. Storm, and if, as you say—"

"Now wasn't that lucky?" said Cliff. "Isn't it lucky that I happened to come here? Don't tell me the world isn't full of wonderful things!"

It went down well, coming from a dying man.

"I do hope," she fluttered, "you will find the room comfortable, Mr. Storm. The bath is not private; but it is very large, and I will say that it is kept scrupulously clean at all times. There are only two gentlemen to share. A Dr. Joseph Bianchi and a Mr. Lawton Archer, who has the room at the back. I am always very, very careful about the people I take in."

"I'm sure you are," said Cliff. "Would they move with you, do you think, if you were to take the other house?"

"Oh, I'm sure the ladies would," she cried. "I have three ladies who have been with me for years."

"I look forward to meeting the ladies," Cliff said with a bow.

"Of course. Of course. Certainly, Mr. Storm. Any time at all. They are all elderly ladies"—too old for all that, her one wild eye was saying—"very refined persons."

Such is the power of hope, Cliff thought cynically as he opened his suitcase and began to take out its contents. He'd have a crack at finding the house of Mrs. Peabody's dreams, if he had time. Otherwise, he'd just stall her long enough.

Meanwhile, he had secured *her* for Edward Reynard's side. For what that was worth. Well, you never knew.

That evening Sherry, knowing she could not sit with any composure under the eyes in the coffeeshop, asked for a sandwich to go and took it to the little park adjacent to the hospital grounds. There she sat on a bench and consumed her supper while tears rolled down her cheeks. It would not make for good digestion, this sort of thing, but that was the way it had to be, this evening, as the sun went down.

Then in the twilight she crossed the street with her face in ruin, hoping she could make it to her little cell without being caught in such a state as this.

She came in at the front door, passed the staircase gleaming now in lamplight, and then saw that man, that Clifford Storm, sitting in the sitting room just as if he lived there.

"Good evening," he called to her. "Hi, Sherry, how are you?"

"Oh, hi. There was a room, then?" said Sherry, keeping her face half turned. "Well, I'm glad. Good night."

But he was too sharp. "What is it?" he said, rising in concern. "Not the little boy?" He came to her, and he could certainly see now that she'd been bawling her head off. "Anything wrong?"

"No, no," she said. "He's all right. It's just . . . everything kind of came down on me, that's all. So excuse me. Good night."

"Don't go. Sit down," he coaxed. "Sit down. Listen, if you go off and cry all by yourself, you're going to make everybody else *miserable*. Don't you know that? Tell me about it."

"It isn't anything . . . Well . . . It's just—"

Sherry knew that the ladies were in their window. They had not greeted her. But their cards were pattering softly now because, of course, they were listening with every pore. She made up her mind suddenly and sat down. She had been weeping from anger; she was still angry; why in hell shouldn't she sit down?

"Johnny's grandmother came to see him," she said, "and that's what's the matter with me."

"Emily herself, eh?" he said at once.

"Oh, you know her? That's right. I forgot."

"Bit of a lightweight in the intellectual department, wouldn't you say?" Cliff lowered his voice.

"I don't know *what* she is," said Sherry, not lowering her voice at all. "But I wish— Oh, damn it to hell! I wish I *had* the great power they think I've got."

"Power?"

"Why is it always *my* doing? Why am I supposed to be able to make other people behave any way I want? Oh, it makes me so—"

"What have you done now?" he said in a drawl that relaxed her at once.

Just the same, she was not going to see the funny side as soon as this. (Cliff caught a flash from her dark blue eyes and found himself bracing.)

"See, Johnny took one look at her," Sherry said, "and went into a fit. He was scared, of course. So he cried. And he wouldn't stop, and that isn't good for him. So the nurses put her out."

"I'll just bet Emily didn't care much for that."

"You're darned tooting right, she didn't care much for that," said Sherry. "So what do you think? *I'd* put him up to it. *I'd* turned him against her. *I'd* fixed it for him to set up a howl at the sight of his dear loving grandmother, who never did anything bad in her whole entire life!" Sherry put her hands over her face, and now she was both laughing and crying. "Makes me so damned mad," she confessed.

"Oh, well," he murmured, "Emily Reynard's a pretty silly woman." (The fair hair was fragrant, he discovered.)

"Oh, she wasn't doing anything bad," said Sherry, wiping her face. "Maybe that's what makes me so mad. Only, she gets it into her head just exactly how somebody else is going to behave or ought to behave, and then, if he doesn't, she won't let it enter her head that things might look different from where *he* sits. Now Johnny is going to scare easy for a while. All right, somebody grown-up did hurt him. He knows that. You can't fool children."

"What grown-up hurt him?" Cliff said softly. He shouldn't have said this, but he wanted to hear her version.

"Oh, *who*, he doesn't remember," said Sherry. "Thank God, and I hope to God he'll never, and that nobody is going to tell him. The one thing he's sure of, it wasn't me. But listen, why would I want Johnny to cry like that for *any* reason? All I ever want is for him to grow up on his own feet. But oh, no. I tried to tell her he wasn't anything but just generally scared. Which he has a right to be. And if she'd just gone at him more slowly— The nurses all knew that. In the beginning they all knew to go slow. They didn't expect him to be instant cozy. And when he wasn't, they didn't turn around and blame me for setting a little tiny boy against them.

"Oh, I am so spitting sick," cried Sherry, "of all this blame, blame, blame! What's the matter with people? Listen, things happen to you. They even get done to you. But afterward *you're* there, aren't you? *You* do what *you* do. Sure you do," she said and sighed deeply. "Look at me, practically throwing a tantrum. And it feels good, too. It sure is great sport to rant and rave sometimes."

"No harm," he soothed. "What's the harm?"

"I don't know," Sherry said soberly.

"Listen, who can blame you for blowing off?"

Sherry's face began to fold into her mischievous smile. "I thought you were listening," she said. "Well, thank you anyhow." She got to her feet.

Cliff Storm put the back of his head on the chairback and stared up at her. "I was listening," he said rather tensely. He felt lost. He didn't understand what she'd just said. This annoyed him.

"Good night now," she said. "Good night, everybody."

The Norns uttered false little cries, as if they had only now noticed that she was there.

Sherry went into the passage and opened the door to her room, put on the light in there, and walked in, feeling a pleasant calm.

It had done her good to blow off to a man who seemed for some reason so easy to talk to, so much her contemporary. He must be Ward's age, but he was older than Ward in a way. It was as if he stood on his feet, and she on hers, and so there could be a free exchange, as between equals. It crossed her mind that he didn't seem to be the same man who had been so wound up in self-pity and the fear of death at noon today.

Well, then, if he was rising up out of a temporary panic, so much the better, and she was glad.

Cliff dismissed his feeling of having been mysteriously hit somehow and began to review what had been said. The three elderly women at their card table had heard every bit of it, he felt sure. Could this be of any use? He had already politely introduced himself to the ladies when he had come in from dinner a little while ago and had assumed the fascinated curiosity in their ancient eyes to be the usual pathetic grasp after a life that had left them behind. (He did not realize that the Norns had not seen a young and personable man settle down to an evening in *this* parlor before and were dying to know why.) Cliff was thinking that Sherry had used a word or two that may have fallen offensively on genteel ears.

He rose and sauntered toward them.

"I hope that hasn't upset you ladies," he said solicitously. "It's just a very unhappy situation."

"You're an old friend of Mrs. Reynard's, are you, Mr. Storm?" said Mrs. Link, patting her coiffure.

"Well, I met her years ago. I know her ex-husband-to-be very well. Divorce is always sad," Cliff said piously.

"Depends, doesn't it?" said Mrs. Kimberly, slapping a card down.

"Of course, nobody on the outside has the right to judge," Cliff said, looking down his nose morosely. "Two sides to everything, so they say." He congratulated himself on two clichés in a row.

"Your friend, her husband, isn't well, I understand," said Mrs. Link. "What's wrong with him?"

"That's hard to say," said Cliff. "He's pretty much an emotional wreck. I can say that. Poor guy. Oh, you can laugh at the cliché 'mental cruelty.'"

" 'The wicked flee when no man pursueth,' " Mrs. Moran said unexpectedly. All the Norns seemed to be nodding sagely.

Cliff couldn't make any sense of the remark, although he thought it sounded as if it might be from the Bible. Probably the phrase was loaded, for these old bodies.

"Ward's father," he told them, "is at least a millionaire, you know. But some things money can't buy."

The Norns seemed to accept this as a deep insight.

"I'm not so much thinking about high temper and scenes," he went on. "There are other humiliations, some I'd hate to mention. I'm afraid there are goings-on today that ladies didn't used to dream of."

"Tch. Tch. Tch." The ladies, all three, clicked their tongues.

Cliff had an inspiration. "A virtuous woman," he intoned, "is more valuable than rubies."

All the Norns bent their heads over the table, as if in prayer. Then Mrs. Moran's old claw scooped up a trick with three hearts in it.

"Shooting the moon, dear?" said Mrs. Kimberly, squirreling her cheeks.

"Oh, you're a sinner," Mrs. Moran said amiably.

"*Mrs.* Reynard is the sinner, eh?" Mrs. Link said so patly upon the other words that Cliff had to gulp as he realized he was supposed to answer.

"Oh, I'd try to keep an open mind," he said in a bit of confusion. "Don't hold it against her, ladies, that she . . . well . . . uses language."

"Who can find a virtuous woman?" Mrs. Moran said in a Biblical chant, " 'for her price is above rubies. She openeth her mouth with wisdom, and in her tongue is the law of kindness.' And now, my good women," she continued in the same tone, "give unto me the thirteenth heart, whoever hath it."

They hooted and rocked, for Mrs. Moran, in the meantime, seemed to have shot the moon.

Cliff drifted away. In a moment he said, "Good night, ladies," and went thoughtfully out of the house.

Mrs. Kimberly, shuffling the deck, said softly, "Hell of a handy thing, money."

"Ladies didn't used to dream about what?" said Mrs. Link. "How does he know?"

"So she took a lover?" Mrs. Moran said with her dainty snort. "Big deal! Couldn't be, could it, she took *another* lover, since his day?"

"Girls, girls," said Mrs. Kimberly, "he's supposed to have his mind on dying."

"Hoo," said Mrs. Moran, "I doubt that's what he's got his mind on."

"Oh, you," said Mrs. Kimberly, slapping her friend's wrist, "getting as bad as the Madame."

They rocked and hooted, and Mrs. Kimberly dealt the cards.

"Sex, does he imagine," said Mrs. Link, "we didn't dream about?"

"He thinks we thought it *was* the stork," Mrs. Moran said glumly.

Mrs. Kimberly had such a fit of the giggles she had to take off her glasses and clean them.

"Why are you *there?*" Edward Reynard said on the phone.

"The point is," Cliff said smoothly, "nothing that happened too long ago is any good. Better be something going on now."

"Yes, I see that. Where is this place?"

Cliff told him and ran down the list of tenants, sparing none.

"Just the kind of place she'd pick," Reynard said bitterly. "Half-wits, alcoholics, senility, perversion."

There was a hollow spot in the back of Cliff's mind wherein he was well able to perceive the workings of prejudice. He could hear the antagonism that twists facts. Even if Cliff were to point out that Mrs. Peabody's rooming house had been Sherry's choice, not because of the inhabitants but because it happened to be cheap and handy, this fact wouldn't even go into the balance. Not that he was going to point it out, of course. It suited him to keep the antagonism going.

He said, "Oh, you're right. It's a pretty rum bunch."

"Both sides have filed suit," said Reynard. "We—I should say Ward—got in first. But her lawyer is pushing for an early hearing. Murchison thinks it will be soon. So you'd better get on with it."

Cliff threw in some evidence of his industry. He said he had talked on the phone with people back East who had known Sherry there. "But then, as I say," he added, "all that would be too long ago." He did not throw in the information that while he was on the long-distance telephone, he had thought he might as well sow, within his excuse for calling, the seeds of discord. That trick about working for the government had been a good one and had borne repeating.

"Can you get something that is useful?" Reynard was barking. "Any progress?"

"I think I have a bit of a hunch," Cliff said cautiously. "I don't want to say until I'm sure. You need solid proof, so I understand."

"What is it? Something important?"

Effective, you mean, thought Cliff. "If I can get the proof," he said, "this should be important enough. But it's . . . well . . . tricky."

"Just keep pushing," said Reynard.

Cliff promised that he would do so and hung up.

The fact was, he had no hunch at all.

He was also irritated to find himself in the position of the expert employee who knew more about the job than his employer did. Edward Reynard's notions of what might prove effective were hopelessly antiquated.

Emily Reynard said to her husband, "Wouldn't it be better to postpone this hearing until Ward is really himself again? Couldn't Mr. Murchison put it off?"

Her husband said, "On the other hand, it would be good to have it settled about John *before* he is ready to leave that hospital."

"Oh, I hadn't thought of that," she said.

"Leave this to me," he said crossly. "I'm keeping my eyes on her."

"Ward's feeling better every day, of course," said Emily, because she wished he were. Immediately she began to sniffle.

"Now, please," said her husband.

"She's just . . . such a horrible mistake. So many *nice* girls in the world, too. I was afraid of her, in the very beginning. Something told me—"

One pale blue eye watched him over her handkerchief.

"He was a fool," Edward Reynard said harshly. "But he knows it now."

Cliff Storm left the phone booth and found a friendly bat cave. He began to think about those old ladies. He had to admit that he had miscast them. He had carelessly taken direction from Mrs. Peabody's script. If they were not the mild old pussycats, prim and refined, that he had assumed them to be, how would he cast them now?

Hm. Three old ladies, with a little salt on their tongues, would make impressive witnesses, wouldn't they? In fact, wasn't that what they were? They watched, and they listened; they were nothing but witnesses. So what sort of episode could he stage for them to witness?

He was very nearly convinced now that he was going to have to frame that girl, that Sherry. He had better bend his talents to figuring how.

Chapter 8

ON THURSDAY MORNING Sherry counted her cash. She had fifty-two dollars and thirty-five cents. Some things from the drugstore she'd *had* to buy. But she had saved on yesterday's meals. A free lunch, and only that sandwich for her dinner. She was now ravenous.

Dr. Bianchi was just leaving as she emerged into the public part of the house. He bade her a breezy hail and farewell, while his quick brown eyes made a fast check of her whole person. Sherry grinned at him.

Mrs. Peabody was alone at her post in the dining room, but almost immediately Elsie appeared with the pitcher of orange juice.

"Good morning," Sherry said cheerfully to them both. "That's a pretty dress, Elsie," she said to the poor girl, unable to resist trying to bring some life into the blankness of that face. "Pink is a good color for you," Sherry continued.

There was no immediate reaction, and Sherry remembered the young doctor's repetition of a phrase. But evidently Elsie *could* hear the first time, and if you waited, she would respond.

"I had feathers around my neck," Elsie said in a moment. "And down at the bottom of the skirt, too."

"Oh?" said Sherry, wondering if this was indeed any kind of reply.

"And they came, and they shot at all the bottles," Elsie said in a childish intonation, but with some animation.

Sherry realized that it was response. She was being offered some token of a willingness to be friendly, too. But she felt lost. She glanced at the mother.

"Television," said Mrs. Peabody, her wild eye sad.

"Hey, I bet that was exciting!" Sherry said at once. "They were cowboys, were they?"

Elsie's face was showing what was almost a glow.

(Cliff Storm, at the archway, held back his greeting and kept himself silent to listen for a moment.)

"I hit one with a bottle. It broke," Elsie said earnestly.

"Did he fall down?" said Sherry.

"Oh, yes, but then they tore my dress."

"Well!" said Sherry, unable to continue the fantasy any further, but marveling that there was this much coherence in the reporting of fiction. She smiled at the girl and picked up her glass.

Elsie opened her mouth to go on, but her mother, insensitive to the fact of dialogue, said, "Pour Mr. Storm's juice now, Elsie," and repeated, at once, the same words. The girl blinked and obeyed.

So now Cliff made his good mornings, and Sherry was a little surprised—and rather amused—to hear Mrs. Peabody coo at her new (and male) roomer. She wondered what Indian sign he had on her. He wasn't any neuter. In fact, he had a kind of dark force that ought to have alarmed the landlady's sensibilities. It was difficult to remember that his health might be in any question at all. He was being yet another person this morning. His manners were just too antique for a man his age.

The Norns arrived, and on their heels came Lawton Archer, wrapped in some tragic garment, invisible, but there for all to sense. Elsie approached him with her mouth a little open, her eyes rounded, and a slight huffing of her breath. The actor only just kept from cringing while she poured juice for him. To this the landlady was sensitive, but accustomed. With a crisp double command she banished her daughter to the kitchen.

Cliff Storm wasn't missing a thing. Sherry, discovering that even limp toast could be absolutely delicious, was happy to see that he was up for examination today. She watched him rising to the test, becoming deferential toward the Norns, as if they were made of old porcelain. Then he sent to Sherry (who had a hunch they were no such thing) the merest twinkle to tell her that he didn't really think so either.

When Sherry left the table, saying that she had an errand, she couldn't help feeling that things were looking up. The addition of Cliff Storm to the group at breakfast was a distinct improvement.

Cliff hurried through the rest of his breakfast, and with a glance at Mrs. Peabody that caused her to flush, he said that he had an errand, too.

When he had gone, the landlady confided in the Norns. There was this house! Mr. Storm just happened to know of it. The whole thing seemed almost too good to be true! But she hoped the ladies had not made firm arrangements for the fall.

Mrs. Link said she really didn't know. She was quite vague. Mrs. Kimberly said she didn't especially want to go to Senior City and perhaps— Where was this house? Mrs. Peabody confessed that she did not know the exact location yet. But Mr. Storm, poor gentleman, had gone off to find out everything. *Wasn't* he the nicest gentleman? And so thoughtful!

Mrs. Moran said he'd get a commission no doubt and added that although she had half promised to go to her son's house, her daughter-in-law would not be offended if Mrs. Moran were to change her mind. Everything, however, depended.

An aura of hope in suspension hung over the dining table.

Sherry went to a jewelry store and offered her ring for sale. The man was reluctant to deal with her; he didn't buy in this way. But he sent her on to another man who might. The other man would, but the price he named was shocking to her. She had always been sure and proud that she wore on her finger a diamond worth eight hundred dollars. But this man said he would pay her four hundred and seventy-five. It seemed much too little. When she said so, he shrugged and said she could try for more, but he doubted she would get much more, and to get *any* more would take long, hard searching. Up to her, of course.

Sherry thought about this and was inclined to believe it. She couldn't afford the bus fares, for instance, to run all around town. So she did arithmetic in her head and decided that she had better take what she could get right this minute.

He was kind enough to go with her to the branch bank next door and see to the cashing of his check—so kind that she began to be afraid she *had* sold it too cheaply. But it was done.

She then bused to an airline office, inquired carefully about taking with her a child not yet four years old. Johnny could go free on her lap. Where else should Johnny be? Sherry thought jubilantly. So she bought and paid for a ticket to New York, tourist class, and tucked it very securely into the deepest zippered recess of her handbag. Now she felt better!

The rest of the ring money she must save to take care of the hospital bills. She thought it would cover them nicely. If anything went wrong in the matter of the savings account or delayed the hearing, Sherry didn't intend to be without the money to pay for Johnny. No matter what, she must have that.

But she must pray that Johnny could go straight from the hospital to the airplane. In New York her best friend, Pat Sims (Anderson now), would take them in until Sherry could get to earning. So if Johnny could travel, and if she could struggle along until then, she just might be all right, without depending too much on anything else good to happen.

She phoned Mr. Jordan to see what was happening. He told her that her suit had become the countersuit, which didn't really matter. He still hoped for a hearing very soon. He was pressing for that, he told her again. He also took the occasion to warn her that the judge was bound (Did she realize?) to make some effort toward a reconciliation between the parties.

Sherry said that was too bad. It would just take up the judge's time.

But as she stood on the curb, waiting for her bus back to the hospital, she had to keep saying to herself with all her might, No! No! No! Ah, but if she only could— There was some little old song. Ward was fond of it. "Blow, blow, thou western wind. That the small rain shall rain. . . ." Maybe that wasn't quite right. But the rest of it, the rest of it, she remembered too well: "Christ, that I were in my bed! And my love in my arms again!"

But no! No! No!

When the bus came, she crept aboard, bent to her sorrow and her loss and feeling a thousand years old.

When she reached the hospital, it was time for lunch, so she went into the coffeeshop, the cheapest eating place she had found handy. She was very hungry, but she chose the low-calorie plate, which cost the least. She might lose a little weight? Okay, call it a fringe benefit.

She couldn't keep her mind off money. She would not touch the rest of the ring money for her own keep, unless she had to or starve. More rent would be due next week, but by then a loan from one or more of her friends would have come in the mail and she'd be fine. Meantime, fifty-two thirty-five, minus all those bus fares (a dollar ten cents), minus this seventy-five-cent meal, and also minus a tip, because Sherry (of all people in the world) couldn't not leave a tip.

Wait! When she had eaten, she sought out the manager of the shop. Did he, by any chance, need an experienced waitress? The man was sorry, but he did not.

Sherry sighed, thanked him anyway, and went upstairs to Johnny. She still had fifty dollars and twenty-five cents. (Quite a lot, she told herself.)

Cliff Storm hadn't been there in the coffeeshop. She wondered if he was elsewhere in the building, taking one of those treatments. Probably it's my duty to cheer him up, she said to herself, and let him buy my dinners. Her mouth quirked. Sure was easy to figure that way. Most girls did. Why had she refused his invitation?

Well, the truth was, Sherry wasn't exactly a girl. Neither maid, wife, nor widow, kiddo, she reminded herself. And there's your limbo for you.

When she got to the ward, a woman she had noticed before, one who visited another child, saw her and started toward her. She was very young, with black hair tortured into an intricate pile that must have taken hours to achieve.

"Say, er, look," she said to Sherry, "there's this man I'm going with, who's got this friend? So we were going out on the town tonight, like about nine o'clock? And I'm supposed to get somebody. So would you want to double-date maybe?"

"Oh, I don't think so, thank you," Sherry said quickly. "I couldn't."

The girl's jaw moved as if she were chewing gum. "Well," she said and shrugged, "I asked."

Why *me?* thought Sherry. That was funny. Out of all the women here, how did she know *I* wasn't going home to a husband and four more kids?

Well, she mused, things get around. Dr. Bianchi could have heard it in the house, about my divorce. He'd have mentioned it to some nurse? This didn't ring quite right, but what other explanation was there? The incident gave her a strange feeling.

She settled down to the long afternoon, thinking that someday, one day, something like this would happen and Sherry would go. But not now. Not at this time. Not for a long time. Do I look, she thought sadly, do I already look as if I'm hunting?

When she went out into the corridor to borrow a stuffed toy from the shelves there, the girl with the high hairdo was talking in a phone booth. She saw Sherry and turned her back. Sherry couldn't sense anger in her turning. There seemed to be caution in it, as if Sherry might be a lip-reader. Come on, said Sherry to herself, what are you, stir crazy?

But it was . . . well . . . funny.

Cliff Storm had a busy, busy day.

As he went out of the house early, he realized that the Norns (he had been told the nicknames current in the place by Joe Bianchi and had found them amusing) were safely in the dining room and Sherry had gone on her errand. So he took the opportunity to slip along the far side of the building and examine carefully Sherry's ex-sun porch from the outside.

Yes, that had been a door. Cliff discovered that it was locked, with the key still there on the inside, but it had also been nailed closed. The nails were not formidable. It might be useful to arrange for Sherry to have available a secret exit and entrance. Then he, the stage manager, could say, "See, you thought she was locked in a box, but she wasn't!" Or he might say, "See, you thought she was out, but she was in!"

He then suffered a revulsion, because he was a creative imagination and not a carpenter, for God's sake. He decided to strike out elsewhere. Maybe he wouldn't have to go to all that trouble.

He got into his car, which he had parked on the street, and, lacking anywhere else to strike, took off for the beach again. Nobody was there, except one of the women, who was sitting, cross-legged, in the middle of the floor in one of the old shacks, wearing a leotard and banging away on a tambourine. She looked at him with strange eyes. She was talking to herself in an excited way. She made no sense to him.

He watched her for a while. Then, craftily, he got out of her at least the nickname for the drug she had taken and, furthermore, the location of her supply. It was right there in the room, a tin box in which there were a number of miniature sugar lumps (each impregnated, he presumed) and also a heap of hard candies. Cliff calmly stole two of each. He couldn't tell whether or not the woman knew what he was doing. At any rate she made no protest. She didn't relate. She didn't react to him. She appeared to be as mad as the proverbial hatter, and Cliff thought this was very interesting.

He didn't know what he was going to do with this loot. He felt rather in the position of the general who was lining up his troops.

Or, perhaps, just a junk collector who never knew what might not come in handy.

He then went to the trouble of visiting a real estate broker in a likely part of town and locating a vacant house of the proper vintage that was for sale. Cliff told the man a tale; he had a buyer. But the deal was contingent on the decision of a couple who might or might not be interested in opening it as a rooming house. He promised to send them around. Would it be possible to make an appointment to show the house in the evening? Was there electricity on?

There was, the man said, and eagerly promised to show the lady and her husband, at any time, this lovely old mansion so-spacious-they-don't-build-them-like-that-anymore. (Or otherwise, this white elephant.) Cliff said he felt sure the lady would make no decision without her husband's approval, but the husband was naturally not always available during working hours. Cliff would call him back.

Later in the afternoon he was delighted to find Mr. Peabody pushing the vacuum cleaner in the upstairs hall, as Cliff came staggering with a case of Scotch.

"How's that," he panted as he put the load down on his bed, "for a hedge against the long chilly nights of April in the Southland?" Mr. Peabody had been drawn, fascinated, to Cliff's door.

"I don't imagine," said Cliff, "your good wife would be too happy about this. Where's a good place to stash it? *Por favor, amigo?*"

"She don't do too much of the cleaning up here," said the landlord, dry-lipped.

"Is that a fact? Well, I hope you're not the man to say I shouldn't have taken advantage of a bargain. Listen, be my guest. We'd better test it out, see if I've been gypped. No ice. Well, so much the better for the real test, eh? Numbs the taste buds, ice."

Cliff handed the man a half-filled water glass, which Mr. Peabody took with no coyness whatsoever.

"You wouldn't believe," Cliff rattled on, "how cheap I got this stuff. So if it's stolen goods, what do I know? The labels look good.

Maybe I'd better get rid of the carton. If you're thinking," said Cliff, sinking down on the bed with his glass in his hand, "that this could speed me to my doom, forget it. What a way to go, eh?"

Mr. Peabody said he was not the man to blame anybody for taking a drop of comfort.

"Say, take a fifth for yourself. Go ahead. Take two. I just happened to think; I may not be around long enough to guzzle all that."

Mr. Peabody looked shocked and drank deep to comfort himself.

"No ladies upstairs at any time, eh?" said Cliff. "Too bad. Tell you who's a two-fisted gal with the liquor. Your Mrs. Reynard."

"Is that so?" said Mr. Peabody. "Well, she better use a good mouthwash, is all I can say. Miz Peabody, she just might throw her out."

"Is that so?" Cliff said sadly. "Too bad. Doesn't go for a man, eh? Or does it? What about you?"

"Me?" Mr. Peabody needed more comfort and got it without words. "Listen, you don't want to think I don't know maybe it's getting a little bit the better of me," said the landlord. "But a man's got to have something." He had sat down on a straight chair; he put his elbows on his thighs, and with both hands, he cradled and caressed the glass. He glanced at Cliff with a touch of shame. "And anyhow," he said with bravado, "what a way to go!" This had now become a very witty saying. They toasted it.

"Listen, Mr. Storm, about this house? I mean, you really do think we might—" The landlord's eyes had become somewhat moist and doglike.

"Certainly," said Cliff. "I saw it again this morning. In a very nice neighborhood, too. And the owner is interested, in a tentative way. The next thing for you and your wife to do is go have a look. See if it suits you. You know your business, I'm sure."

Mr. Peabody's eyes filled with tears. "Listen," he said, "with my poor kid and all, the heart's out of me. What *I* do is, I do the heavy cleaning. That's about what *I* do. So I'm the janitor, you might

say. *That's* my business." Mr. Peabody seemed headed for a crying
jag.

"I don't want you to take this amiss," said Cliff, "but have you
ever thought of putting your girl—Elsie, isn't it?—into some
school? Seems to me there are such places, where she'd be happy."

"Oh, she's happy." Mr. Peabody wept. "All she does is watch
television, but she's happy. Oh, them schools. Listen, they cost
something fierce. We went into that one time. Miz Peabody, you
know, she don't want to ask the state or the county. But these
private places, what they call prevocational? It's too much. See,
Elsie is just . . . well, I mean, she's not *crazy*. I'll tell you, Mr.
Storm, I sure wish we could do that for her. She don't learn a
thing, hanging around here. Augh, it's pitiful to me, all that
TV. Well, she's *got* no life. She's got no life.

"But then again, Mr. Storm, I'll tell you what scares the liver
out of me. I mean, you know, she's getting to be— She's older
now. I guess you noticed the way she moons around after the
fellow in the back room? Of course, *he's* safe. I guess you got that
figured."

"Right," Cliff said comfortably. "I've been trying to figure how
come your wife lets him live here."

"It could be," Mr. Peabody said gloomily, "she don't know. All
she knows, she thinks he's a gentleman. The way he puts on and
the way he talks and all that. And she can see how he don't *like*
it. She thinks that's nice. But still and all, not everybody is going
to be that safe."

"I know what you mean," said Cliff, "and you're right. It is
dangerous. I've read somewhere that girls like Elsie are too vulnerable. She'd have no defense. Wouldn't even understand, poor
kid."

Mr. Peabody was sobbing in an accomplished way.

Cliff refilled his glass. "Man, you need it!" he said. "Yes, I guess
those schools train such people, and then they place them in
some job they can handle, and that would be a whole lot better,
I agree. Now the thing is, I happen to know a couple of fairly
prominent— I'm just wondering if I couldn't pull a couple of

strings. I have a hunch Mr. Edward Reynard could help that way. He's a big contributor to lots of good works around town."

"You're a good man, Mr. Storm," said the landlord when he found his voice. "I don't see why you're taking this trouble for a couple of perfect strangers. A *good* man! May heaven bless you, Mr. Storm."

"Hey, knock it off, *amigo*," said Cliff. "I'm not going to believe in heaven till I get to the gates. Still, I might not make it that far, eh? Maybe it's smart to be on the safe side, in case the rules are what they say."

He was judging Mr. Peabody to be on the safe side now, all right.

After a while Lawton Archer came out of his room and went into the bathroom, which was halfway along the hall. Cliff called to him as he emerged. "Care to join us?"

Archer said he would take a very small shot and lap it up gratefully. He was as gloomy as usual, with his raven locks awry and his voice richer than life.

"How's the theatah?" said Cliff. "Or is it the cinema?"

He was turning in his mind the fact that he would soon have the power to hire an actor. But this was different. He was afraid he couldn't use Archer. After all, business was business. Cliff didn't intend to risk *himself* or anything of *his* in this gamble. Poor Archer was too much. His tragic pose was probably the way he handled his basic problem, but Cliff couldn't afford to feel too sorry for him.

"Did you know," he said idly, "that you have a fellow Thespian in the house? Sure enough. Sherry Reynard used to be in show biz, as I recall."

Archer's dark eyes lit briefly. "I must say it would be pleasant to talk one's own language on occasion," he said stiffly. "Not that there's much chance here."

"Doesn't Mrs. Peabody ever go out?" Cliff said jovially. "I mean, what she doesn't know can't hurt her, can it?"

The landlord was too soggy by now to deny that he was inclined to agree. But he then pulled himself into a remembrance of loyalty and said that they were kind of stuck, a lot of the time, because of Elsie.

He then cast an odd glance at Archer, gripped a full bottle of whisky firmly under his arm *and* sweater, and departed damply.

"I can't help noticing how our Elsie tends to swoon in your presence," Cliff said to the actor. "You watch that, I suppose."

There was no note of sarcasm in his voice, but the actor nevertheless stiffened.

"I think I shall be forced to find other living quarters very soon. It has become an embarrassment and a harassment. Poor misbegotten creature," he went on. "One ought never to be kind to such people." His eyes shot defiance. *Don't be kind to me,* they warned. "That's a pity, if you like," he continued, his lids swooning, "but it doesn't do."

"Hey, what am I missing?" Joe Bianchi was grinning at the door.

This sent Archer scurrying to his hole, and Joe came in, still grinning, and was offered a drink.

"Why doesn't he go where they are?" said Cliff. "Who does he think he is, a martyr?"

"You hit it," Joe said cheerfully. "He's got it in his head the whole world's against him. Well, that gives him something to think about, you know."

Cliff was deciding that Archer wasn't going to be of any use to him in his schemes.

"Well, now," he said lazily, "speaking of the opposite sex, how are the chances for luring, say, our little blond grass-widow-to-be up here, like in the wee hours?"

"Fer-git it," said Joe. "The Madame's got cat's ears. And believe me, she can diagnose every creak in them stairs, like you wouldn't believe. She's a pretty innocent woman, the Madame."

"I see what you mean," said Cliff. "Don't get much pay, you fellows, eh?"

"You're wondering why I stay in this dump," said Joe. "I guess you got it pinpointed."

"Need a loan?" Cliff said carelessly.

"Nope," Joe said promptly. "Not me. I figure to keep all my ill-gotten gains, once I start to ill-get them." In a moment he said, "How are you feeling?"

"No particular pain," said Cliff, who had been drinking along with his guests all the way.

"Who's your doctor? Elwood?"

Cliff was alerted. "Aha," he said, faking to seem deeper in his cups than he actually was, "nothing doing. My insides shall re-main—and that's a good word, too—a secret between him and me. Who needs any bright-eyed little punk like you trying to read the score?"

"Okay, okay," Joe said genially. "I was only wondering if he wanted you every hour, on the hour, and if so why. By the way, what did you mean about a loan?" he added with curiosity.

Cliff was beginning to think that Joe Bianchi was a little *too* bright-eyed and decided that the young doctor was not going to be useful either. "Oh, I dunno," he drawled. "I'm overflowing with good deeds these latter days. Say, how many decks of cards do your friends, the Norns, go through in a year?"

"Who's counting?" said Joe.

"Never go out of the damn house, eh? Except to eat?"

"Why, sure they do. They organize a big expedition to the movies, like once a month. Oh, it's a project. They go to the five o'clock show; no standing in line, see? On the other hand, they don't want to faint from hunger, so"—Joe was enjoying him-self; his eyes shone—"they scarf up what they call a bite before they go. Then, of course, afterward, since they didn't count that, they go eat dinner. *They* don't suffer, believe me. I don't know. They're kind of great old gals."

"I still don't know why you're living here," Cliff said absent-mindedly.

"Likewise," said Joe promptly. "Gets me, when you run a car like yours, why you want to hang around this dump."

"Oh, I've got my reasons," Cliff said drunkenly. "Maybe I need to suffer. Superstition's in it. If I suffer enough, I don't got to die."

"Well, like I say, enjoy yourself," Joe said indulgently and went away.

Cliff thought sullenly: I don't have to fake going over to the damn hospital today, do I? Didn't I say every other day?

He lay back, brooding. He supposed he ought to call old man Reynard again, keep him on the hook. But he felt too lax to bother. He'd just been flubbing around all day. Funny, though, how things work out.

What the hell, he thought (his mind veering), was the matter with Sherry baby, that she'd let herself get off on the wrong foot with the Reynards? She must be plain stupid. Surely, she could have done better out of the deal. Why not live in their big house and be served by their servants? And toil not? Why couldn't she have had her cake and eaten it, too, as the saying goes? He didn't see why Sherry couldn't have done about as she pleased if she'd gone about it tactfully.

If, on the other hand, she took any serious stock in the prospect of Ward's ever becoming any kind of successful writer (for God's sake!), then she had to be stupid. What was the idea of plugging away in poorly paid jobs, harnessed in that lousy routine, night and day? What did she think she was? Noble? Selfless?

So where was she now? She was on quite a spot, she was. Flat broke, with a sick kid to take care of, nowhere to turn, and feuding with power. Locking horns with such as Edward Reynard, who was ready and willing and eager to put her down. She'd got herself pretty far down, with no help from anybody. Little fool!

Cliff went into a fantasy. He made up a scene in which Sherry was hysterical, using bad language, screaming, raging, in some judge's presence. Denying, denying, driven out of control by some outrageous lie.

Yeah, lie. Cliff squirmed and sat up. All right, so he had a bit of a hunch. Got it cheap, too. Price of a little Scotch whisky. Always pays to be thorough. Starts up the creative processes. Bits and pieces begin to fit together.

A wild idea! Wild, yeah, because no red-blooded young American fellow was going to believe it for one instant. Still, the people in this house would. Edward Reynard would. And it was very possible that some judge would, too. Oh, it had its possibilities.

But he wasn't going to push it. Not now. He couldn't see how to work it out, not yet. He wasn't sure he'd even try. It was just comforting to have thought of *something*.

He sighed. First thing, he thought, whatever I do, is to fix that damned door into her room from the yard. How am I going to get in there and do it, making noise and so on, unless I figure to clear the house of people?

Ah, now, there was a nice little problem. He had already worked on it some. He could, for instance, move the Peabodys at any time he chose. (It should be at dusk, he thought.) But what about the Norns? They went out for their dinners erratically. He couldn't trust to that. No, he needed them out of the house early enough and long enough to give him some time before Sherry Reynard came in. He knew she came in at about seven. He knew she was locked into the hospital's rhythm. *That* was reliable. So it entertained him to settle down quietly and work out a way to clear the people out of this house, and all simultaneously, for his convenience.

After a while, taking great pains to purify his breath, he went down to the sitting room to tackle the Norns. He had the germ of an idea of what to do with them. He trusted himself to improvise.

Chapter 9

ACROSS THE STREET three ambulances had just come in on one another's heels, and the Norns were sure there had been some really bloody accident. They were counting the victims and assessing the chances of each. Cliff had to wait until the last scurrying of white coats was over before he got their attention at all.

But when they beamed in on him, they wanted something. They wanted to know where this house was, the one he knew about.

"I bet it don't have a window on the front, like this one," Mrs. Link said with a sigh.

"Won't be across from a hospital, either, I'll bet," Mrs. Moran said with a toss of her head.

"I'm betting it's in a nice suburban residential area," Mrs. Kimberly said with faint sarcasm. "Maybe a little run-down?" She fixed her bright old eyes on his face.

Cliff couldn't help feeling tickled. He also felt pleased with himself for having located a house that he could now describe. Oh, attention to detail paid off, all right.

"I believe," he said, "there *is* a quite cozy little room that would be ideal for cards." This statement did not cause the ladies' expressions to brighten. Cliff began to lie. "It looks out on the street," he said and saw that this went down a little better. But he began to chide himself. Why was he fooling around, aimlessly playing a silly game with these old souls? Game? he thought. Ah, there it was again. How interesting to notice his natural ingenuity pick up these trifles!

Meantime, thinking of something else, he said truthfully, "There is a church across the street."

At this their faces took on a hopeful thoughtfulness that he could not help seeing. He was puzzled, briefly.

"Deal the cards," Mrs. Moran said with a sigh.

But Cliff had his plan. "I take it," he said, "that you ladies don't disapprove of a little playful bet, here and there. With all your talk about *betting* this or that." He took care to be teasing.

"That depends," said Mrs. Kimberly, her eyes leery.

"Tell you what I'll do," he said, reaching for a straight chair to pull to their table. "I'll buy the Canfield deck. How does it go, again? I buy for fifty-five. You pay me back five for every card I get out. One of you at a time, that is. Anyone for Canfield?" He took the cards from Mrs. Link and began to shuffle.

"Once through the pack, one card at a time," Mrs. Kimberly said instantly.

So Cliff made merry about who was to cut, dealt out, and played three gambling games of Canfield against each of them in turn. The ladies hooted and rocked and seemed vastly entertained as he managed to lose the games, all three.

So Cliff leaned back and said, "Unlucky at cards, lucky in love, that's what they say. Well, now, let's see. I owe Mrs. Kimberly . . . I got out six cards, didn't I? Times five, that's thirty. So I owe you twenty-five. Mrs. Link didn't do quite so well. I owe you twenty, ma'am. And Mrs. Moran. That's the time I nearly made it. All you get, madam, is ten dollars. Sorry."

They all began to squeal. No, no, not dollars! They had thought he meant pennies. Oh, no, no, Mr. Storm! We can't afford to gamble for dollars! They were in a great twitter.

Cliff said, "Believe me, I've learned a valuable lesson. What a sucker's game that is, eh? So how about a compromise? Let me pay off—in full, mind you—by treating you ladies to a movie. Any show you like. Whenever it would be convenient. I'll be getting off cheap. Don't forget."

Finally, they said that if he would be sure to remember his lesson, they'd allow him to do this on . . . well . . . perhaps Saturday? They usually went to the five o'clock showing.

"Fine," he said, "and that includes refreshments. I insist." After some further banter about the difference between dollars and cents, he got them to accept, each, a ten-dollar bill.

Then he went out of the house and phoned the real estate man. The tenants he had in prospect, Cliff said, would be able to inspect the house on Saturday, around five thirty or quarter to six. Was this possible?

"Saturday!" the man groaned. "This fellow works Saturdays, does he? How about Sunday?"

"I don't think so," Cliff said sternly. "They're church people. Try to make it latish Saturday, will you? Meantime, you might be getting the papers ready for escrow. Looks like a pretty sure thing to me. These people are bound to see the possibilities there, unless, of course, they see something else before you can get together with them."

"Oh, I'll be glad to show it Saturday, if that's the only time they can make it," the man said. "Have I got the name of your, uh, buyer?"

"That's a Mr. Edward Reynard," said Cliff.

"Oh, I see," said the man. "Now I believe I quoted you a price—"

"But seeing it's Reynard, you might up that a couple of grand," Cliff said gently, "between the two of us."

"Weddings," said Mrs. Link, clicking her upper plate pleasurably.

"Christenings?" said Mrs. Kimberly. "There should be a few anyhow. But of course, services and suppers."

"Choir practice and funerals, don't forget," said Mrs. Moran. "A hell of a lot goes on around a church. Hoo. Hoo." Her plump shoulders shook. "I suppose," she said, sobering, "there'd be something to see."

The cards slapped.

"He don't know the cards," burst Mrs. Link. "Three times with me, he missed putting the right black on red, so's he could get a king space."

"Ho, with me there was a three of spades and a four of diamonds he never put out at all," Mrs. Kimberly said with animation. "I had to laugh to myself."

"He didn't fool so much with *me*," said Mrs. Moran.

The cards fell, pit pat.

"Turned out to be a great kidder, didn't he?" Mrs. Moran said thoughtfully. "What happened to his company manners? Who wants to bet he ain't a deep one?"

When Sherry came in, as usual, at seven o'clock, she found a letter on the table under the mirror. It had been mailed locally. Well, there hadn't been time yet for a reply from New York. She came into the sitting room and greeted the Norns, tearing open the envelope at the same time. There was a check in it from Mr. Dodd at the Club. The check was for eight dollars and fifty cents.

She made a face at it, smiled at the ladies, told them that Johnny was feeling well enough to be naughty, offered them hard candy from the small box she had bought at the coffeeshop, and went into her room. She ought to wash her hair and do a bit of light laundry. But she sat down on the bed and stared at the wall.

Cliff Storm, at the moment, was in the kitchen talking about the house. He asked what the rent was here (while he surveyed the Peabody private domain) and announced that he felt sure the other house could be had for somewhat less than that. Mr. Reynard would redecorate, of course, and he might make at least some small alterations.

Now, could the Peabodys go see the house late Saturday afternoon, say about six o'clock? The agent, who had the keys, was a very busy man, and this was his earliest convenience. Oh, yes, both of them. Mr. Reynard would want their decision to be a joint one. Cliff had told the agent that Mrs. Peabody was an experienced housekeeper and Mr. Peabody an experienced maintenance man. *They* were not to deal with the agent at all. Cliff would arrange any contact with Mr. Reynard.

He was a little sorry, he said, that on Saturday he would not be able to go with them, but after all, he didn't know the house. Was it a date?

Mrs. Peabody's eyes rolled in their slightly diverging directions. She did not know about both of them leaving the house at the same time.

"You're thinking of Elsie?" asked Cliff. He could see, from where he was, through to the small room (ex-servants' room?) that had evidently become dedicated to television. Elsie was there. She had a low chair drawn up too near the set; her outsized head was motionless. This was the life she had.

"You know," said Cliff, "I believe I *can* arrange to be here until you get back, which shouldn't be too late. By eight o'clock, I'm sure. Why couldn't I keep an eye on things? After all, what could happen? Won't she be watching some program or other?

They said that, of course, she would. Elsie was a very good girl—obedient, and no trouble. It was only that they worried about some emergency. In case, for instance, of fire, they didn't think Elsie would realize her danger. But she usually stayed right where she was now. And if Mr. Storm didn't mind . . .

Cliff was reminded of people who owned dogs. He could remember being introduced by an owner to a watchdog as one who need not be watched, who was a friend. Just so, the Peabodys introduced him now to their daughter. From now on, he realized, she would obey him, especially if he took care to speak twice, as her mother and father always did.

He was careful to put on an avuncular attitude that was on the stern side. But he thought this solved any problems with Elsie. She would do what he told her to do. And he would use her; he must use her. She was human clay and given into his hand.

The Peabodys went on to proclaim that Mr. Storm was the kindest person they had met in a long time and a true friend indeed.

Cliff fended off the praise. Then he said, "By the way, speaking of being friendly, maybe I ought to tell you something about Mrs. Reynard. I'm afraid she has been running up a lot of bills around town. Her creditors can't find her, at the moment. But I shouldn't think her credit rating was so hot. Just in friendship, perhaps you ought to keep that in mind.

A dig here, and a dab there, you never know, he thought to himself. Something about money was working in the dark of his mind.

It took time to shake off further effusions. Finally, he made it back to the sitting room.

The ladies spoke up at once.

"She's in," said Mrs. Kimberly.

"She's already eaten," said Mrs. Link.

"She had a letter," said Mrs. Moran, "with a check in it."

Cliff simply stood there, staring at them. At last he stirred himself to say, "Oh! Oh, you mean Mrs. Reynard? Well, thank you, I'm sure." He put on a mocking smile (he hoped), said, "Good night, ladies," and went fast out of the place.

How had he given away his primary interest as clearly as that?

Augh, the hell with it!

Sonia said, "Now, listen, Buster, what makes you think *you* can come barging in—"

"Because I can," he said.

He was right, of course. Sonia was an uncomplicated character. The woods were full of Sonias.

In her tiny cell Sherry was feeling depressed. The eight dollars and fifty cents had depressed her. And the sale of her ring depressed her now. Once you cashed in what you had thought of as your security, then you didn't have the security anymore.

She told herself that she would just have to go back to work.

Back to the Club. The tips there would carry her through, and why had she been thinking, anyway, that Johnny needed her by night? He was well taken care of where he was; she wouldn't even have to hire a baby-sitter. She could be with him by day, just as before. Okay, she'd call up Mr. Dodd tomorrow. Of course, it wasn't fair to ask for just a few days on the old job. She would have to leave very soon. But he might understand.

Now she remembered that she still owed Miss Erskine nine dollars. She looked at the check and thought: So I'm only out fifty cents. But then her mind rebelled. Let Ward pay that bill. He wasn't dead, was he? He was still Johnny's father.

She let herself fall over and put her cheek to the cheap cotton spread. He wasn't dead. She wished she knew how he was. One reason she'd been so mad at Emily Reynard was Emily had refused to say a word about how Ward was.

Sherry hadn't thought she had better telephone the house to ask how he was. It might only start things that had better not be started. She could be tempted to go back. No use pretending it wasn't a temptation. It was possible to call Johnny's involvement a kind of accident. It was possible to imagine going back, even to that house. She knew Ward needed her, didn't she? She could pretend that she just had to be drawn back to him by his need. She could even admit that she needed Ward. She *could* get out of this awful lonely limbo. To try again? Try again? Once more? Oh, it was a temptation to think that this was the right and loving thing to do.

But she must not go. Was she right about that? *Yes*, she was right about it.

Sherry began to cry. She cried for a long time, because it was rough, the way things had to be. It was pretty rough, all right, and it wasn't going to get any better for a long while yet. And maybe not a whole lot better, ever.

Cliff said to Sonia in the dark, "Say, toots, one of these days would you make a gag phone call for me?"

"What? What?" said Sonia lazily. "To who?"

"I'll give you the number and the name of the dame. And I'll write your lines."

"It better be something mean," she said. "A dame, you say?"

"I'm not going to give you the name of the game," Cliff said. "But rest your mind. It'll be plenty mean."

"Good. Why not, then?"

Cliff sighed and rolled over.

Creaking up Mrs. Peabody's stairs at 4 A.M., Cliff recalled the fact that at dinner, among his peers and rivals, he had let drop intimations of a deal cooking. It wasn't so much what he had said, but the revelation in his manner that he anticipated the acquisition of power. Nobody believed this, of course. Hints of power to come were always discounted in the industry. In fact, they were often taken as a sign of real desperation. That was what made it so sweet—so sweet!—when such a hint turned out to have had the truth in it.

He thought to himself that he had managed to put a little sugar on the prize.

He'd better call Reynard again in the morning. And also get on with it. It began to look as if he ought to give some hard thought to that wild notion and take a crack at working out the details. He *had* Elsie. Elsie *was* vulnerable.

Because if not that, then what? What else could he do?

Think backward from the desired result. He wanted Sherry Reynard to seem to be or seem to have done what some judge, some cold-minded (remember this) representative of Society (with the capital letter), would reliably condemn.

But what the devil was that? What did Society condemn these days? It was one thing if she was either physically or mentally disabled so that she obviously could not care for a child. But Cliff couldn't maim her physically. Mentally, he could throw her, at least temporarily, off balance with a drug, of course. This had been in the back of his mind all along. But there had to be more to it than that.

What if she were in jail? Yes. Good. That dragged Society in.

A crime then? Yes, but this meant that a crime would have to be committed. And Cliff was not interested in committing a crime himself in order to frame her as being guilty of it. That was entirely too much to ask of him. For that matter, what crime did Society reliably condemn these days?

Beating up old people in the streets? Burning down buildings? Don't be silly. Wait a minute. It might have to be a crime against property at that.

He got into bed; his mind was clear and sad.

But at the same time, he mused on, he ought to turn against her some powerful emotion that still existed in the public breast.

What would that be? A fear? Of the bomb, for instance? Well, he couldn't shanghai her and ship her off and say she'd defected, although there was a reliable disapproval of a traitor. What else? Cliff couldn't think of a thing.

But there used to be such a thing as the pressure of public disapproval. Some deeds used to be "not done," not so much from fear of the law, but because the perpetrator would lose forever what had once been considered valuable—his reputation.

Cliff tended to think that the public still frowned on some crimes. Kidnapping, for instance, was viewed with great horror.

Well, forget it. He couldn't make Sherry into a kidnapper. Still, he had hold of a thought here.

He had a flash; a freakish notion popped into his head. Hit and run! Hit and run! The sacred automobile!

This tickled him so much that he fell abruptly into sound sleep.

Chapter 10

AT BREAKFAST on Friday morning there was a series of small conflicts.

Dr. Bianchi, as usual, escaped early, and Cliff was not downstairs. But when Elsie came to pour Lawton Archer's orange juice, in her trance of adoration she happened to spill a few drops on his shoulder. Whereupon Archer pushed his chair away from the table violently and said in a voice suddenly pitched an octave higher, "Mrs. Peabody, I'm sorry to have to tell you that I am making other arrangements. I must give you notice that I'll be leaving here within the week."

"You'll be leaving here within the week," Mrs. Peabody said nastily, with her left eye darting anger.

But now, since it had been repeated, Elsie got the message. She threw her big head back and began a soft howling sound, like a dog to the moon. It was shocking, distressing, disgusting, pitiable, and unbearable.

Archer got up and simply fled. Mrs. Peabody got up and snatched Elsie out of the room, taking her to the kitchen. In a moment Mr. Peabody appeared, reeling, and, of all things, sat himself to preside drunkenly over the coffeepot. But Mrs. Peabody reappeared within seconds and sent him back to his place with one sharp command.

Through all this commotion the Norns sipped and chewed in an alert silence, while Sherry gaped.

As soon as she had sat down again, Mrs. Peabody spoke to Sherry.

"Mrs. Reynard"—she sounded furious, and Sherry thought to herself: Hey, what did *I* do?—"I will require another week's rent from you today, if you please."

"Today?" said Sherry. "But it hasn't been a week."

"I realize that," the landlady said coldly, "but if you wish to remain in the room for still another week, I'll ask you for the rental now. Otherwise, I can't promise that I will hold it."

"Yes, I'd like to stay here at least another week. So I suppose it doesn't matter." Sherry swallowed hard. She never moved these days without her purse close beside her because of the ticket and the ring money in there. In there was also the check. "Would you take part of it in a check?" she asked. "Made out to me?"

"I would prefer not," snapped Mrs. Peabody.

So Sherry counted out two tens and five single dollar bills and handed them to the landlady, who thanked her in a chilly manner.

"I don't suppose I need a receipt," said Sherry, who was somewhat angry herself. "These ladies will be my witnesses."

"I will bring you a receipt, of course," Mrs. Peabody said furiously. She rose and flounced off to the kitchen.

"Now what did I do to make her so mad at me?" Sherry said to the Norns.

The Norns did not answer. Uncannily, they continued to sip and chew in silence.

Well! Sherry had a phone call to make, for sure now, but she wasn't going to use the phone in the front hall.

She went over to the hospital, adding and subtracting on the way. She had had forty-eight dollars and ninety-five cents, after her meal last night. Plus eight fifty (although there was the problem of cashing that check). But now, minus the horrendous sum of twenty-five dollars! The balance came to thirty-two forty-five.

She used the booth in the hospital to call Mr. Dodd. To her astonishment not only was he not especially glad to hear from her, but he did not want her to come back to work. Although he hemmed and hawed and evaded, he made that perfectly plain.

But not *why* not.

Sherry hung up, wondering what was happening. What was going on? (She now had only thirty-two dollars and twenty-five cents.)

Johnny would be in the midst of the morning bath at the moment, so Sherry went out into the daylight and walked slowly to the little park adjacent to the hospital grounds. She ambled along the paths for a while. She had mailed her airmail letters to New York on Wednesday. They would have arrived there on Thursday, surely. It was possible for her to receive a reply today, this being Friday.

The mailman came by every morning on almost the dot of ten, so just before that hour Sherry went directly back to the house.

The Norns had not yet settled to their post. Sherry could hear the vacuum running in her room. Her door stood open. Elsie, under her mother's ever-present direction, did a good deal of the cleaning downstairs. They both must be in there.

So Sherry sat down in the sitting room. Very soon Mr. Peabody came, in a rolling gait, out of the dining room and hailed her with a comradely leer.

"What do you know? All alone, eh? Say here's your chance, little lady. How's about a friendly little drinky with the old man?" He had an almost full bottle under his arm. "Go ahead," he encouraged her. "Lots more where that came from."

She could see in his eyes his sad knowledge that this day was gone; he had already lost his grip on it. But he also seemed convinced that, even at this hour in the morning, Sherry must be dying of thirst.

She refused, with thanks, as inoffensively as she could. But he persisted. So Sherry finally retreated, stepping behind the screen into the area forbidden the landlord as male.

Mrs. Kimberly, at the moment, appeared farther along the passage on the other side of the screen. Mr. Peabody seemed to begin to sob. Mrs. Kimberly's face put on a haughty look. Sherry went into her own room. Mrs. Peabody was wielding a dustrag, running it with downward strokes all around the lampshade. Elsie was pushing the vacuum cleaner back and forth, with an entranced air about her.

"Oh," said the landlady. "Come, Elsie, Mrs. Reynard wants the room now." With her foot Mrs. Peabody switched off the machine. As its noise died, Elsie looked up stupidly.

"Oh, let her finish," said Sherry. "I'll just sit in the corner. I'm only waiting for the mail."

"I see," said the landlady. "But after all, you have paid for your privacy." She flounced out of the door and away.

Sherry could recognize the woman's compulsion to go on being cross, especially if she'd had no real excuse for it in the first place. But Sherry's ears stretched to hear whether the man still sobbed out there. If he did and if he were to say that the "little lady wouldn't drink with him" or anything *like* that, there would be demonstrated Sherry Reynard's "evil power." Oh, would it not! She held her breath to listen, and jumped as Mrs. Link, going past the door, glanced in.

There was an unwritten law (Sherry had discovered) that the ladies did not chat in this wing of the house. This wing was for privacy and relief from chatter. So she didn't speak, nor did the stout old lady. But Sherry soon realized two things; the man must have gone away; she herself was acting exactly as if she were guilty of something.

She shook herself and saw Elsie still standing there, dumb and forgotten. "It looks very neat and clean, Elsie," said Sherry, smiling. "Very neat and clean."

The girl's face brightened, and Sherry thought: Poor thing. If somebody took a little more trouble with her, I wonder . . .

Then the landlady was at the door, ordering Elsie out, as if this had been Sherry's request and had offended Mrs. Peabody mightily.

So Sherry sat there alone and reflected. She couldn't help feeling that something odd was happening all around her. It felt as if people were turning against her. "Whoops! Hold it, kiddo," she said aloud. She knew very well that this was the kind of thing you had better not feel and must never admit that you were feeling. Paranoia? Delusions of persecution? She had better be careful.

At ten o'clock she emerged. The Norns were established in the window. They turned bland faces whose eyes seemed very bright with suspicion.

No, no, they are *not,* Sherry warned herself. She told them she had been waiting for the mail. Had it come?

Yes, it had come. But there was no letter for Mrs. Reynard.

"You are expecting something important?" said Mrs. Kimberly, arching her neck, pulling her small chin down, and causing another to appear.

"Yes, I am," said Sherry. Then, hitting out blindly at the clouds that seemed to be gathering around her, she said, "Do you *mind?*" She was sorry immediately. "I'm sorry, Mrs. Kimberly," she said in a different voice. "Yes, it is important to me. I am expecting a letter from a friend."

"That's the best kind," Mrs. Moran said aloofly.

"Yes. Excuse me."

Sherry went out and crossed the street. How many times had she crossed here, on this narrow beat? And how many more times must she go to and fro, in and out, up and down, on the same track? Could she endure? *Was* it getting her down?

She was inclined to agree with Mr. Peabody. This day was lost. It was going to be Blue Friday.

In the window, Mrs. Kimberly failed to duck taking the queen of spades. She was distraught and undoubtedly somewhat miffed. Her cronies said nothing. At last Mrs. Kimberly, with the flesh of her face rising up in her smile, said, "How old am I?"

"Old enough," Mrs. Moran said affectionately.

"Everything matters too much to the young," Mrs. Link said lazily. "Poor things. Deal the cards."

When Cliff Storm finally levered his hangover out of bed, at 11 A.M., he left the house without even putting his head around the corner of the wall to greet the ladies.

On the sidewalk, he started to his left, caught himself, changed course, and walked slowly and suddenly much less vigorously toward the crossing to the hospital, changed his mind, and did not cross.

"Something's up," said Mrs. Moran, putting it in a nutshell.

When the doctor came in at noon on this Blue Friday, Sherry couldn't get him to say anything definite about Johnny's release. They'd be getting him out of bed soon. Then they must see. The doctor was pleased with Johnny. That was all he could say for now. Well, Sherry supposed that it wasn't the doctor's fault that he couldn't give her a day and hour.

Nor could she get any firm estimate out of the hospital office about what her eventual bill here might be. Unable to give them the time span, she had no way to press them. It wasn't their fault. It was just rough on Sherry.

She had the low-calorie plate for lunch, knowing that it was silly not to eat, although it was frightening to be so low in personal funds. She kept feeling that if she dipped into the ring money for herself, she'd risk being caught short when she must not be.

What else did she have that could be sold?

Sherry didn't own a watch. She had no other jewelry of any value. She began to rummage in her mind over the contents of her former residence. Was there anything there she could claim and turn to cash? An appliance? she wondered. The toaster, for instance. That had been a wedding present. Pat Sims (now Anderson) had given it to her.

Sherry thought she had better ask Mr. Jordan first, although it would cost ten cents to phone him.

Mr. Jordan said that he was a little upset about the things that had been in the house.

"*Had been?*"

Yes, it seemed that Mr. Edward Reynard, with a somewhat high hand, had simply arranged, without consulting anyone, for the stuff to be taken off to storage. The landlord had wanted it out of the house or another month's rent paid. The storage charges would be somewhat less expensive than paying the rent on a dwelling where nobody dwelled, but Reynard had no right to do that. His lawyer, Samuel Murchison, had been upset, too. He had phoned Jordan and guaranteed that his client would be totally responsible for the storage cost. So, on the whole, it might work out to Sherry's advantage. Now if she really wanted to get at those objects, signed permission would have to be procured and so on.

"No, no," said Sherry. "I was thinking of selling something that's mine, because I'm awfully broke. But I wouldn't get enough to be worth so much fuss, I'm afraid."

The lawyer was alarmed. What did she mean? How broke? Was she all right, basically, for food and shelter?

Sherry said honestly, "Oh, I have money that I'm saving to pay the hospital. Outside of that, I mean, I'm really getting pretty low."

"I see," he said. "I was going to suggest that the Reynards ought to know it if you are in real distress. They would just about be forced to do something about it. And actually, I can't believe they would want you to be suffering in any such way."

(*I* could believe it, Sherry thought.) She said, "I'd rather not go to them. I can always use that other money. I mean, I won't starve. And I've asked some friends to help me. I could hear from them as soon as tomorrow. But do you really think I can have some of the savings money? Can I *count* on that, Mr. Jordan?"

"Certainly," he said. "On half of it, absolutely. It may not be all yours legally, but morally it well may be. You earned it, didn't you? I am almost positive that any judge, in view of that and of certain behavior by the other side, will award you all of it and whatever the furnishings bring besides."

"You know," she said thinly, "I don't know what I was worrying about."

"By the way," he said, "I have some good news. The hearing has been set for yesterday a week."

"Oh, really!" A load rolled from her shoulders. "Do you mean Thursday? Next Thursday?"

"That's it. Two thirty in the afternoon. I'll call for you, of course." He continued with a few instructions.

"Whatever you say." Sherry sighed. "Wow, that helps a lot. Now I feel as if I could put up with anything."

She hung up and did her arithmetic. Thirty-one dollars and twenty-five cents (since lunch and a phone call). Okay. Dinner tonight; lunch on Thursday . . . Six more days' worth of meals then. Hey, not bad, to have more than five dollars and twenty cents per day! The low-calorie plate came to a dollar (with tip), and in the evening there were at least two choices she could have for a dollar and a half (with tip). My gosh, thought Sherry, I can even squander two dollars and seventy cents every single day! Whoopee!

She whirled out into the corridor smack into Joe Bianchi, who promptly put both arms around her and would not let her go. The situation developed into what was, beyond any doubt, a real pitch of woo. A hugger-mugger ensued.

But Sherry, recovering from surprise, soon slipped away expertly without giving offense. Joe was expert enough in these matters to accept the message quickly, without taking offense, either.

"So solly," he said. "A little misunderstanding, maybe? How you doing, doll?"

Sherry grinned at him and said she was fine and hoped he was the same. She walked away.

But sitting beside Johnny's bed while he entertained himself with crayons, seeming only to need to see her there, she couldn't help turning several things over in her mind.

Funny! How come the young doctor had approached her so

abruptly, without any skirmishing? How come, earlier on, Mr. Peabody had been so sure she was a fellow lush? How come the landlady had jumped on her for rent in advance, as if Sherry might be some kind of deadbeat? Was somebody putting out snide rumors about Sherry Reynard?

Aw, now, come on, she told herself. You'd better be sure the whole world is *not* against you. You're not that important for one thing, kiddo. Things are a little rough right now, sure. But you'd better *not* let them get you down.

She decided that Mrs. Peabody, having been upset by Archer's sudden notice, had just taken it out on Sherry, as people do. The poor woman had her worries in the financial department.

As for Mr. Peabody, he hadn't known what time it was. Just a friendly drunk. And Joe Bianchi had to conform, didn't he, and make like a regular intern or lose face among his peers? And the Norns? Well, they were curious about her because they were curious about everything. They had nothing *else* to be. So it all was explained, and Sherry ought not to have snapped at Mrs. Kimberly; but otherwise, what was there to worry about?

In a moment she got up and went down the ward to where the girl with the fantastic black hair was leaning over a small patient.

"Hi," said Sherry. "Did you have a good time?"

The girl's jaw moved.

"Last night?" Sherry prodded.

The motion of chewing stopped. "Oh. Yeah. I guess so." She grimaced suddenly. "We didn't go."

"Why not?" Sherry said bluntly.

"I dunno. It was going to be on this fellow's expense account."

"Whose expense account?"

"Listen, *I* dunno. Your name's Reynard? Right?"

Sherry said, "Where did he want to take us?"

"I dunno," the girl said. "Just some place for laughs." Her eyes fell. "It gets boring," she said, "when you're divorced, and your kid's sick all the time, and you never have any fun." Her face fell into sullen lines. She turned away.

"I guess it does," Sherry said in a moment.

She went back to her own place, telling herself to watch it now. You could look guilty when you weren't. Sherry ought to know.

She settled down, resolving that she would be very careful indeed. She'd stay in that ex-sun porch by night, that sterile prison. And by day she'd stay in the hospital, which was sterile enough. It wasn't for much longer. Once she had the interlocutory decree and custody and her own money, then everything would be easier. She ought to be able to endure until next Thursday. She sure wasn't going out on any risky blind dates. That would be just too stupid.

So endure limbo? Endure time, that went in such slow scallops? Peaks of pleasure to see Johnny improving. Yet hours of attendance on a child, gearing speech to his vocabulary, and too much jolly, jolly beaming around the ward at other mothers, who were keeping up their spirits, too. And on other children, little children, who were unhappy often and sometimes in pain, and Sherry couldn't help them.

Sherry would rather, she thought, have been out digging a ditch with her bare hands. Or she wished she could be, if not a nurse, at least an aide. But her job was Johnny. Some things she could do for him that nobody else could do. The trouble was, she seemed to be unable to do *anything else*.

Couldn't afford to telephone one of the girls she'd worked with, or meet her for lunch, or shopping, or bus around town. Must stay in this street or nearby. Couldn't really get away by day.

And the long shallow loops of nothingness in between. The nights, the evenings . . .

In the evenings she couldn't even read. Mrs. Peabody's dusty volumes in the glass-doored bookshelves were just too ancient, all slow-paced, second-rate Victorian stuff. She couldn't abide it. She'd left her library card behind, and the library was a bus fare away anyhow. Didn't want magazines. She'd read all the hospital's magazines. Had no radio. Couldn't even do her nails over. Couldn't afford the polish remover. Didn't even have so much as a deck of cards.

She was reminded of the Norns and felt weirdly in sympathy with them. All right, she could walk in the park, sit in the hospital lobby, or in the sitting room at the house, and she could watch other people live.

But, oh, she was young for that. Young and yearning and wishing and wanting, but stuck. Hung up in this limbo. For a while. For a while. The thing about time is that it goes, she told herself. The world turns. This won't be forever.

That evening Cliff Storm greeted her with exasperation. "How many days ahead do I have to ask you to go to dinner with me? Do you own stock in that coffeeshop, or what? Every time I catch you to say one word, you've just eaten."

"Well, I'm sorry," Sherry said. "Glutton that I am." But her heart jumped up and almost sang for the fun of this.

"Why don't you ask her for tomorrow night?" Mrs. Kimberly said tartly, from the window.

Sherry was startled. She knew it was the Norns' policy to watch and listen, but seldom butt in.

Cliff Storm was snapping his fingers. "Nuts! Tomorrow night I can't make it. How about Sunday?" He was beaming at her. It all seemed so pleasant.

"Thank you," said Sherry, "I'll be glad to." She felt a great relief. Oh, why not? There was no risk with this man. "By Sunday, I warn you," she said mischievously, "I may be down to skin and bones."

"Not really?" he said quickly. "Now, look here—"

"No, no, not really," she reassured him. Sherry sat down. No harm to kid around a bit, talk awhile with a contemporary— especially here, where three chaperones listened to every syllable.

"Can I do anything?" Cliff sat down on the same sofa, but a good four feet away. He knew better than to crowd closer. What he wanted to know was how much money she had.

"Could you cash a check for me?" she said, suddenly inspired.

"Of course."

She endorsed the check, and he gave her eight dollars and fifty cents. She thanked him heartily. He took note of the sum, so little. Her left hand, bare of all but the simple wedding band, had been under his eye, but he had not noticed.

He said, "Sherry, do you mind if I ask a question that's none of my business?"

"No," she said. "Of course, maybe I won't answer."

"Why aren't you rolling in filthy money? Old man Reynard isn't down to his last hundred thousand, is he?"

"That has nothing to do with me," she said slowly.

"But I can't see why not. Why don't you let Reynard pay the hospital bills, for instance? Why don't you—I'm sorry, but you've more or less got me baffled, Mrs. Reynard."

She was looking at him thoughtfully.

"What are you so afraid of?" he said impatiently.

"You must have seen them," she said. "So I guess you can guess."

Cliff said quickly, "Listen, Sherry, aren't you going to have one heck of a tough time raising that kid all by yourself?"

"I sure am," she said pleasantly, but he almost literally squirmed under that dark blue gaze.

"I know it's none of my business," he said, looking away, "but when you stop to think of the education, the travel, the privileges they could give that child. All right, a pack of clichés. Don't they mean *anything?*"

"Of course, they do," she said gravely.

"But you're not going to give him up," Cliff said emphatically.

"No, I'm not," she said quietly.

"Listen, for the sake of argument," he went on, drawn by some personal curiosity, "don't you imagine you'll ever want to marry again?"

"I probably will," said Sherry, looking ahead in sad calm.

"Sometimes," he said, "men would rather not . . . well . . . not tangle with the responsibility of another man's son. I don't mean to— Sure, I'm being damned nosy and obnoxious. But I'm thinking of *you.*"

"Do you think so?" she murmured. Sho looked amused. (She made him feel like a jackass, damn it!)

"Oh, it's a feeble effort I'm making to try to see your point of view," he said testily. "But what about a career? You could go roaring back into show business, if that's what you always wanted. Do any damned thing. Because, quite seriously, I think you could get about as much money as you'd need to keep the wolf from the door for years to come."

"How could I do that?" she asked.

"Just tell Ward that under certain conditions he could have the boy."

(If he *talked* her into this, it would count, wouldn't it?)

She surprised him. "Does Ward really want him?" she said mournfully.

"Naturally," said Cliff.

"I hoped he didn't," she said. "How is he?"

"As a matter of fact, he's flat in bed. Emily was reading aloud."

He saw Sherry's eyes fill with tears.

"Do you really think," he said, mysteriously infuriated, "that there's something evil about people wanting to spend money on a child, buy him the good things? Why are you so suspicious and superior? The old man and Emily are devoted to the boy, aren't they?"

"So is Ward," she said in a broken voice. "You don't understand." Her lids hid those eyes.

"It's true," he said dryly in a moment, "I've never been a mother."

"I can't give Johnny to Ward," she murmured. "If I could, I wouldn't have to."

"Oh, hey, now, cheer up!" he said, bewildered. "I shouldn't have opened my big mouth. Come on, let's go out someplace and kick things around. Other things. If we don't, it looks to me as if you're going to bawl."

"Well, it's rough," she said. "I have to admit."

"Why, Sherry?" Cliff shifted closer.

She straightened her body and drew it slightly away. She knew and acknowledged the wave that went between them and projected to him clearly the message that it wasn't going to mean a thing.

She said, "I wish I could stay married to Ward. Didn't you know that? But I can't."

"Why not?" Cliff said keenly.

"Didn't he tell you?" she said. "Please, I'm sorry, but I will not talk about it anymore."

"Okay," he said at once. "Then we'll skip it. Now, how about my bright idea? Let's—"

"How was the treatment?" Sherry interrupted.

Cliff blinked. Damn, he'd almost forgotten. Furthermore, he had better not lie, because the Norns would know. He had not gone through the front door of the hospital, and there was no reason on earth for him to have gone through any other entrance.

"They start tomorrow," he said. "And I don't want to talk about them. Have we got a deal?"

"Did they tell you the hearing's going to be on Thursday?" she said inconsistently.

"No," he said, startled. "No, they didn't."

Sherry got up. "You'll have to excuse me," she said, "because for now I can't think of anything *else* to talk about. I'll do better on Sunday," she promised, and said good night to the Norns, who chorused replies. She went to her room.

Cliff, who had risen politely, jingled change in his pocket. He strolled over to the card table. "She's a puzzlement," he said ruefully.

"I'm willing to believe," Mrs. Moran said severely, "that you've never been a mother."

"No, no," he said. "I understand that. That isn't what baffles me. Those people are good sound people of means and all. And now—you heard her—she says she doesn't even want the divorce. So something's wrong."

"Personally," said Mrs. Link, "I never heard of a divorce action where something wasn't."

"But you know," Cliff said dreamily, "I can't help wondering what it was her husband didn't tell me."

"Oh, no, you don't!" Mrs. Kimberly said in a glad cry, slipping the deuce of hearts under the trey in the trick on the table.

"You're quite an old gossip, aren't you, Mr. Storm?" Mrs. Moran said benignly.

A siren came screaming. The Norns bent to concentrate on the lighted area of the emergency entrance.

Cliff left them. He felt tired. He felt, in fact, discouraged. Better hit the sack, he supposed. He must be getting old.

The idea that had come to him in the wee hours had needed embellishment, of course. He had thought of working his two notions into one device, but no scheme would quite jell in his mind. The notion of hit and run would involve him, physically, too much for his taste. And his other notion—or any notion, for that matter—would involve his telling, personally, some flat lies against Sherry in direct confrontation. Well, they had to be lies, didn't they? So what was the matter with him? Actually, the more fantastically unbelievable his machinations, the better.

But he wished he could get his plot clear. It didn't click yet. He had not got it yet.

He went along the upper hall and saw the door of the middle room standing open. There was a light, but nobody there. On the floor stood the doctor's little black bag.

Cliff thought: How about Sherry's turning up in possession of narcotics? That was a crime. And what if the narcotics had been stolen on top of it? So how about Cliff's removing something interesting from Joe Bianchi's bag and planting it in Sherry's room? (To which he planned to achieve a private entrance by tomorrow night.) Joe could easily be stirred up to suspect her. Cliff could play the part of the indignant defender of the innocent and so arrange the search. Maybe this wasn't such a bad idea. Simplicity! Ah . . .

He went into Joe's room.

The bathroom door swished open. When Joe hailed him, Cliff was standing at the dresser.

"Greetings," said Joe, politely unsurprised.

Cliff's wits grabbed for the first thing he saw. "Can I have the loan of your scissors," he said, "since, now that you're here, I don't have to snitch them?" He picked them up from the dresser top. They looked somehow meanly and cruelly surgical. "Or are these, all the time, sterile?"

"Be my guest," said Joe. "That's a flawed pair."

"You don't say," said Cliff. "Gads, what eyesight!" He ran the points under a fingernail idly. The black bag was now in touch with Joe's foot. "What have you fellows got in those bags anyhow?" said Cliff. *He* didn't know. He hadn't had time to look.

"Band-Aids," said Joe. "What else?"

"Little nightcap?" said Cliff, with an inviting jerk of his head.

"Don't mind if I do," Joe said.

Carrying the scissors, Cliff led the way to the front bedroom. He'd been stupid. Joe wouldn't be carrying hallucinogens. A user of old-standard narcotics could be spotted by science. And likewise so could a nonuser. Cliff must keep science in mind.

After a while Joe said, "By the way, your timing was off, Brother Storm. Our Sherry's not getting that restless. Maybe someday, but not yet."

"Okay," Cliff said furiously. "So she's Rebecca of Sunnybrook Farm! She's the *Belle Dame sans* whatever she was *sans!* She's Sister Bernadette!"

"Well, well, well," Joe said mildly.

"Yeah," said Cliff, recovering artfully. "If I wasn't a dying man—"

"So suffer some more," Joe said blandly. "Then maybe you don't got to die."

When he had gone, Cliff opened another bottle.

One sure way to win the prize had just occurred to him. He could murder her! Trouble with him was he was too smart.

"Don't want to be bothered, raising another man's son, eh?" Mrs. Link said in her languid way, stroking a wisp to lie flat behind her ear.

"Looks ahead, don't he, for a dying man?" said Mrs. Moran, giving her friends a Look. "But not taking her *out* tomorrow night."

"Mr. Peabody's going to get the DT's," Mrs. Kimberly said briskly, "if Mr. Storm don't quit feeding him whisky. He's not going to know which way is up when he goes to see that house."

They hooted together, but only mildly.

"I think girls," said Mrs. Moran, "we ought to eat one good hearty meal before the show."

They all nodded sagely. Something was up. Right here in the house. What sport!

Chapter 11

THERE WAS no mail for Mrs. Reynard on Saturday morning.

Walking in the park turned out to be a lonely business. Maybe it took practice to settle for watching other people live. No one spoke to Sherry. She spoke to no one. She saw one person she knew, but was not seen. It was a very small park. She could stroll all the way around it, she discovered, in about ten minutes. She also discovered that walking in the open air made her hungry.

In the afternoon (lest she blow her top, she told herself) Sherry went to the drugstore and bought nail polish remover, assorted implements, and a new bottle of pale polish with the same guilty delight any female feels when she buys what she can't afford and does not absolutely need, but simply wants.

That evening, according to her routine, after Johnny had been read his story and patted down for sleep, and Sherry had had her dismal meal, she came back to the house and could not imagine for a moment why the sitting room looked so bare.

Then she realized that the Norns were not in their window nook. This made the whole house seem deserted. At first she thought: Oh, marvelous! But soon it began to seem uncanny.

What now? she wondered. For a moment she even found herself ready to dash back across the street to the safety of the hospital lobby. What's the matter with me? she thought. How silly! What's there to be afraid of? What can happen? Nothing! Unless I'm dumb enough to let it.

She went into her room and came out again immediately to choose the love seat in the sitting room, where she could sit and see both the opening to the entrance hall and the arch into the dining room. She somehow did not fancy anything coming up, unnoticed, behind her. She listened. Music afar? Elsie's TV? Well, then, one living soul was here.

Cliff Storm, standing at the top of the stairs, made no noise. Peering past the sign on the porch roof, he had seen Sherry come out of the hospital. He had heard her come into the house. He knew that she was down there now, alone.

There was no one else in the house but the landlady's daughter, the other side of the kitchen. Archer had not yet returned from the appointment Cliff had set up for him with a man in the industry who might, Cliff had said, offer him a part. Archer had gone gratefully.

Cliff had spent the last hour reviewing his great achievement. All right. He had moved the people, directed them to go away from here, as he had wished them to be away. He had done it by devious methods, by telling many lies. He had done it, in fact, rather arduously.

But what had he succeeded in doing, after all?

It had taken him seven minutes, all told, and in full daylight (because he had been too jittery to wait for the light to fade) to go into Sherry's room, pry the nails out of the door to the yard, return to the nail holes some mere nailheads, test that the door would now open (not too noisily), lock it, take the key out of the lock, and pocket it. And thereafter to search through all of Sherry's possessions.

He had opened the suitcase on the floor of the wardrobe and found it full of little boy's clothing. The garments hanging from the rod were few and had no hidden pockets. The dresser drawers held nothing mysterious, except the usual feminine mysteries. The other suitcase, standing in the corner, was empty.

What had he got out of all this? Kicks, he thought morosely. It was true that he had been excited the entire time, with his pulse fast, his throat dry, his breath shallow, feeling the delicious terror of the child thief. And listening all the while for Dr. Bianchi, casting him as the grown-up menace. As if Joe would have paid the slightest attention to some far-off scream of a nail leaving wood! Joe was erratic in his comings and goings, however, and was the one person whose whereabouts Cliff had not been able either to predict or to dictate.

But during the long seven minutes Joe had not happened to visit his room. So Cliff had done what he had planned safely, and in a very short time. And ever since he had been asking himself whether these antics were fitting for a grown man and future executive.

So now he could enter Sherry's room unseen, and she could (theoretically) leave or arrive in secret, too, although she, of course, wouldn't know this. But the accomplishment did seem disproportionate to the effort.

Come on, milk the situation for a little more. How could he use Sherry's presence, down there all alone?

He heard a key in the front-door lock and drew back. Lawton Archer came in.

Cliff heard Sherry's hail.

"Oh, good evening, Mrs. Reynard." The actor hesitated. "Where is everyone?"

"I wish I knew," said Sherry.

Cliff realized that Archer was walking through to the sitting room, so he tiptoed down as far as the landing.

Now he could hear Sherry saying, "Are you really moving out, Mr. Archer?"

"Oh, yes. Oh, yes. That's imperative."

"You've found another place, have you?"

"Not definitely," Archer said. "I am considering the possibility of going back to New York."

"*I'm* going back," she said warmly. "Just as soon as I can get away."

"Is that so?" Archer was evidently settling down for a chat. "I can't say I blame you. One can't afford to lower one's standards. That doesn't do, does it?"

"Surely not," said Sherry. (What was there about her voice? Cliff wondered. The man was such an ass. She couldn't be taking him at his own valuation, could she?)

"I've trained myself on the classics, you know," boomed Archer. "Out here, there is very little respect."

"Isn't there?" said Sherry. "It's such a big city. I should think there must be all kinds of theater."

"Oh I suppose there are a few little theaters that do attempt serious classical drama, but they are absolute cliques, you know. And this person"—Archer used the noun as if it were a dirty name—"who offered me a part, just now . . . Can you imagine what it was? A one-shot bit in a TV series. I was to play that tired old stereotype, the Mississippi steamboat gambling man."

Cliff thought to himself: The casting's not impossible. Nothing like a genuine phony.

"You didn't take it?" Sherry was saying sympathetically.

"Oh, no, no, no, no," said Archer in the British manner. "I daresay there would have been money in it. I could, perhaps, have qualified myself to be *the* Mississippi steamboat gambling man around this town, available whenever such is needed, which is altogether too often. Mr. Storm was very kind to send me there, but I'm afraid he didn't quite realize—" Archer sighed and became thoughtful of her now. "I hear that you have been on the stage yourself, ma'am. In New York, was it?"

"Oh, no, I wasn't," said Sherry. "Not really."

"But someone . . . Mr. Storm, wasn't it? I think he said show business."

"Oh, *that* I tried," said Sherry. "I guess."

"I suppose one ought not to be discouraged by the values of today, but it's difficult, isn't it?"

"Well, in my case," Sherry said cheerfully, "I just wasn't good enough."

"Oh, now, come." But Archer was suspicious.

"Listen, all I wanted to do was dance in a nightclub chorus line. But wow! Did I ever find out, the minute they got going in rehearsal, I'd zig when I was supposed to zag—every time!" Sherry began to laugh.

Cliff, listening on the stairs, remarked to himself that he had not heard her laugh until now.

"Boy," she said, "some of those routines! It's worse than being in the Army."

"I may have misunderstood," Archer said in an aggrieved way. "I was given the impression that you had been a dramatic actress."

"Oh, gosh," Sherry said merrily, "not me. Even if I could do it, I don't think I could stand that kind of life."

"May I ask," Archer said with an ominous courtesy, alert for insult, "what you mean by 'that kind of life'?"

"Well, I mean it's awfully hard, isn't it? All that training. Your voice and the way you move and your brain and your whole self. And then you have to work like a dog. Although," she went on, "I never can figure out why people say that. I never saw a dog do one single stitch of work that I know." She was laughing again.

Then Cliff heard a strange sound. It was the tragedian, trying to join her in laughter. Cliff could even hear how the man experimented with changes of pace, with a variety of notes on the scale. He was first astonished, and then it struck him funny, and he doubled over the rail.

He was startled by a crooning sound somewhere below. There was a flutter, out of his line of sight, and then here came Archer, flying for the stairs. And then Elsie Peabody, who never moved fast, came lumbering after him.

Archer leaped upward, bumped into Cliff, and darted around behind him without apology. He vanished above.

Cliff stifled his need to howl with mirth and went down.

Elsie was hanging there on the newel-post. She was obedient. She was forbidden the upstairs. But she was still crooning after her adored one.

Cliff said to her, "Come on, Elsie. Come on back in the other room."

The girl, with her delayed reaction, took the message, blinked, and walked ahead of him into the sitting room, obeying. (His creature.)

Sherry was perched on the edge of the small pinkish sofa. "Hi," she said. She wasn't laughing anymore.

Cliff sobered himself completely and shook his head sadly behind the half-wit's back. "Don't worry about a thing, Elsie," he said. "Sherry wants to talk to you. Don't you, Sherry?"

"Why, I certainly do," Sherry said at once. She held out her hand as if to a toddler. "Come, sit down and tell me . . . Where is your mama? Where is your daddy?"

Elsie, swinging her too heavy hips, walked toward Sherry.

"They're out," Cliff said softly, remaining where he was, standing near the mirror, "and damn, I promised to keep an eye on her. I'm sorry. I thought she was watching television."

But Sherry could see Elsie's colorless lashes wincing in a curious way. She suddenly had a vision of a double consciousness here. The girl must have heard Archer's voice. She must have very keen hearing. There must be a faulty connection between the sensory perception and the brain's reception of the news. Or was it only the brain's *reaction* that was slow? Did the poor thing know more than she could seem to know, understand more than she could ever express? Was there a quick animal sense of the world there, with a heavy lid on it, so that it was impeded, it was frustrated, it was disabled, but yet in existence? An exquisite torture, she thought. Like Ward's? Her heart hurt. Oh, poor thing. Poor thing.

"Do you want to watch more television, Elsie?" Sherry said tenderly. "Or would you rather just talk to me for a while? Talk to me." Sherry patted the other half of the little sofa's seat. "What did you see on television tonight?"

Elsie's face took on some animation, as it had before. She had tilted her head; her ears seemed to yearn after a particular chord. She sat down beside Sherry. "Oh, I was singing," she said. "I was singing." She began to make the arm motions of the popular singer.

"Whoops!" said Sherry, ducking and laughing. "Hey!" She reached for Elsie's hand to stop the motion. Elsie seemed to think this was pleasant. Her broad hand tightened.

Sherry thought: Her sense of touch, too?

"What was the name of the singing lady?" she asked.

But Elsie, even after Sherry had repeated the question, didn't seem to have a grasp of names. She settled back into the upholstery. "Singing," she crooned, and began to swing Sherry's hand.

Sherry was listening hard, wondering if the girl had a voice. "Do you like to sing?"

"I was singing," said Elsie.

Cliff Storm, fascinated, absorbed in watching them, was genuinely startled when the front door opened behind him and in came the Norns, Mrs. Kimberly atrot, Mrs. Link with heavy tread, and Mrs. Moran in her mysteriously swift shuffle. Their ancient eyes lit at once as if (aha!) they had caught him out somehow.

"You're early, ladies," he said politely.

"We skipped the second feature." Mrs. Kimberly squirreled her cheeks; her bright eyes were hopeful.

"Excuse me," said Cliff. He felt annoyed, for some reason. He went quickly to Elsie and took her other hand firmly with a lifting tug. "Now be a good girl," he said. "Be a good girl, Elsie. That's enough. You'd better go back to the other part of the house now. That's a good girl. Your mother is coming soon. Your mother is coming."

She was docile to his authority. He took her away through the dining room, and he heard Sherry say, "Poor thing! Doesn't she ever get to go anywhere and see anything and have any fun?"

He didn't hear the Norns' answer.

They hadn't answered. Sherry, feeling for some reason flustered, kept smoothing her skirt. A strange mood had been created by somebody.

The Norns homed to their table. They were twittering out of their wraps.

"It certainly seems lonely around here," said Sherry, "when you are away."

They all looked at her solemnly.

"Did you have a good time?" she went on stubbornly.

"We saw a show," said Mrs. Moran.

"Very entertaining," sighed Mrs. Link.

"Parts of it," said Mrs. Kimberly.

Then they sat staring at her like owls.

Sherry got up not quite steadily and said she ought to go do her nails; she'd say good night.

She didn't know what they were expecting of her. Some entertainment?

At this moment the Peabodys came in. Mr. Peabody kept right on rolling, in his seaman's gait, through to the dining room. He gave Sherry a somewhat sullen glare as he passed her. Mrs. Peabody seemed excited. "Oh," she said. "Well! Yes. Fine! Good night." Her odd eyes evaded all other eyes, and off she went.

Sherry went into her room; she spread out her purchases; she removed her old polish, then filed and neatened the bare nails. But when it came to putting on the new polish, she found her hands were too shaky.

Caught in the kitchen, Cliff was forced to listen to Mrs. Peabody being enthusiastic about the House. (It now wore a capital *H*). He said he was glad they had liked it, and he promised to talk to Mr. Edward Reynard as soon as he could. The basic difference in levels here—Mrs. Peabody's burning interest, because to her the House represented her economic future, and Cliff's disinclination to talk about it anymore, because he was well satisfied with matters as they stood—began to grate on each other.

Cliff now switched the subject to Elsie, saying that he had gone upstairs for a bit, but Mrs. Reynard had been there, so Elsie had been well looked after. The landlady scarcely glanced at the back of her daughter's head, but she muted her impatience to be sure of the House. She had to thank Mr. Storm several times more, and Mr. Peabody, although making up for some dry hours, kept chiming in.

When Cliff got away at last, he found the Norns obviously waiting for him. They chorused their thanks for the pleasant evening. Then they sat there, each with her wrap on her arm, each clasping a handbag in a lizard-textured hand, all three pairs of eyes expecting something of him.

He sat down and said softly, "Our Elsie is heading for a crush on Mrs. Reynard, I see. I guess there's no harm." He watched them. They did not react at all. He cocked his head, inquiring of their silence.

"How was the house?" Mrs. Moran said at last.

"Oh. Oh, very satisfactory," he said.

"Are they taking it?" said Mrs. Link.

"I would imagine so," he purred.

Mrs. Kimberly gave her friends a Look. "Well, girls." She rose.

When they had disappeared, Cliff realized vaguely that the news of the house was important to them. But he was listening for voices, beyond that screen, in the women's quarters.

He could hear nothing.

Cliff went out of the house by the front door. Damn and damn. He couldn't feel sure of his control. He wasn't at all sure that the Norns weren't on to the fact that they had been manipulated and, furthermore, suspected that the Peabodys had been, too. And if they were speculating about all this, was Sherry Reynard listening?

Well, what of it? Suppose she were to become aware of his machinations? Might not really matter to the results, he told himself. So why was he uneasy?

He had intended to go to Sonia's, but he discovered that he didn't feel like it and fled to a bar. Damn and damn. Here he had set the board (to use the chess thing) and moved the pieces, but the pieces wouldn't stay. Some of them had moved out of turn, and (he couldn't help feeling) unfairly.

How could he know what went on in the restricted female quarters?

Nothing went on there. The ladies each had her cell and in it kept each to herself. So did Sherry Reynard.

Chapter 12

ON SUNDAY MORNING, while Emily was at church, the doctor came. After a while he took Edward Reynard downstairs to the study and talked for quite some time. Upstairs the male nurse crouched in a chair, watching. Downstairs the father seemed to turn to stone. A little later Reynard called Murchison at home and got some honest answers.

He then phoned Mrs. Peabody's rooming house and asked for Clifford Storm.

"I want to know exactly what, if anything, you've turned up," he said harshly.

"All right," Cliff said promptly. "I'll meet you in your office tomorrow morning."

"I want to know *now*."

"It's inadvisable to talk over the telephone," Cliff said. "And you'll have some papers ready, I believe, that I'll need to see?"

"In the morning," Reynard said grudgingly. "Without fail."

They set the hour. But Cliff felt oppressed. He didn't like being nagged.

Reynard said to his wife, who had just come in from church, that he was afraid Ward was in for a longer illness than they had anticipated.

She looked at him with terrified round eyes.

"Now, now," he said impatiently. "For pity's sakes, don't cry. You know perfectly well he has the best doctors there are, and they will do everything that ought to be done. Crying won't help. Be patient."

Her mouth trembled. "He'll be all right," she said. "I *know* that!"

"By the way," he said, "would you care for a little Sunday afternoon game? The Tandys were more or less hinting."

So now Emily knew that the illness was very bad indeed. It was worse than he had told her.

But she said brightly, "Oh, that would be nice! Shall I call Geraldine?"

It was much easier this way. He needn't listen to her weeping. And Emily needn't weep. Thus, obliquely, they spared each other, pretending she didn't know.

Sherry came briskly into the house that Sunday, an hour earlier than usual. If it was six o'clock here, then in New York it would be nine. Not too late. Not too early.

The low telephone rates were on all day on Sundays, weren't they? She thought she could place a long-distance call for only a dollar, wasn't it? Or, on the other hand, if she called collect, she would be out nothing. But she wasn't sure that the low rates prevailed if the call were collect.

She shook off worrying about the rates. She had to know, and she was broke, so she would simply telephone collect. If money was already in the mail, fine. But if not, she could try to hurry it up. Funds could be sent by wire. When they came, she would move out of this place fast. Find some small furnished apartment to which she could, if it became necessary, take Johnny. And if Mrs. Peabody wouldn't give back the twenty-five dollars, Sherry resolved that it didn't matter very much, on any sensible scale.

I have been stupid about money, she told herself. Obsessed with it. That's just silly. What have I been doing? Occupying my mind with a little puzzle in arithmetic so as not to have to think?

She went to the phone in the hall and placed a collect call
for Mr. Cornelius Fowler. He was the oldest friend she had, and
since he had been best man at her grandparents' wedding, he was
as good as family. He was also the one to whom a loan of five
hundred dollars would seem the least important. He had retired
long ago and lived well, although he was not in robust health. But
that made him also the one of her friends the most likely to be
found at home.

He was at home. He answered. Sherry could hear the operator's voice asking whether Mr. Fowler would accept a long-
distance call collect from Mrs. Sherry Reynard in Los Angeles.
To her total astonishment she heard his thin old voice saying,
"No, I will not. No, I want no communication with Mrs. Reynard."

She felt stunned. He had hung up. She thought, I should have
spent the dollar. But what was the matter with old Mr. Fowler?

She could sense some shadow presently overhead. She looked
up. There was Cliff Storm, hanging over the banister above her.

He said, "Excuse me, I don't want to disturb you," and came
down the stairs and swiftly passed her, going into the sitting
room.

Sherry took her purse from under her arm and examined her
change. All right, she had five quarters and also the necessary
other dime.

People did get old and crotchety, she supposed. She placed another call, this time to her old roommate—best friend, who was
now Mrs. Roy Anderson.

It wasn't Pat who answered. It was her husband.

"Roy, this is Sherry. Sherry Coleman, that used to be."

"I see." His voice was cool.

"Listen, I wrote Pat. Could I speak to her, please?"

"She's not here."

"Then listen, Roy, did she get my letter?"

"I guess so," he said coldly.

"Well, I wanted to say that I need what I asked her for pretty

bad and pretty quick. So could she *wire* it to me, do you think?
And I'm coming East myself, just as soon—"

"Pat doesn't care to answer your letter."

Then Sherry distinctly heard Pat's voice in the background.
"Roy? Who is that?"

"Let me talk to Pat, please," Sherry said.

"I don't think so," Roy said. "If you got yourself mixed up with
the wrong kind of people, Pat's not going to have any part of it."

He hung up.

Sherry put the phone on its hook. Her money had gone clang-
ing away.

But it wasn't the money. (Remember that, she said to herself.
You worry too much about money.) Just the same, her heart was
sinking. Where was she going to take Johnny when she got him
to New York, if Pat had been turned against her?

"I don't believe it," she said aloud.

"Trouble?" Cliff was standing there.

"I feel," she said slowly, "as if somebody is trying to cut me off
from the world." She smiled at him. "Isn't that silly?"

He said, "We're going out to dinner, aren't we?"

"Of course. I'll be ready in fifteen minutes." She spread out
her hands and looked at them. "I was going to put some polish
on, but I think I'm too darned hungry to wait for it to dry."

"Steak?" said Cliff, leering a little. "Roast beef? Or, if you must,
orange duckling?"

"What kind of wrong people could *I* get mixed up with?" she
said, drawing her eyebrows together.

"Lots of kinds." He was looking down at the top of her head.

She moved, slipping away and dancing around the end of the
wall. The Norns sat clutching their cards.

"Guess what I just found out?" said Sherry joyously. "The way
to get rich is to stop *worrying* about money." She beamed on
them and danced off to array herself for her dinner date. She was
starving! And somebody else was going to buy.

Cliff jingled his change. He strolled back into the sitting room
and sat down to wait.

The cards slapped. When the Norns had finished a hand, Mrs. Kimberly put down the score in silence.

"Who's winning?" Cliff called to them, missing the usual hooting and chirping.

Mrs. Link touched her hair. "The game's not over," she said.

" 'Better is a dinner of herbs where love is,' " said Mrs. Moran, " 'than a stalled ox and hatred therewith.' " She seemed to think she'd been saucy.

"Deal the cards," said Mrs. Kimberly. She nodded her head several times. "There's luck in the cards," she said.

Cliff thought: Poor old *nuts!* They've had it!

"Good luck to all," he said genially.

"That's right," Mrs. Link said mysteriously.

When Sherry appeared, he could have sworn that the three of them were trying to give her Looks. But Sherry was merry.

He had chosen a good and very quiet restaurant, not too far away. He put Sherry Reynard into the coziest corner of the corner banquette and ordered cocktails.

She was wearing the black dress; he remembered it from her wardrobe. On the hanger it had not looked as elegant as it looked now. She had made up her face skillfully. She carried herself confidently. She didn't look like a country girl.

He couldn't figure out what the devil she meant by not worrying about money. Cliff knew what blows she must have received on the telephone. He knew who had cut her off from those people. He'd done it himself, with his little hatchet.

But Sherry seemed relaxed. She drank her cocktail with relish and refused another with no strain. He couldn't help thinking she must have come to some decision. Maybe she was going to take the money and let the child go. If so, he had better know it and find out how he could seem to have been the influencing factor.

So he asked how Johnny was. Johnny was doing very well. When would he be able to leave the hospital? She wasn't sure.

Cliff said he might drop by to call on the boy one day. Would that be possible? Of course, it would. Did Cliff like children? He had to admit he didn't know many.

Look here, did she need money? Certainly not, enough was as good as plenty.

He could not figure her out. He couldn't imagine what kind of world she thought this was.

He began to ask questions about Ward's ambition to write. "Did he really have talent, Sherry, do you think?"

"Well, of course, I thought so," she said. She smiled. The food came. It was excellent, and the portions were lavish. Sherry sampled it and said with gusto, "This is marvelous!"

He said he was glad, and he was glad. What pleasure to feed a truly hungry woman!

But he wasn't here to enjoy himself.

"What's your talent? Interest? Hobby? What do you do that's creative, I mean?" he queried.

"Oh, gosh," said Sherry, "not a thing. Everybody doesn't have to be an artist. In fact, everybody'd better not be."

"You mean to tell me," said Cliff, tickled in spite of himself, "that you're not one of the seventeen million housewives who are taking up ceramics? How are you ever going to express yourself?"

"The trouble with me is," she said with her mischievous grin, "I can't see how in the world you can help expressing yourself. What could you do that didn't?"

"Oh," he said, "come on. You know the story. You can be too timid to let out your true self or your deepest thoughts. Scared not to conform and all that."

"Yes, I know," she said. "Sure, you express your timidity, if that's what you've got."

Cliff had to laugh.

"Well," he said, "you take this fellow, Race Rhode. (And what a moniker *that* is!) Now there's self-expression for you." Rhode was one of the men at the beach, the sculptor, as Cliff recalled. "Is that phony?" he asked her.

Sherry kept on with her roast beef. She was comfortable. The food was good and her appetite better. But it began to appear that when she had shucked off an anxiety which might have been more an evasion than a reality, when she had cleared her mind of that compulsive arithmetic, now her mind was at work adding up another sum.

Here was Cliff Storm mentioning Race Rhode. So add this in, too. Add it in with the events of yestereve and other events, as, for instance, yesterday morning.

Yesterday morning, walking in the park, she had seen Cliff Storm come out the hospital's back entrance and go racing along the street at the far side of the park. She had wondered at the time why he had come out that way when his car was parked in front of the rooming house. She had wondered why he didn't cut through the park to reach it. She had concluded that he didn't want or need his car at the moment. But she hadn't been able to help noticing that wherever he had been going on foot, he had been going at a fast clip. There had been nothing feeble about his movements, nothing even cautious. She had thought no more about it then.

She was thinking about it now.

Cliff had been to see Ward. He must also have seen Edward Reynard. Had he been to see Race Rhode recently? Now he wanted to see Johnny!

Cliff Storm's intense interest in so many things to do with Sherry Reynard was beginning to seem not altogether flattering. Also, Lawton Archer had told her that Cliff was the one who had mentioned her abortive foray into show business. So Cliff Storm *had* discussed her in the house. He was, in fact, the only person who could possibly have put ideas about Sherry into people's heads there, since he was the only one of them who had ever seen her before in his life.

Was all this adding up to something?

As for yestereve, she knew that Cliff had treated the Norns to the movies. Cliff had arranged for the Peabodys to go see some house. Cliff had sent the actor to an interview. Had there been any purpose in all this? Had he been clearing the house of people for a *reason?*

Well, the whole world could not possibly be against her. But there was one man in it who definitely was. Edward Reynard was her avowed enemy. And here was Cliff Storm, old family friend, so very, very interested, so very, very curious, so very, very intent upon her.

Could it be that Edward Reynard was using Cliff Storm's accidental presence in the rooming house? How? Was Cliff supposed to keep a watch on Sherry? What good was that? Or was he supposed to make trouble for her?

Well, that was an awfully mean thing to be thinking about anybody. Yet last night Cliff Storm had fixed it so that all those people had had somewhere else to go. What might have happened in that emptied house? Maybe, she thought, poor half-witted Elsie, barging in so unexpectedly, had spoiled whatever plan there had been. Something to do with Sherry's being alone with Lawton Archer? Oh, surely not! It couldn't be that. Archer himself may have come back too early. But wait! Who *had* been in that house (not counting Elsie)? Sherry Reynard and Clifford Storm.

Here now, what kind of thinking was this? How come she sat here, in this fine restaurant, eating his food and making up fantasies of conspiracy and persecution?

But she couldn't keep from remembering his moving figure yesterday, that careless vigor. She thought to herself: Okay, it may be stupid to think you're being persecuted if you're not. But what if you really are? There was a kind of half test she could apply. If he had really had that surgery and was now really being given treatments that might really be frightening, then his presence in the rooming house was a consequence of his having run into her that day, and nothing could be proved by it. But what if he were lying?

Oh, no! How could he be lying? Yet, *if he were,* then that would be pretty darned peculiar. And she would conclude, she thought (yes, she would!), that he was an agent of Edward Reynard's and, therefore, her enemy, too.

She winced at the thought. But Cliff himself could not feel hostile toward Sherry Reynard. He doesn't know me, she thought. He may not know what it's all about. He's human. What if I told him?

She said, to answer his question, "I don't know whether Race Rhode's a phony. I'm not too sure what that means. I don't know those people very well at all. I sure wish Ward had never taken up with them, though. Did you know"—she looked at him—"that Ward's been playing around with drugs for quite some time?"

"I didn't know that," said Cliff, and thought: But I'm not surprised. He pulled at his wits and said, "Have *you* experimented?"

"Oh, gosh," she said, "I'*d* never."

"Why not? I don't mean go overboard. But just to try?"

"I'm not curious to know how it feels," she said. "The whole idea just doesn't attract me."

Nor me, Cliff thought, with a flash of pleasure. "Why did it attract Ward, I wonder?" he probed.

"I don't know. It attracts an awful lot of people. The story is, they want to be themselves, or free themselves, or expand themselves."

"I guess that's the story," Cliff drawled, and she turned her face to him and smiled suddenly.

"Do you get the point?" she said. "I don't. I simply cannot see their point. Who wants to be a rag doll?"

"Now, what do you mean by—"

"Oh, I see in my mind. Listen. If you're a rag doll, then anything can throw you down, and you flop where it throws you. You *have* to. You've got no bones. Well, with those drugs, maybe you see more or hear more and so on; but you give up your bones, and I don't want to do that. I can't get it through my head that this makes you free or more *you* even. It's a way to be nothing, it seems to me."

A strange notion was creeping into Cliff's mind. He thought she was absolutely right. He felt exactly the same way about drugs. They were not attractive to him and never had been. In fact, he wasn't a lush either. He watched the sauce, and every once in a while he laid off. He didn't like things getting a hold on him. Drugs, especially the addictive ones, were in his opinion exactly what she called them. "A way to be nothing."

But what was strange, he'd taken a notion that Sherry must be more his kind of person than she ever was Ward's. Ward was weak. But she was— Well, damn it, she was tough. In her own way, Protestant ethic or whatever, she was. And so, of course, was Cliff Storm a tough-minded fellow.

"I couldn't agree more," he murmured now.

"It's semantics, of course," she said, astonishing him. "They mean they want to *feel* free. But I mean I want to *be* free. There's a little difference."

"Could be," he murmured.

"You know, I'll bet it does feel free, to get rid of any bother, get rid of time and strife, just flop whenever any old thing happens to drop you or kick you, because you're so busy flitting around inside your own consciousness. Oh, gosh, I would hate that."

"What do you call *being* free?" he asked her.

"Choosing," she said promptly.

"Free will, eh?" He smiled at her.

"Ward says that's only a delusion," said Sherry. "So I say okay, then I'll *choose that* delusion." She looked at him mischievously. "I used to mix him up sometimes." Her face saddened. "Well, I guess we got so we didn't talk an awful lot."

Cliff put cream in his coffee. "All right. Look here. What if you choose to be a rag doll?"

"Come on, that's no fair," she said. "Sure you can—once or twice. A living man can choose to be dead—once. But then it's the end of the line."

He said nothing; his face didn't change; he was thinking: I agree, damn it.

Sherry said, "Oh, listen, listen!" She swayed toward him. "I'm sorry! What an idiot I am! I shouldn't have said that."

"Why not?" he said, surprised, and saw her face change and knew that he had just made a mistake.

"Sometimes there is no choice, you'll have to admit," he said and shrugged. "No use to complain."

"No," she said, "no use to complain. There sure is no choice, about some things. Being born, for instance. A member of the species."

Damn and damn. Cliff was fuming to himself. He'd forgotten again that he was supposed to be in terror of an early death. But why did she bring that up about being born? And the *species*?

He asked for the dessert cart to be brought. Sherry hesitated over the goodies. Then she smiled and ordered a large piece of rich cake, loaded with cream.

"Last chance," she said and looked at him sideways.

He played with his spoon. "So you're going to struggle and slave, and take the boy back to some hole in the wall in the dirty old city, and work and work, night and day. This is being free?"

"I didn't think it *was* a choice," she said. "But as you pointed out the other night, there may be an alternative. I could give Johnny up, and he could have all that expensive education, the privileges Ward had." She looked sideways again. "And Ward *might not* kill him."

Cliff felt as if the top of his head were coming off. "What do you mean, '*kill him*'?"

"I mean I think Ward's done himself a permanent damage," she said flatly. "There was this girl at the beach . . . Oh, she's a goner. You see, Ward did hurt Johnny. Yet he didn't choose to. It was the drug that did it. So poor Ward, I'm afraid he might not have any choices anymore."

Cliff whistled softly and leaned back. (Damn and damn!)

"I realize you've never been a mother," she was saying, "but have you ever been a father?"

"No, no. And I'm not going to argue with you," he snapped.

"Good," said Sherry. Demurely she ate cream.

In a while he paid the check (she watched him tip). They went out to his car. He asked listlessly if she would like to go to some place of entertainment. He had had some places in mind. But Sherry thought she'd rather (being so pleasantly stuffed!) go home now. Cliff didn't argue. He thought the game was over.

When he pulled the car to the curb, they could see the Norns in the window.

"Thank you," said Sherry, "for a delicious dinner. It's done me good."

"Thank you for the sermon," he said politely.

"What?"

"On the meaning of freedom."

"What makes you call that a sermon?" she asked indignantly.

"Figure of speech."

"Wow," she said, "freedom! That's only the beginning."

"Really?" he drawled as insultingly as he could.

"You still have to *make* the choice," she said flatly. "You know that."

"Aha," he crowed. "Now comes in the sermon? All right. I'll bite. On what basis, granting there may be a choice, do you make a choice?" He was needling her now. They both knew it.

Sherry said slowly, "Are you asking me *why* I don't want Johnny to be beaten up or terrorized or even killed by his own father? I don't know why. But I'd rather he wasn't. I'm darned sure of that."

"Blind instinct, eh?" he sneered. "What you'd rather? And that's what freedom comes down to?"

She was getting angry. "Oh, you can't do much about your blind instincts," she said, "except choose *among* them. Or did you think I had only one?"

Cliff didn't answer.

"How do *you* pick and choose among them?" she went on. "I mean, when you're not worrying about your health?"

He got out on his side and went around to open the other door and bow her out.

Sherry said, "You don't settle for sensation now, do you?"

"Why not?" he said coldly.

"You operate in time," she said angrily. "I *know* you do."

"I don't understand you," he said, putting up a wall.

"Yes, you do," she said. "You're a chooser, too."

She went up the walk, and he followed her. On the stoop he reached around her to use his door key, and she shrank away from him insultingly. Cliff thought that if he could now choose to do what he'd rather, in the moment, he would, then and there, wring her fragrant little neck.

They came into the sitting room. The Norns gave greeting. "You're early," said Mrs. Kimberly.

Cliff flung himself into a chair sullenly.

"I wish I hadn't let her talk me out of going somewhere where we could get a drink," he complained. "Of course, I've got a bottle upstairs, but I suppose the sky would fall—"

"You must have quite a supply," said Mrs. Link. "Keeping up with Mr. Peabody, too."

Cliff gave her a hard look, but her face was as bland as usual.

Sherry said, "I wonder how come Mr. Peabody thought *I* was perishing for alcohol at eight thirty this morning."

"He didn't!" said Cliff, playing amused.

"Who would *bother*," she said scathingly, "to tell my friends that I'm mixed up with the wrong kind of people?"

"When you're not, eh?" he said.

"I'm not sure about that," she said darkly.

In another moment she said good night and went to her room. Cliff, looking black and not bothering to conceal it, jingled his change and felt the key to that room at his fingertips. *No.* And the hell with it! In a moment he flung himself away and banged up the stairs.

"Are they in love?" Mrs. Link said dryly.

"Certainly. And one of these days," Mrs. Kimberly said briskly, "one of them is going to kill the other one."

"Deal the cards," Mrs. Moran said gloomily.

Cliff thought it was all over, never begun. Never *been* any chance. No gamble. All Sherry ever had to do was to say what she had said to him to some judge. Any judge. Ward could never qualify for custody, and unless there were to be some special safeguards set up to keep the father and the child apart, neither could his parents.

So there it went. He wondered about Edward Reynard. If this was the truth, surely Ward's father must realize it.

Wait. Why had Cliff believed Sherry, at once, without question? She couldn't know that Ward was as good as insane or (you might say) better, because his condition was irreversible. How could she know that? Ignorant little country girl at heart. No, no. She'd dreamed that up because she wanted out. She admitted she didn't know why she did as she did. Well, few do. But Cliff Storm understood human motivations better than most, and in the end he remembered the kid would get the bulk of *all* the Reynard money. So if Ward was as good as insane *and* dangerous, then naturally she'd play it safe and go for the long wait. Nuts! Here he was, back to believing her again.

The trouble was, he did.

Chapter 13

"SATISFACTORY?" said Edward Reynard.

Cliff looked up from the papers at the small tyrant enthroned behind his office desk. The agreement, in Cliff's hands, would *give* him Storm and Savage. He had been reading with intense concentration, hunting for loopholes and ambiguities. He complained now of one paragraph.

Reynard said, "Pencil in the changes you want."

At last Cliff put the papers down on the desk between them.

"Well?" said the man.

"There are a couple of questions," Cliff said mildly, although the agreement had excited him and his wits were probing and prying for some way to win yet. "I'm going to have to ask you about Ward's condition," he continued. "Did you know he had been taking drugs? Do you know to what extent? And are you sure how they have affected him?"

Reynard's gray face turned a somewhat lighter gray. "I know all about it," he said sharply. "He keeps having recurring spells when he more or less goes out of control and evidently hallucinates. The doctor tells me that some people are especially sensitive to certain substances, and Ward seems to have been one of them."

"I'm sorry to hear that, er, confirmed," Cliff murmured.

"Who told *you?*"

"Sherry suspects there has been permanent damage."

"She does, eh?" Reynard blazed. "She's damned right! I hope she's proud of what she—" Reynard made an effort. He leaned forward and said, in a different voice, "Do you see what this means to me? Outside of the fact that my only son has been driven to this, I cannot now ever have another grandchild. Ever! There is only that one little boy. Only the one. Now tell me how I'm going to get him away from that woman."

"I don't know," Cliff said softly. "It may not be possible at all, unless— What does Ward's doctor suggest be done for him? If you intend to keep him there in the house, at home, I doubt— It seems there might be physical danger for the child. Sherry will say so to the judge, I'm afraid."

Edward Reynard held his forehead in one clutching hand. "All right," he said, "I've faced up to that. I am prepared to give Ward over to some institutional care, for John's sake. If we have to do that, then we will do that."

Cliff thought: Well, this begins to sound a little better! But then he heard himself blurting, "Why don't you take them both in?"

"Both?"

"Sherry and the boy."

"Because that leaves *her free!*" snarled Reynard. "What are you trying to say?"

"Only wondering." Cliff shrugged, wondering to himself why or whether he had *chosen* to say such a thing.

But now Reynard was settling his thin shoulders. "Did you enjoy your dinner date last night?" he said acidly.

Cliff's eyes rolled. "I see. You've got somebody else working on this thing. Well . . ." He moved as if to get up and leave.

"Just a minute. Naturally I've had a man keeping an eye on Sherry. Making sure she doesn't run off. I told you."

"No, sir, you did not," said Cliff. "I had assumed that was *my*

job. Has your other employee come up with something . . . useful?"

Reynard's jawline was hard.

Cliff laughed. "Or did he tell you that she's as pure as the
driven snow and has the strength of ten, and you haven't got a
prayer?"

Reynard came as close to frothing at the mouth as Cliff had
ever seen in what is known as "real life." "So she got to you,"
he cried. "I thought so. I don't know what reward you're getting,
but I hope it's worth it." He reached for the copies of the agreement. "I ought to have known better than to expect *you* to resist
that kind of woman."

"Hey!" said Cliff, alarmed. He stood up and leaned over the
desk. Reynard's hands stopped, just as they were poised to tear
the papers. "Have I said I couldn't or wouldn't do the job for
you?" Cliff demanded.

He was thinking fast. I see! I see! He knows (and may have
known all the time) that he has to have her framed. And for
that, I'm his boy. He dassn't hire that done. Dassn't even suggest
it, because who knows? The private investigator might be honest.
But me he trusts to do the dirty work. He is hiring me (and he
has a plum for me) to frame her. But does *he* know that's what
he's doing?

"Can you do the job for me?" Reynard said angrily.

"Oh, I imagine so," Cliff drawled, and waited to see whether
the man would now admit what the job was.

But Reynard said, with a brighter look, "You're onto something
then?"

"I could be." Cliff kept wary.

Reynard flattened the papers on the desk and reached for a
pen. "I'll tell you what I'll do," he said. "You guarantee me that
you can and will produce evidence that should . . . that by all
reasonable expectations ought . . . to prove to any decent man
that the child must be taken away from her. Tell me *that*, and
I will sign this agreement now."

"Sign it," Cliff said quickly.

Reynard signed his name to five copies and even initialed the changes. He then capped his pen and turned it in his clean pale hands. "Now we come to the sequel," he said nastily. "If you do not meet that guarantee, you may as well anticipate that I'll break Storm and Savage into little pieces and throw the pieces down the sewer. Down the sewer, that is, of a wide-open investigation of your moneymaking venture of a few years ago. I have copies of three films you shot for the dirty people, and I have proof that you were the boy genius who produced and directed them."

"Somehow or other," said Cliff, "I don't seem to be surprised."

He sat down and rubbed his chin. With his other hand he reached for the top copy of the agreement and rolled it up. He held it in his fist like a scepter. He felt a touch of pitying condescension for a man who thought it was as easy as this to throw somebody else down the sewer. Oh, Reynard might be a nuisance, digging up this part of the past. But let Cliff, in power at Storm and Savage, acquire money and prestige in the present tense, and he had no doubt that he could continue without much bother. The old man didn't seem to realize how fuzzy such things could get in these days.

Still, let him think he had a powerful threat here? Use it to force some admission out of him?

"I'll ask you," Cliff said coldly, "to get in touch with whoever is the director of admissions at the Sherman Prevocational School for Mentally Retarded Juveniles. I want an appointment with this director for Mrs. Peabody, to discuss the admission of her daughter, Elsie, into the school at a *minimum* fee, tuition, or whatever it is called. This comes under expenses."

Reynard said, "Nothing wrong with that. All right."

"I want the appointment on Wednesday evening. Give the man my name. I'll set it up with him just when I want it."

"All right."

Cliff was still wondering whether Reynard was fully conscious of what he was doing. He said, "Nothing much will happen, you see, unless this woman is out of the house."

"But if she is out of the house, then something will happen?" Reynard said sharply.

"I have reason to believe so," purred Cliff.

"Cuts it close, doesn't it? Wednesday?"

"If you want this done," Cliff said boldly, "then you'll have to let me be the judge of how and when it can be done."

"All right," said Reynard. He shut his mouth tight. He wasn't going to come any closer to admitting anything.

"Do you want to know the details?" Cliff said seductively.

"No, no," said Reynard, admitting everything.

So Cliff tucked the agreement, rolled as it was, into his inside pocket and patted his jacket. Feeling pleasantly powerful, he got up and said, "By the way, call off your other man or men, will you? They're not necessary, and they might interfere. I don't want them around."

"All right," said Reynard. His eyes were cold.

Cliff went down in the elevator and out of the office building. He got into his car. Now he was for it! Now he had to solidify some scheme and put it into the works and make it work.

His car was a year and a half old—not too much to sacrifice. He could figure, roughly, how to get Sherry Reynard *seemingly* involved in a hit and run. That was possible.

What he needed to do was to work in the sexy overtone. He would use *Elsie*. That should be shocking. Of course, he wondered to himself whether this sort of thing really had much bearing on a young woman's fitness to be a mother. He did know that human beings punish other human beings not necessarily and perhaps never in reasonable ways. All he needed was the shock of revulsion at the proper time. The timing was important.

It occurred to him that a sneak preview was sometimes revealing. So he changed course and drove to Miss Erskine's cottage.

He paid her the nine dollars. Then he began to hint, accusingly.

The woman stared at him. She put her hand over her eyes,

and Cliff braced himself for an outburst of hysteria until he realized that she was trying not to laugh.

He said, "Well?" quite sharply.

"Oh, Mr. Storm," she gasped, eyes brimming. "Really! You *can't* believe that! You can't *possibly!* Sherry Reynard! Haven't you ever seen her? Have you seen her in the same room with— I thought you *knew* her husband? What are you *talking* about?" Now she sputtered out laughter. "Even if it were so, what would she want with the likes of me? Oh, dear! I'm sorry." She was trying to stop laughing for the sake of politeness. "Did you think I hadn't been to see her because of some great emotional— No, no. *I* was worried about being asked for money." She began to use her handkerchief on her mirthful tears. "I'm sorry it struck me so f-funny," she said. Now her dried and faded eyes were pitying him. "I don't suppose you'd understand these things too well," she said kindly. And blinked, and said, *not* kindly, "What are you trying to do?"

Cliff got up. "Well," he said, concealing his rage as best he could, "I guess you've answered my question. I'm glad. And thank you very, very much. It's a relief," he lied. "I didn't *really* believe it, of course," he added truthfully.

He drove off, feeling sour. He would have expected her to shed tears all right. But not that kind. He couldn't have been that wrong. The very hint of such an accusation should have been enough to set her outraged innocence screaming. How innocent was Miss Erskine? How innocent was anybody?

He went to where he had his cache. He opened the large metal box and fingered the cryptic titles. Shocking stuff, he had always supposed. (Not to him, of course.) What would Sherry Reynard want with the likes of Elsie? Then it leaped into his hand. Ah! *This* was what had been haunting the dark of his mind. Of course. Of course. Of course.

He took one particular can of film to his apartment. He wanted to run it off, remind himself. But he remembered well enough. He remembered the one significant thing useful to his purposes.

They paid money. Cliff was acquainted with quite a few groups in the city to whose odd tastes he had, from time to time, catered. But this group had a taste for something that really was, he thought with amusement, not only old-fashioned, but *ancient*. And for what they needed, they were willing to pay quite well.

He sat down and went to work and figured the whole scheme out in detail. When he finished, he thought he would like some-day to let Miss Erskine know how much she had helped.

The male nurse said, "It's not such a good time, Mrs. Reynard."

"Oh, dear," said Emily, "I never seem to see him these days. You're sure he's been taking his medicine regularly?"

"Oh, yes, ma'am."

"It's discouraging," she sighed.

"Yes, ma'am. Excuse me." The bedroom door was firmly closed in her face.

Ward said to his nurse, "She's gone?"

"She won't bother you."

"I love my mother," said Ward, writhing, "but she drives me crazy." Then he looked the nurse in the eye. "Or she would, if I wasn't crazy already."

"Come on, now. You don't want to talk like that."

Ward said, in a soft singsong, " 'Christ, that I were in my bed . . .' "

The nurse, who had never heard of the song, was glad his patient was making *some* sense, anyway.

Emily wandered disconsolately along the blue carpet of the upper hall and into her own huge bedroom. No one had yet told her directly that Ward was probably never going to recover fully or be himself again. Even the doctor avoided the subject with her.

She sat down at her dressing table and looked at her frightened blue eyes. Never mind. Never mind. It wasn't *her* fault. It wasn't *her* doing. Things happen. Awful things happen, even to nice people. Even to nice girls, like Emily. In a way she had long ago got her reward. When Edward had been saved. Of course, in those days, there hadn't been this dreadful drug business. She didn't understand it. Still, there was a thing Edward often said. Sounded so coldly businesslike, but it must have merit: "Cut your losses."

Emily closed her eyes and began to plan. The room that had been fixed up for a nursery after Johnny had been born would not do. No. He would need more space than that. A little boy had to have his things, his shelves of toys, and so on. She thought: The garden side of the house, the big guest room? Yes, but there was that staircase down from the balcony, over the back terrace. Emily felt a shiver of fear. Kidnappers! No, perhaps it would be better to give Johnny a room at the front of the house and put his nurse next door. Her mind began to select colors. It might do no harm if she were to begin to look around some of the finer children's furnishings shops.

She would do absolutely everything she could for the dear little boy.

He wouldn't be much trouble.

Monday was, comparatively speaking, a good day for Sherry. In the first place, she had enjoyed that dinner, had managed to beat down both her anger with Cliff Storm and her shame at having been rude to him so that she could digest it. It had done her good, restored some energy. In the second place, her resolution not to worry about money held, to a degree. She still had twenty-two dollars and fifty cents, and although she certainly wasn't going to throw money around, here it was Monday already.

Then Johnny's doctor was pleased to say that he could imagine no reason why Johnny could not go immediately from the hospital to an airplane. Riding in a jet was not, the doctor felt, physically strenuous. Sherry was encouraged by this news and felt sure she could solve the problem of what to do in New York before she took off for that city. If Pat Anderson was lost to her, not everybody was. Her young husband might have thought he was protecting her, thought it his duty. Sometimes Sherry wondered what she was supposed to be. A member of the Mafia? A spy, maybe? Well, no matter. She wasn't either.

During the morning the black-haired girl took her own small child away. She said to Sherry, going by, "Good luck. And listen, take it easy."

Sherry was cheered by the sight of a patient who had been healed.

At noon she bought a box of crackers and some cheese and ate in the park, delighted to escape the low-calorie plate. She drank from the public fountain, watched the people and the pigeons and the healthy children, who bobbed along the grass under gay balloons.

But there was the long, long afternoon and Johnny sulking. He couldn't be disciplined firmly until he was all well either. And there was the same dismal dinner. By the time she got back to the house, the good shine of the day was tarnishing.

She did not linger in the sitting room. The Norns were there, and she might have enjoyed a chat with them. But Elsie Peabody came to her with the tale of something Elsie had experienced, in her vicarious way. Sherry put her off gently and went into her room, where she busied herself with her costume for the big event. What would she wear, and was it in good order? When ought she to wash her hair to have it at its best?

She had seen no sign of Cliff Storm all day long and did not want to see any. She did not want to think about him. Or Edward Reynard. Or Ward. Or herself, much. So she thought about her grooming.

She did not want to think about the importance of Thursday in a suspenseful way at all. She would not even *imagine* losing Johnny. It wasn't going to happen. All she had to do was keep steady, keep steady, go right on, keep being what she was.

She had chosen her instinct to keep Johnny safe and to raise him well. *That was it.* She had canceled out her instinct to stick to Ward, to keep on hoping foolishly and kidding herself, because she wanted him so much to be what he was not.

She had also to give up her fierce desire to come to a blazing showdown with this man, Cliff Storm. To demand to know what he thought he was doing. To rage at him, if he was her enemy.

To be rid of her nasty suspicions and to beg him to forgive them, if he was not.

But *this* she could not afford at this time. All this she must suppress and skip over and only keep herself steady, on her own feet and her own path.

Chapter 14

WHEN CLIFF came down to breakfast on Tuesday morning, an electric antagonism jumped between him and Sherry Reynard. But he greeted the company casually and announced that Lawton Archer seemed to be in the process of packing his possessions.

Not until Sherry rose to leave the table did he address her directly. "Did you ever find out what your friends back East were told about you?" he said, eyes crinkled.

"No," she said, looking at him steadily. "Don't worry about it," she added a bit too kindly. "It doesn't matter."

(It matters to me, thought Cliff, because I'm going to use your third friend, Sherry baby, the one I now know you never did call.) He watched her walk away.

Sherry was thinking: How would he know my friends are back East? Oh, yes, he heard me placing those phone calls. But that was *after* they'd been told something or other.

Maybe he didn't do it, she thought sadly. How could he have done that? Maybe I am crazy!

When Sherry had gone, Cliff asked Mrs. Peabody to arrange, if possible, to meet a certain man on Wednesday evening. He went on to describe the school and the excellent chance there was of getting Elsie into it, at a much reduced and reasonable cost. The landlady reacted with what seemed to be astonishment. She was overwhelmed. She became almost dumb.

The Norns, sipping and chewing, listened and said nothing.

Later Mr. Peabody came in pursuit of Cliff up to his room. He seemed ready to weep. He couldn't believe it, he said. Couldn't believe it! "Well, now," said Cliff, "it may not be the right place for her. And you may not approve of what they do there. You may not like the people. Or they may, when they see Elsie, decide that they can't help her, for all I know. But it's worth a try, wouldn't you say?"

Mr. Peabody's agitation seemed to subside. He said it certainly was, and now he broke down a little, so Cliff saw to it that he was comforted and provided him against sorrow for some time to come.

Cliff had figured out what pieces he needed to move on Wednesday. Archer was no factor; he was leaving. Joe Bianchi was no more movable than before. He wasn't much of a risk. Joe evidently lit in his room or, for that matter, in his own bed, as infrequently as possible. The chances were, he wouldn't be crossing the street at an awkward time.

The Norns were going to be witnesses of a sort. Mrs. Peabody was taken care of. Cliff had decided that the landlord could just as well spend another sodden evening in his wicker chair and know nothing about what was going on in the world, near or far. Cliff could manage Elsie easily, when the time came. There remained the problem of causing Sherry Reynard to go where he wished her to go, at the time he chose.

In the kitchen the wicker creaked. "I guess it's worth a try," said Mr. Peabody, sighing. "I know there's some people who like to make you happy; they like to hear you say how wonderful they are. They always promise they'll get it for you wholesale."

Mrs. Peabody said, "I know what you mean. It makes me nervous, too. The House is different. We know the work. We could save it from getting all run-down. That makes sense. If we could only get the House! Elsie's happy enough, just staying home."

"The point is," said her husband, "maybe Mr. Storm is thinking about getting into heaven, but what's up with Mr. Edward Reynard?"

"I wish we could meet that man and talk about the House. I wonder . . . After all, Mrs. Reynard must know him."

"I don't think she's in so good with him," said Mr. Peabody. "And I don't think you and me are in so good with her either." He opened the bottle.

Mrs. Peabody said, "I don't know that Mr. Storm is going to get himself into heaven by catering to a man's weaknesses."

The landlord's hands stopped moving; they shook only a little. "I don't either," he said seriously, sighed, and poured.

Sherry had only just greeted her son that morning when an aide told her that a man wanted to see her in the corridor. She went out of the ward, bracing herself against the sight of Edward Reynard, but the "man" turned out to be Lawton Archer. He seemed terribly upset. "I'm leaving," he said. "I simply can't stay another hour in that terrible house. But I had to speak to you before I go, Mrs. Reynard."

Sherry held out her hand. "Good-bye then, and good luck."

He took her hand and held it nervously a moment. His voice lost its depth and resonance. He began to chirp and twitter. "I have been insulted so fantastically, I can't be expected to keep quiet about it, and I don't intend to keep quiet. I came to warn you. After all, you are the one person who seems to have any conception of the enormous demands of my profession. I—"

"What's the matter?" she said in astonishment.

"Your father-in-law *is* Edward Reynard?"

"Yes."

"I was summoned—summoned, mind you!—to his office late yesterday afternoon. There was the hint of something to do with my career, you see. So, of course, I went." Archer was getting back

to his normal voice. "Now, he promised . . . he held it out to
me . . . He *said* that he would employ on my behalf one of the
most expensive and successful personal publicity men in town.
He said that he would not insult me by offering money. Oh, no,
he was more subtle than that!" Archer was chewing the scenery
now. "He said that I must realize this man could and would get
me about where I wanted to be in the cinema. He meant com-
mercially, of course. What does he know about where I want to
be? He thought I would do anything at all for cheap *notoriety!*
For my name in the papers. Like that horrible girl with the tattoo,
do you remember? Some gimmicky kind of attention-getting—"
Archer seemed about to explode.

"Yes, but—" Sherry tried to steady him.

"What he wanted me to *do*," said Archer, "was to gossip about
you. That is what he thought he could bribe me to do. Spy on
you."

"He . . . actually said so?" Sherry stared at the man.

"Oh, did he not!" raved Archer. "As if I would sell my honor
for mere 'success'!"

Sherry knew suddenly that this man was terrified of any kind
of success. He couldn't have borne it. He would lose his pre-
occupation. She said gently, "Then I'd better thank you for not
taking the bribe."

"No, no, don't thank me," Archer said passionately. "How could
I do otherwise? This is a terrible world, Mrs. Reynard. Knives in
people's backs. Nobody is kind anymore, or good." He was ready
to bawl. "Or understanding. And although I try, I sometimes
don't know why."

"Don't worry about me," she said gently. "Thank you for
telling me."

"He thinks, you know," Archer said violently, "that you and
Clifford Storm are having an affair!" His lips drew back from his
teeth. He looked wolfish.

Sherry's mouth dropped open. A hoot of laughter came out of
her throat in sheer surprise. She sobered quickly. The actor was
in no mood for laughter. It was beyond him. He had done what

he considered honorable and right and had done it in the face of a universe that he believed held him in perpetual contempt and derision. He needed her praise, and Sherry thought that, on his own terms at least, he probably deserved it. So she comforted him, and at last he walked away, a tragic figure, his skinny little frame wrapped in noble woe.

But then Sherry tried to make sense of what he had told her.

She was not surprised to learn that Edward Reynard was this ruthlessly her enemy. She had been feeling it. But it was strange that he suspected any such relationship between her and Cliff Storm. Maybe he's just hoping, she thought wryly.

On the other hand, might this not mean that she could believe Cliff Storm was not on Reynard's side at all?

Well, she could be sure of one thing. Somebody was Reynard's agent. Somebody had been, was, or soon would be "spying" on her, at the very least. Was it Cliff?

The little test came into her mind. Okay, she'd snoop around and find out for sure about that. Here she was in the hospital, which was the place to snoop. She considered ways and means, thinking rather sadly that she wasn't being particularly honorable. But she needed to know, so after asking many questions, she finally found Joe Bianchi. He was busy. Energy steamed out of him, but he paused to greet her kindly and ask what he could do.

She told him.

Joe made a long face. "You want to know did Storm have surgery here not too long ago? And is he getting a course of treatments currently? Right? Well, I guess I could find out if I really tried. Not that I can figure why in hell he'd want to lie about it." Or what business it is of yours, if he does? Joe's eyes added.

"It's about the custody of my little boy," Sherry told him a little sadly, because she thought she could guess his coming reaction. "My father-in-law has been setting spies on me."

"How do you like that?" Joe said softly. "Why, the louse! So that's why Cliff Storm is living over there and pretending he's scared he's going to die. Just to spy on you, right?"

Sherry had expected this.

"Tell you what," said Joe. "Why don't you and I go have us a bite in some spaghetti parlor tonight? Okay? And you can tell Uncle Joe all about the bad mans."

Sherry grinned at him. "Not while I've got to hang onto my good name," she said fliply.

"Oh, I don't know," said Joe, jolted enough to speak less condescendingly. "Might do you good to talk and all that. Get it off your mind." Oh, he was watching her.

"That's a darned nice offer," she said, "and thanks a lot. But what I really want you to do for me is check it out. Otherwise, how do I know I'm not having a delusion?"

Joe gave her a hard look. He cocked his head. "Right," he said in a minute, grinned at her, and went off to his work.

Sherry went away, not quite sure he would try to check it out for her, wondering whether she ought to have quoted Archer, thinking: No, better that I didn't. The last thing I'd better do is go into any screaming fits, trying to make people believe I'm being persecuted. Because then they surely won't.

She had a meager picnic lunch in the park again. As she went to put some debris into a trash receiver, the balloon man spoke to her. He was a small, lean, much weather-beaten man who haunted the park, pushing before him a stand whose long folding legs had wheels on the ends. Now the cloud of many colored balloons swayed with him as he leaned over his tray of wares to say to her, "So I see you lost your shadow, miss."

"What?"

"The fellow that's been watching you every day, he's gone, eh?"

"Who?"

"What they call a tail? No offense," he said.

"You've noticed somebody like that? Is he tallish and dark-haired?"

"No, no. A kind of light-haired fellow, about five eight? You don't know him, eh? I didn't think so. Well, cheer up. He's not here today."

Sherry was not cheered up. She felt chilled and frightened.

She said, with chattering teeth, "Thank you for telling me. I'd buy something for my little boy, but I can't afford it."

"That's okay," he said. "Any time."

She could see his thoughts going around. Now he was sure she had something to be afraid of. He was right! Sherry walked back fast to the hospital.

When she came out, at seven o'clock, it was dark. She scurried across the street and walked the few yards to the rooming house as if, in the shrubs to her left, there were sleeping dogs or perhaps nervous tigers. She ran up the stoop and went in, breathless.

The ladies, at their table, gave greeting as usual. Sherry was very glad to see them. "You're not going out anywhere, are you?" she said impulsively.

No, they told her. They'd had dinner. They were in for the night.

She sat down and began to try to conquer this physical fear, as well as to shake some sense into her frightened spirit.

"Did you enjoy your dinner date with Mr. Storm?" asked Mrs. Kimberly.

Sherry was startled. "Oh, the food was wonderful!" she evaded.

"He's a very generous man," said Mrs. Link. "Do you know that he is arranging something to do with a school for poor Elsie?"

"Oh, is he? That's very nice."

"Mrs. Peabody has an interview tomorrow night," said Mrs. Moran, "the hell-and-gone across town. Oh, you sinners! Now I can't shoot!"

Mrs. Link picked up the trick with one heart in it. "My sacrifice," she sighed.

But Sherry's heart had jumped in alarm. "You ladies aren't going out tomorrow night, are you?"

"No, no," said Mrs. Moran. "We'll be doing business at the old stand. Hoo hoo."

"We are not going *anywhere* tonight *or* tomorrow night," Mrs. Kimberly said firmly enough to intimidate wild horses.

Sherry found herself sighing with deep relief. They were listening. They were watching her. She knew they were. She said,

"I missed you. It made me so nervous the other night when you were gone."

Now they all frankly stared at her.

"The hearing, about my divorce and the custody, you know, is on Thursday." Sherry told them. "I'm just hoping I can last till then."

"In what way, dear?" said Mrs. Link. "Time flies. I should think you'd last."

"Is it money?" Mrs. Moran said in her shrewd fashion.

"No. I have enough. I will have plenty," said Sherry. "It's—" But then she swallowed her voice. No, she must not tell them how she was sensing enemies around her. What would they make of that? Who would believe it?

She heard somebody in the dining room; she got up quickly, said, "Good night," and hurried to shut herself away, safe in her cell, where she could slide the bolt and cut off the one and only entrance and endure. Endure.

Cliff Storm was coming away from another session *en famille* with the Peabodys. Except for his checking survey of the exits and entrances in their quarters, the meeting had been a bit of a strain. They had fluttered, and they had flattered; but they had kept bringing up the matter of the House. He had been forced to soothe and promise and reassure; this had been a bore.

He saw Sherry's flight; he raised his brows at the Norns.

"Tell me," Mrs. Moran said somewhat uncannily, "this house the Peabodys are going to take, it belongs to Mr. Edward Reynard, did you say?"

"I believe it does," Cliff said smoothly. "Why?"

"So interesting," said Mrs. Link, "the coincidence."

"I do hope," Cliff said gallantly, "that you ladies are going to grace that house with your presence."

"That depends," said Mrs. Kimberly. "How are you feeling these days, Mr. Storm?"

"Do you know," he said, "I think I may live after all?"

"Then you'll be leaving here?" Mrs. Kimberly said promptly.

"I imagine so," he said.

"On Friday, eh?" said Mrs. Moran.

He was startled, but he said, "I don't know that I've decided. Why Friday, ma'am?"

"Coincidence," murmured Mrs. Link, picking up a trick.

"I understand," Mrs. Moran said sourly, "that among the young there is a disposition to more or less carry on over the weekends."

Cliff laughed, saluted them all, and left for Sonia's.

The rhythm of the cards was slow.

"She missed us," Mrs. Link said with wry lips.

"We didn't grace this house with our presence Saturday night, you see?" Mrs. Kimberly said with her cheeks squirreled high.

"Flattery will get them nowhere," gloomed Mrs. Moran.

"I think she *is* nervous," Mrs. Link said thoughtfully.

"I think he pretty much forgot about dying and all," said Mrs. Kimberly. "Whose side are we on, girls?"

"That depends," said Mrs. Moran.

Chapter 15

WEDNESDAY DAWNED no differently from any other day at Mrs. Peabody's until Sherry, dressed for the morning, came out of her room and found Joe Bianchi lingering in the entrance hall, peering at himself in the mirror there, and whistling softly. She stopped in her path to breakfast and looked her question.

"Nope," said Joe. "Nothing. Never was. Isn't now. A phony." He was giving her a hard, straight look, with respect in it.

But Sherry stood still and closed her eyes. Her hands had clenched, and she tried to relax them. Watch it! So now you know. But don't blow your top! Just keep quiet. Put it aside. Out of your mind. Stick to your *own* track. Don't let him push you around, even as much as to be so furious!

When she had control and opened her eyes, meaning to smile at Joe and thank him, he had gone.

She thought she was just as glad that Cliff Storm was not in the dining room. She consumed the meal. But then, perversely, Sherry found herself lingering a little longer than necessary, in case he would yet appear. She was so damned mad at him for putting her on, for sticking his nose in her business, for . . . for . . . *One dirty look*—just *one!*—would have done her a world of good!

But he didn't come, and finally, she left the table.

The Norns, who were naturally just as disappointed as she, slipped their eyes sideways, giving one another Looks.

The day wore on.

Cliff went over his script twenty times. He scouted some locations. He had instructed Sonia. She alone would help him, not knowing why. (The Sonias of this world needn't be told anything. They were like trained seals. They did what you asked, and you gave them fish.)

Late in the afternoon he did what he had to do to his car. He drove it into the mountains and found a deserted spot. Then he took a sledgehammer to the right front fender. He bashed it in suitably; he broke his right front headlight, although he carefully removed the bulb first and replaced it afterward. Cliff wasn't going to drive so much as a mile after dark in a one-eyed car. He wouldn't (for a while—later on) be in a position to afford to be stopped. He took a few whacks at the right end of his front bumper, keeping the wonders of science in mind as best he could. When he had finished, he thought the car certainly appeared to have hit something.

Cliff's imagination was daring enough, but he didn't like taking personal physical risks. He'd been afraid to try a real collision. In fact, he was terrified there on the empty mountain, and he threw the hammer down the hill with great relief.

He didn't like having to drive the car back into town, but he had to do it. He came into the wrong end of the block and U-turned to the curb at the spot where he could snub the damaged fender into a shrub and leave the car in the deepest available shadow, once dark came down. It was well out of the range of the Norns in their lookout, too. He couldn't risk *that*.

By this time it was six twenty o'clock.

The sequences were rolling. Cliff went, with relief, into the next one, which was all talk.

He came into the house and waited for Mrs. Peabody's scheduled exit. She was prompt. Dressed to the eyebrows, she appeared in the sitting room, all aflutter. She drew Cliff aside, her one wild eye wilder than usual.

"Oh, Mr. Storm," she said, "I hate to ask you to do us any more favors, but I'm afraid . . . The minute Mr. Peabody finished his supper he . . . well . . . he isn't as alert as he ought to be. I wonder . . . Are you going to be in this evening?"

"More or less," Cliff said.

"It's such a long drive to that school," she said. (He knew! He knew!) "I was just wondering if you could keep an eye on things, a little bit? And if I'm not back by, say, nine thirty . . . All that you'd have to do is tell Elsie it's her bedtime. She'll do as you say."

"I understand," Cliff said in his benevolent-uncle role. "You mustn't worry about a thing. I'll be happy to keep an eye out. I'm sure everything will be fine."

"I just . . . I can't . . . I don't believe. I *will* go," she said valiantly, "and I *will* talk to this man. But I don't dare hope—"

"You'll see," said Cliff. Then he adjusted his hold on this pawn. "By the way, I have an appointment with Mr. Edward Reynard tomorrow. I wonder if you and your husband would like to go along. To meet him and settle the business of taking over the House?"

He saw the balm flowing over her nerves. She went away happy.

(He thought she *would* be the one to go along tomorrow, in all probability. That is, if she didn't collapse.)

As soon as she had departed, he winked at the Norns and went off to the kitchen to check. The landlord was snoring in his chair. Elsie was already at her post before the television set. Mrs. Peabody had stacked the supper dishes.

Sherry was due in from the hospital at seven o'clock. So Cliff began to speak softly to Elsie. He repeated and repeated. At last he could see the bloom of understanding and a certain joy on her face.

"Here comes Sherry now," he said. "Here comes Sherry now."

The pawn moved. He followed quietly and stopped himself in the dining room to listen.

Sherry had greeted the Norns and was regaling them with a tale, causing cozy laughter at a cute saying of Johnny's.

Elsie barged into the scene.

"You're going to take me with you to the party, Sherry?"

Sherry said, in honest surprise, "Why, I'm sorry, Elsie, but I'm not going to any party."

"You're going to take me with you to the party, Sherry?" said Elsie, repeating, as if she thought this was the way all people must communicate.

"No, no," said Sherry, and then she added, "I don't go to so many parties these days."

"Take me with you to the party?"

"No, no."

"Go watch television, Elsie," said Mrs. Kimberly, cutting in calmly.

"Go watch television, Elsie," Mrs. Link said in the same way.

"Maybe there'll be a party on television," said Mrs. Moran. "Go watch television, Elsie."

So Elsie turned, obedient and no more bewildered than usual. As she walked past Cliff, where he stood, hidden, he heard Sherry saying, "I guess any experience is better than none. But it seems so sad. Her one and only life—"

Cliff, stepping softly along after Elsie, thought that he couldn't have written better lines, or any more fitting to the prospect.

"The truth is," said Mrs. Moran, in the sitting room, "if you can't take the poor girl on and do a real piece of work with her, best you don't begin."

Sherry said, "I suppose that's so." She thought: I don't like not being able, but it's true, I'm not. She grinned at them. "You ladies don't watch much television, do you?"

"I may come to that," Mrs. Kimberly said with a small sigh, "in the fall."

"God forbid," said Mrs. Moran.

Cliff, in the kitchen, was busy with the next step. He gave Elsie what he wanted her to consume, and as soon as her poor dim wits began to dim still more, he took her out the back way into the newly fallen darkness. He had no trouble guiding her to his car, putting her down on the back seat, covering her with the blanket, and ordering her to do what the drug was already suggesting. "Sleep, Elsie."

He slipped back into the Peabody property on the kitchen side of the house, a little ahead of his schedule. Sonia wouldn't call for ten more minutes. Cliff went around the back of the house and crossed the unkept yard until he was creeping cautiously nearer the old sun porch.

There was a light in the room. In the center of the nearest glassed side was the door. He had the key to it in his pocket. He stepped into the shadow of a tall shrub that grew in the corner where the porch jutted forth from the house proper.

Sherry Reynard was in there now, living her one and only life that he, Cliff Storm, was about to alter drastically.

Openly they called themselves The Hoofers, the group did. They were supposed to amuse themselves with some corny dance lessons. Secretly they had another name, and where they met and what they did there were secret, too.

They were preponderantly female, all youngish and all very rich. They had always "had everything," including the kicks that money could buy. Their leader, a chap of mixed blood who never went near them by day, had told Cliff that they desperately needed religion. But, of course, they had to have it backward. Cliff thought that they all were mad, and the man the maddest, and strong-stomached though he was, they made *him* a little ill. He had once been paid to photograph their idiotic ritual, the slaughter of birds, the masks and the drums and the blood. He knew the secret name. He knew the meeting place.

He was pretty sure that the police would recognize the name and be glad to know the place, although, unless they were to walk in on one of the ceremonial horrors, Cliff doubted the police could do anything much—even though the group had already tortured one poor child too long; she had not survived their altar.

Her body had been found on a vacant lot and was down in the books as an inept and butchered abortion. But unsolved.

Still, the police always knew more than the police were accustomed to say. And if they did not know that sometimes this jolly group needed a virgin, for which rarity they would pay quite well, then Cliff (who knew it) could quote them the going price. For instance, on the likes of Elsie Peabody.

The shrub waved its leafy wands over his head; he could hear traffic afar; somebody slammed a car door. He heard Sherry cry out, within the room, "For *me?*"

Sonia was on schedule. He could hear Sherry's footsteps departing.

He put the key in the lock and opened the door quietly. He took three swift steps. Her purse was lying on the dresser. He'd thought so! He had been right! She wouldn't take it to the telephone. Now he could find out what he needed to know. What was in it? His hands were slippery on the clasp. The door to the rest of the house was slightly open. He was taking a risk. His pulse pounded. Kicks, eh? What did he need of drugs or the Devil? He could always take up burglary.

But he had time. He knew that Sonia had a long speech. He'd written it.

There didn't seem to be anything in the purse—no piece of paper, old envelope—on which *this* address was noted. Good. There wasn't much money in the wallet. Fine. He zipped open the side compartments. Nothing. Wait! To his astonishment, here was money, a mass of bills! And here, in this envelope, was an airplane ticket!

Wouldn't do! She shouldn't have so much money. He put it in his pocket. Plane ticket? Oh-oh! He put the ticket in his pocket, too. He zipped up the compartment and closed the purse and put it back where it had been. He had taken his three steps and was outside, crouching low, not daring to risk the turning of the key to lock the door again, while his pulse was making so much noise in his ears when he knew that Sherry was back in the room, sensing, without hearing, the rush and the power of her presence.

He hadn't meant to take that ticket. But he was sending her to the airport, and she mustn't fly away. No, no, he was getting mixed up. Come on, steady now. He was only seeming to send her to the airport. No, she would be seeming— Never mind. He *had* had it clear.

He could hear her now, flying around in there, getting ready to go. Moving like a good little pawn, the queen was.

And *he* must move. The next part was the tricky part.

He crept around the house, not, of course, through the Norns' line of sight. They would see and hear only what he chose them to see or hear.

He would offer to drive Sherry to the airport. He would also offer to lend her his car, if she preferred to drive herself. He would take care that the Norns *did* hear this.

The illusion was going to be that Sherry drove away in Cliff's car, free to do what she liked, go where she liked, and take whom she liked along.

But, in fact, Cliff would persuade her to let *him* drive. He knew how to do that. He understood the universal female mind. The rest of it would take a drug, finally. That was the only way. So he'd offer her the piece of hard candy. He'd do that in such a way that she couldn't refuse.

She wouldn't notice Elsie in the car. He would drive off, and the Norns would not see which of them was driving. As soon as Sherry was in that state of incoherence and confusion (he remembered the woman at the beach), he would send his car, at an awkward and illegal angle, into the curb in some dark spot. (He knew about where.)

And, after a few touches, he would leave it, and he would be safe. It would have been accomplished.

Somebody would tell the cops there was a car parked so as to impede traffic. The cops would come at once, traffic being sacred.

They would find one female under the steering wheel, obviously unsafe to have been driving. They would find fresh damage to the car, one headlight gone (he'd have smashed the bulb), and it would look like a hit and run. They would find, doped, in the back seat one female minor. (And sooner or later they would discover that she was feebleminded at that.) They would find no address that would lead them to this house, the rooming house, but in Sherry's purse they would find, where he would put it, that name. The secret name. (The Cloven. Pretty cute, Cliff thought it was.) And they would find the address of *their place*, and a whole lot of it would begin to fit together.

What could the cops do but take both females off to the pokey? They would have the handy charge, driving while under the influence. (A crime.) They would suspect not only a hit and run (a crime), but the reason for running. Contributing to the delinquency . . . Or even *kidnapping*. (Crimes.)

Sherry could explain nothing. She'd make no sense for quite a while. When Elsie came out of it, she'd say that Sherry was taking her to a "party."

Meantime, Cliff would have been long back here, discovering the absence of Elsie (whenever he thought best), fanning up consternation and alarm. He would most probably be the one to call the police, find out what had "happened," and go fetch poor Elsie back from jail or wherever.

And comfort the parents in their hysteria.

And then tomorrow . . .

Sherry's lawyer would probably bail her out and bring her to the hearing. There she would come, emotionally disheveled from a night in a cell, accused of heaven knew what! (And if heaven were too slow in speaking up, Cliff Storm would explain.)

Let her say *he* had driven the car. He could "prove" he had not. Let her say she had *not* taken Elsie with her. Elsie would have been with her. Let her say the name and address meant nothing to her. Why then were they in her purse?

Let her say she had never heard of The Cloven. Cliff would say, sadly, he was afraid she had. She had been telling him about them at dinner only last Sunday evening.

Meantime, for atmosphere, the Peabodys would be hysterical, since it might well be a powerful human instinct to care what happens to one's child, for all Cliff knew.

Reynard ought to be pleased. He would no doubt say that he had always suspected great evil. If Ward disagreed, he would be credited with a tragic and mistaken gallantry. Besides, he'd be doped up pretty well. He wouldn't count.

So Sherry! Reduced to screaming and sobbing and denying, denying, denying. Damning Cliff Storm in hysterical rage! Damning Edward Reynard for his persecution of her! Not very "fit," surely, and out on bail in the bargain.

All this, thought Cliff, must follow if now he could only go through with this next bit and do it perfectly.

He came in, as if only now returning from the kitchen, and the Norns obliged him with some news at once.

"An old friend of Mrs. Reynard's is flying in tonight. Somebody called, and Mrs. Reynard is going to the airport," said Mrs. Link.

"International?" said Cliff. "That's a long ways."

"She didn't say," said Mrs. Kimberly, "but it's American Airlines. Flight One Seventy-four."

Cliff assimilated this rapidly. So Sherry had mentioned the flight number? A bonus? Use it later on? When Sherry tried to swear that she had had a phone call. But knew no surname, no number, no address for the caller, so could not prove *from whom*. Cliff intended to hint, sadly, that the phone call might have confirmed that the "party" was on, the merchandise expected, the pay ready. Now he could also mention how odd it was that she had quoted a flight number which must be wrong.

He was keyed up. He could hardly wait for her to come. And then she came.

She was wearing her beige suit, looking flushed and vivid and happy.

"They told me," Cliff said at once. "When is the plane due in?"

"Eight forty-two," she said. "Excuse me?"

"Let me drive you to the airport," he said enthusiastically. "You're going to have to take God knows how many buses. Let me do that?"

"I don't think so, thank you," she said coolly.

"Okay, you take my car." He pulled out his key ring and dangled it. "Go ahead, take it, please."

"Oh, no, I couldn't," she said. "Thank you just the same."

"Honey, you're not going to make it on buses," he said, pursuing her as she started through the hall.

"Yes, I am," she said. "My friend will wait if I'm a little late. Don't worry about me."

"But listen—" Cliff followed her out of the house.

The Norns watched them as they went down the path, talking, and walked away, still talking.

"Where did he leave his car?" said Mrs. Link.

"Must be parked that way," said Mrs. Moran. "I missed that."

"Can't see!" fumed Mrs. Kimberly.

Mrs. Link used both hands on her back hair, removing hairpins and reinserting them with vicious stabs.

No doubt of it, the Norns were feeling letdown.

Sherry had to go two blocks to a bus line. She had to walk, here, on this dark sidewalk. But she didn't like his touching her arm, and she swayed away.

He said in her ear, "Sherry, I have a confession. Listen to me, please? I've been keeping an eye on you because old man Reynard asked me to do that."

"Yes, I know," she said.

"Well, I'm sorry," he went on. "I'm really sorry. It wasn't a very nice thing to do. But please listen. I didn't understand. Now I've told him, and I'll tell him again, that he's been dead wrong about you. That you are a great girl. The kind of mother a little boy ought to have."

Her feet had lagged. She stopped walking now, and she could feel her eyes stinging. He was beside her, bent over her. He seemed to be anxious. His voice was pleading. "So I wish," he said, "you would forgive me. I truly am very sorry. So I *wish* you would let me do this one little thing for you. Let me drive you to meet your friend. It's only—what?—forty minutes by car. Just so I'll know you understand. Please let me do this."

Sherry blinked to clear her vision. She couldn't see him very well. It was too shadowy here, where they stood.

He said, "Ah, good girl," and moved toward the curb. A car was parked there.

It was her inclination to forgive him. She did understand how this should be done. She ought to let him be helpful. It would also certainly be a lot more comfortable for her to be driven, in a private car, to the airport to meet Jessie Holmes.

And yet, and yet, Sherry had things to think about.

It came to her, with perfect clarity, that she was all right now. Jessie Holmes was coming, dear old soul. Here and now, standing up in her own shoes, Sherry Reynard was just fine. And tomorrow was *the day*. So all in the world she had to do now was stay just fine.

Why should she risk anything else? Lawton Archer had said that Edward Reynard had a notion about her and Cliff Storm. And the balloon man had told her that *somebody* was watching. Why should she now go off in a car with this man alone? Under somebody's eyes?

She said gently, because he *was* appealing, "I'm sorry."

She took a step, and he caught her arm. "Don't be," he groaned, "don't be so mean, Sherry. Please! That's one thing I found out about you. You are not mean. Are you?"

He seemed to be asking her to prove it.

But I don't need to prove it, she thought. I know I'm not mean. And I don't need him to drive me to the airport either. I'll get there. I can't afford to be so generous and forgiving that I let him take me anywhere. Not right now. It doesn't count enough on the scale.

She said, "I can't afford the luxury."

He said quickly, "What do you mean? Tell me as we go. Please, Sherry! Or I'll never forgive myself."

"Aren't you being silly?" She drew away. You forgave yourself, by *yourself*—or so she reckoned. "It's not the end of the world if I don't let you drive me to the airport. Good night."

He seemed to gasp as if she had hurt him. He took something out of his pocket. It looked, in the dim light, like a roll of hard candies wrapped in waxed paper. The package was ripped open, at one end.

He said, "Would you please? Just anyway? Be a flower child? Let me give you *something?*"

He was holding out the candy.

But Sherry could feel herself turning very hard and cold. He was acting like a huge baby. He was being ridiculous! Sentimental! Whimsical! This seemed to her to be insulting. She said severely, "We are not children. You know that."

She turned away. She walked away. She went swiftly and very steadily. She was under the streetlight. She was crossing the street.

Cliff stood still. How could he have grabbed her and forced her into his car? How could he sprint after her now and argue anymore? So he stood here, like a jackass? What was the *matter* with her? Didn't she *have* any female psychology? She *had* to forgive him!

But, no, she'd knocked out the whole sequence, *just like that!*

He thought he saw her graceful figure going in and out of another swathe of light. His anger built; the pressure rose. *All right, damn her to hell!*

He got into his mutilated car. He drove down the street. He passed her and did not stop, nor did he look. *And damn her to hell!*

He drove, with no special caution, to his apartment. He parked at the back, and he took Elsie in at the rear. He was too angry to notice whether anybody was watching. He tossed Elsie down on his sofa. He battened down his windows with shades and draperies. He took out his equipment and set it up.

Improvise, then!

He had Elsie, this stupid lump! He could do what he liked with her. And she didn't know life from the movies, Elsie didn't.

So this might be even better. Simplicity? Ah! He'd make Elsie into a weapon. Yes, a bomb for him to explode whenever he chose. It wouldn't take long. He had time. Sherry would find nobody at the airport. It would take her long enough—lost in the crowds, on public buses. She'd never prove that she had been there.

He began to slap Elsie's face. "Come on. Snap out of it." His mind was busy picking up bits and pieces of his plot and fitting them together with a new twist.

Damn Sherry Reynard! (He wasn't even thinking about his prize.)

Chapter 16

As SHERRY walked on, her feet seemed to grow lighter. She had seen Cliff drive by. So he's mad at me? she thought. Too bad.

But God bless Jessie Holmes, oh, God bless dear old Mrs. Holmes, from home! She didn't get turned against me, thought Sherry. Oh, she's a real home person, next door to Mom and Dad for forty years. So I'm just fine, now!

Sherry had twelve dollars and fifty-five cents in her wallet. But she didn't care how little that was. She thought it was a lot. Enough!

The strange female voice on the phone had sounded young and pleasant. Did Mrs. Reynard remember Jessie Holmes? Well, this was a sort of niece of hers speaking. Carolee was her name. Mrs. Holmes was actually flying into LA this very evening. She had asked Carolee to please call Mrs. Reynard. Could Mrs. Reynard meet the plane? Mrs. Holmes was very anxious to see Mrs. Reynard just as soon as possible. She had said to say that she was worried and wanted to be in touch right away. Mrs. Holmes had called Carolee just before boarding. It was a sudden visit. Carolee's husband had gone to meet the plane, too. He'd checked, and it was on time, and he'd gone right from his office. Maybe Mrs. Reynard would like to come to their house afterward? Carolee would be so glad to meet her.

Sherry was glad already. She came to the second corner and danced into the drugstore. It was true, there wasn't a lot of time for catching many buses. So caution to the wind! She phoned for a cab.

She was thinking, both seriously and joyously, about home. Why couldn't she take Johnny to the old hometown? And not to any dirty old city? There'd be jobs there. Jessie Holmes would help her. Sherry might even finish going to college. Whole new vistas opened. She felt happy and excited. It seemed to take no time to get to the airport.

The cab cost six dollars. Sherry paid cheerfully, tipping a dollar, and hurried into the building. Although she had arrived early, she trotted along the tiled corridor, too full of bouncing energy to bother with the moving walk.

When she came to the upper area and inquired, she realized that she must have got the flight number wrong. It developed that the estimated time of arrival was wrong, too. No such flight. No such arrival time. She was dashed. This was a bit of a blow. Then she had got the *airline* wrong.

She went to the telephone and poured dimes into the slot, trying to find another flight on another airline, but there was no such number that to any degree coincided with the arrival time she had been given. She had *not* got it wrong either.

Abruptly Sherry gave up. She walked into the concourse, her heart thudding. She looked at the big clock. Suspicion had been seeping in; now it flooded and became conviction.

The voice had lied to her! *Somebody* had pushed her around! Why? If somebody had wanted her out of the way, then she had better get back quick. This was her hunch. She sat down and opened her purse. There was five dollars and five cents left in her wallet. She unzipped the pocket to get at her emergency funds.

The pocket was empty.

All right! Sherry sat up, with iron in her soul. *All right!* This was absolutely not the time to burst into tears of outrage and frustration. There were better uses for *this* energy.

She surged to her feet. Her feet began to carry her fast. She sailed down the stairs and began to run in the long echoing corridor below. She rushed out to the pavement. There, right before her, was a cab that had just discharged some passengers. Sherry shrieked for the driver's attention, got in. She said, "Seventeen sixty-four Morelli, Beverly Hills. Wait a minute. First, you tell me exactly what time it is right now."

He told her.

Sherry wrote down the time, and then she wrote down the driver's name.

"Okay. Now get me there as fast as you can." The cab lurched, and she fell back in the seat.

All right! She was tired of creeping around the world trying to be good, damn it! Or meek. Or inoffensive. She was weary of just waiting. She'd had enough of this cowering and hoping for the best.

"Wasn't Mr. Storm supposed to keep an eye on Elsie?" said Mrs. Kimberly. "Where is that man?"

"Elsie's watching the pictures," said Mrs. Link. "Leave her be, poor child."

"He's hanging around the airport," said Mrs. Moran. "Of course, in my day, people kept their word."

"Times change," Mrs. Kimberly said with disdain.

Then in the street there came a screeching motorcycle, followed by a private car. Both swerved gracefully into the well-lighted emergency area. Nobody got out of the car. White coats were getting in.

"Must be a baby!" cried Mrs. Link.

"Don't care where it gets born," said Mrs. Kimberly, beaming. "What does *it* care?"

All their heads bent, and their old eyes strained, and their faces seemed to smooth over with remembrances.

"Times don't change so much," said Mrs. Moran.

The cab bounced to a fast stop in front of the Reynards' door. Sherry got out, saying to the driver, "Just wait." She said it with command and assurance. She put her finger on the bell button and held it there. When the houseman opened the door, Sherry said to him, "Please pay the cab, Michael." She swept in past him.

"Yes, ma'am, Miss Sherry," Michael stuttered with surprise.

But Sherry walked fast, going deeper within the wide entrance hall. When she was opposite the opening to the large living room, she saw four women seated around the table in the card corner. One of them was Emily, who gasped and struggled to rise.

Sherry felt sure that she must have met the other women at one time or another, but she couldn't bother with names. "Good evening," she said coolly. "I want to see Ward, Mrs. Reynard. Don't bother. He is in his own room, I suppose."

She swept on to the stairs.

Emily Reynard came tripping into the hall, and Michael said, "Mrs. Reynard, ma'am? Should I pay the taxi driver?"

"Why, certainly, certainly," Emily said in a great fluster. "Excuse me," she said over her shoulder to her friends. "We didn't expect—" She began to climb the stairs as fast as she could, after Sherry.

But when she came to Ward's room and could see in, Emily staggered and held onto the doorframe. It was as if the wind blew and the world cracked open with a terrifying blast.

Ward, wearing his dressing gown, had been sitting in a chair. Now his book was on the floor with its pages rumpled and crushed. Sherry was on her knees, and her cheek lay against his shoulder. Ward's arms were tight around her, his cheek on her hair. Neither moved, neither made a sound, and on both young faces there was a look of such uncanny bliss that Emily Reynard had to dig her small plump fingers into the wood until her hands ached.

Ward began to murmur, "Oh, Sherry. Oh, Sherry. Oh, Sherry . . . I thought I'd never . . . Oh, Sherry . . ." And still they did not move, and yet they moved and seemed to melt into one creature.

Emily Reynard, aged fifty-four, knew she was seeing something she had never seen before. It was and was not a manifestation of the flesh; it was and was not what she would have called love. It frightened her very much.

Then Ward moved to be able to see Sherry's face. "Johnny's okay, isn't he? Oh, God, Sherry, forgive me? Listen, I know. I remember. I know. I know. I know."

Sherry's head tilted back; her face yearned. But she said, "He's okay. He'll be all right. I forgive you. You know I do. But you know what I can't do?"

"I know. I understand. I know that. But listen, darling. Could *you*, sometimes— Only sometimes?"

Sherry lifted herself away a little more. "I don't see how," she said in anguish. "I can only say 'maybe.' I have to take him back East, Ward."

Ward said, "Don't talk. Don't talk. Let me hold you. Don't talk." But he went on talking. "If we could only . . . if I don't have you, *sometimes*, I'd just as soon be dead and be done with it. I've been trying to think. I was thinking, if we watched out and never let me be in the room with him. But that won't work. I know. Never mind. Let me hold you now. Oh, Sherry—"

"Are you any better?" She put her head back again to search his face, the face she knew so well and had loved so much. She looked for the truth in his face, his eyes, and it was there.

"It keeps coming in on me," he said. "They don't know what to do. I'm not taking any more. I never will. But it doesn't seem to matter. I don't know what to do. Sometimes I think— Sherry, if *you* were here?"

Now she could see the clouds going over the truth.

"Wouldn't I be all right," he said in pleading, "if I had you?" Then he let her go suddenly and raised both fists to the sides of his head.

Someone stirred, and Sherry looked and saw the male nurse watching closely. She thought: Oh, no. Not now. Don't let him go off . . . into whatever . . . please!

She said loudly, "Ward, I haven't any money left. I came to tell you. Because it wouldn't be fair, if you didn't know."

He kept on holding his head in that desperate way, but his eyes were intelligent. He said, "Where are you staying, Sherry?"

"In a rooming house, across from Johnny's hospital."

"Where?"

"Mrs. Peabody's."

"Peabody's?"

"Ward, did you hear me?"

"Why haven't you got any money left? What happened to the money in the bank?"

"I can't touch it, because it's contested. Oh, I can, I think, by tomorrow. Only somebody stole what I had in my purse. I came to see if you knew about it."

"Well," said Ward, "then . . . why don't you . . . . Is the bank closed? Sherry, listen, *everything* is *yours*. Who said it wasn't?"

"I thought it wasn't you," she murmured. He took his fists away from his head, and Sherry took one of those fists in both of her hands and began to stroke the tight fingers open. Maybe? she was thinking in temptation.

He said, "If there isn't any way, why should I stay alive?"

"Maybe, maybe," she crooned. "They might find something. Just endure. Endure. Just wait . . . and maybe . . . If I *could*—"

In the hall Edward Reynard took his wife by her shoulders and said, "What's going on here?"

Emily, for the first and last time in her life, stiffened and made herself a barrier to him. "Let them alone," she croaked in a voice not like her own.

"*What!*" He put her aside.

Ward was saying piteously, "Oh, Sherry, what happened anyway? Help me?"

Edward Reynard marched into the room. "What are you doing here?" he demanded.

Ward looked up at his father; his face crumpled. He put his hands over his face and rocked in the chair. There was no strength in him, to match that strength.

Sherry sat back on her heels. Then, using both hands on the arm of Ward's chair, she got clumsily and wearily to her feet.

The male nurse darted forward and picked up her purse from the floor. She thanked him and took it.

"I came," she said to Reynard, "to tell my husband that I have no money."

"Your husband?" hissed Reynard.

"As of now," she said evenly.

"You want *money*? I see."

"No, you don't," she said. "That's too much to ask."

She then dismissed him from her mind and leaned over Ward. She couldn't say the word "good-bye." She ran one hand over his hair and down to the back of his neck, his warm neck, where her hand lingered a moment. Then she turned away and, blind with tears, went toward the doorway.

Ward began to cry out loud, like a baby boy.

Reynard sent a hard look at the nurse, who stiffened, signifying that he knew his duty and would do it, although his face was somewhat awed.

Emily melted out of Sherry's path, so Sherry, dashing the tears away with the back of her hand, walked along the blue carpet, away. She felt as if she were all alone on the planet Earth. But she was not.

"Follow me," Edward Reynard said curtly. "My study. I want to know the meaning of this visit." He darted around her and started down the stairs fast.

Sherry took a moment to steady her vision and then began to go down slowly. Emily seemed to be teetering along behind her.

At the bottom of the stairs Sherry stopped moving.

"This way," the man said sharply.

But Sherry wasn't going with him into his study. She set her heels into the carpet and said in a hard clear voice, "I was going to ask Ward to call you off. But he never could. So how could he now?"

"Not here," he said impatiently.

Emily said, "Oh, please, Sherry. Not here."

Emily hadn't forgotten that three women sat in the living room not far away. They were silent. Sherry remembered them not at all.

"I don't understand," she said to her father-in-law, "how you can be so cruel. I would like to be cruel to you, Mr. Reynard, but I can't do it. It would make me sick. The man you sent to spy on me stole all my money. Did you tell him to do that?"

"Are you out of your mind?" he snarled.

"No," she said. "Count it. I have five dollars and five cents. That isn't even enough for a cab. Will you give me cab fare back? I don't know whether I can walk as far as the bus from here."

"Oh, my dear!" cried Emily. "No *money!* But, of course, you should have money. You should have said so!"

Reynard said, "What did you really come here for? Trying to call off the divorce, are you?"

"No," said Sherry. "I can't afford that either. Never mind." She began to walk. (All right, she could if she had to.) She glanced in and saw the three women. "Good evening," she said.

Reynard may have only now become aware of their presence. He moved. "Just a minute. Now what is this nonsense? Somebody stole money from you? It wasn't I. If you came to see Ward, all right, you have seen him. Now you need money?" He had his wallet in his hand. "How much," he said nastily, "do you maintain that I have stolen from you?"

"It comes to four hundred and seventy-five dollars," she said quietly. "The price of my engagement ring."

"Here's a hundred on account," he said dryly, "although I really don't need four hundred and seventy-five dollars, as I think the judge will agree tomorrow. That is, if you intend to appear at all."

"I have to appear," Sherry said wearily. She took the money. It was in two bills. "On account," she said. "Will Michael phone for a cab?"

"Oh, Edward," said Emily. "The poor . . . so upset . . . I hadn't understood . . ."

"Neither had I," Reynard said thoughtfully. "But she certainly is in no condition to be on the streets at night alone. Michael, get out my car and drive Miss Sherry wherever she wants to go."

"Yes, sir," said the houseman, scurrying.

"Will you sit down and wait, Sherry?" fluttered Emily. "Will you take some coffee? You remember Nona Parkes and—"

Sherry said, "No." She began to shake her head. "I can't do it," she said sadly. "I can't be as hypocritical as you are or as cruel as he. I can't pretend anymore in this house. But I can't scream at you and tell you what I think of you either. It would only make me sick. So I'll wait outside. By myself."

She walked on, past the living room, to the front door, which she opened herself, and then she stepped out into the cool dark air.

Emily was, of course, crying. She stumbled into the living room and sobbed to her friends. "Oh, I'm sorry. I'm so sorry."

"Michael will see her home safe," Reynard said soothingly. "What a state she's in! Such insults. Wild accusations."

"How sad, really!" said one of the women, and then brightly, "Paranoia?"

"Oh, it *is* sad." Emily wept.

"I'm afraid," said her husband, "that there is very little we can do for that girl. And Ward just simply cannot put up with her anymore. Now, Emily, try to look ahead. After tomorrow we will be responsible for little John."

He went away into his study, where he phoned the hospital, from which some half-amused and half-exasperated voice told him that there was absolutely no chance of a child's being kidnapped from these premises during the night.

"Emily, dear, maybe we should take our coffee now and not try to play. We can chat about pleasanter things."

"It just breaks my heart," said Emily.

"But Edward is right, dear."

"Yes, he . . . is, I suppose." Emily braced up and brightened. "Edward never did like that girl, not from the first."

"He may have had an intuition."

"Well," said Emily, half laughing, half crying, "I suppose he *had* been around more than I."

Chapter 17

AT TEN O'CLOCK Cliff Storm sat on the sofa in the sitting room with his eyes cast down toward his paperback, but he was allowing the Norns to perceive that he was not reading. He turned no pages. He kept himself tense and solemn; he was well pleased. He had improvised brilliantly!

By George, it had been a bit of a tour de force, but he had pulled it off. He had a reliable little bomb ticking away, out there in Elsie's room. All he had to do now was wait for Sherry to come in. He would then decide whether to explode the bomb tonight or wait for morning.

He was rounding up his cast in his mind. All his players were in place; everybody was where Cliff wanted each to be. And in the wings Sonia was standing by, to give him an alibi for any time he had taken.

Mr. Peabody, who had snoozed the evening away in his wicker chair, would wake to deep guilt. He would have no notion that the director had arranged for him to be more reliably oblivious than usual. Cliff thought to himself smugly that if he had to become addicted to drugs, this was the way. Give them to *other* people!

Mrs. Peabody was in position. She had come in, very high on

hope, about fifteen minutes ago. Such a charming man had shown her around the school. Marvelous, the things they did there. Elsie was to be brought for an interview. The fee, if she were accepted, did not seem bad at all. The man had spoken highly of Mr. Edward Reynard.

At this point Cliff had hustled her off through the dining room and paused in the pantry for more talk.

He had promised the Norns that he would, of course, tell the mother. The Norns had been very firm about it, reminding him that he was not a mother, whereas they each had been, so he had agreed and, furthermore, had said that it was definitely *his* responsibility. The ladies had had enough exertion, had done all that they ought to have done, and so on. They had assumed that he would tell the mother, but he had not, nor had he intended to. Not yet. Cliff preferred to be in control of the timing.

Mrs. Peabody had said that if she found out for sure about the House tomorrow, then the Peabodys would really be on top of their lives, thanks to Mr. Storm and, of course, to Mr. Edward Reynard.

Cliff, basking in her good graces, nevertheless was leery of her excited mood. He didn't want her stirring things up either inadvertently or independently, so he set himself to work to sober her. He said, in a sad hushed way, that he was afraid Mr. Peabody had been as good as unconscious all evening. Cliff understood, of course, and she must, too. It was only the anxiety. Cliff felt sure that the landlord would straighten up and fly right, now that his affairs were looking so much more hopeful.

Elsie was safe in her room now, he said, as Mrs. Peabody had desired. He then said, a trifle too enthusiastically, that the school might be an excellent solution to the problem of Elsie, and he did hope it would work out—and soon. As for the House, Cliff hoped that Mr. Peabody would feel steady in the morning. Of course, it really depended on *her*.

By this time Mrs. Peabody was filled with nervous uncertainty. So Cliff told her that she looked very tired. She had, after all, so much on her own frail brave shoulders. Why didn't she simply leave the man where he was, in his chair? He wouldn't know the difference. Elsie was safe abed. So there was no reason why Mrs. Peabody could not rest and be refreshed, so that on the morrow, when she went at last to meet the fount of all good things, Mr. Edward Reynard, she would be feeling and looking her very best. She must think of herself for a change, he chided. He guaranteed that this was, in fact, the most unselfish thing that she could do.

Now Cliff thought he must have pulled out all the right stops, because no hysterical cries had arisen in the kitchen wing. He could feel sure that none would until he so decreed. Mrs. Peabody must have taken his kindly advice and was no doubt adorned with hair curlers or plastered with cold cream, indulging in whatever cosmetic devices she affected, against the excitements of tomorrow.

It was funny, in a way. He noted with amusement how the Norns were behaving. From time to time their three backs bent like the legs of a tripod, and their three heads gathered, almost touching, while mouths muttered and breath blew on adjacent cheeks.

Oh, they must be in a terrible twitter!

He had returned, just now, from his chat with the landlady and reported only that he had done what he ought to have done. He had kept on this grave tension.

The trouble with the Norns was that they did not really know what had "happened." Naturally, they would never know that, he corrected his thought, but they did not yet even know what was supposed to have "happened." They knew that Elsie had been mysteriously lost for a while. They also knew that Cliff was, very obviously, not telling them everything he knew. It must be maddening to the old gossips, he thought with a touch of glee.

Let's see, from their point of view, what had happened so far?

Sherry had told her tale about meeting a friend at the airport. She had departed. She had not, as Cliff had long ago told them, taken his car, nor had she let him drive her.

The fact was, he had said, some idiot had run into his car, probably in some parking lot, and his headlight was busted. So

Cliff had mooched cautiously along to his girl's place. He had
needed comforting, he said. But Sonia hadn't been feeling too
well, so he'd come back early, as they knew.

(They didn't know how carefully he had scouted this house
before he had whisked Elsie in, the kitchen way, and sent her
sternly to her bedroom. He had been very stern with Elsie, pretending to have caught her doing what her mother wouldn't like,
but promising he'd never tell if she'd go to bed now, quickly. He
could handle Elsie. He had her exactly where and how he wanted
her to be.)

The Norns had been atwitter in the sitting room when he had
come in, so innocently, "from Sonia's." It seemed that they had
bestirred themselves to check on Elsie not too long ago, and Mrs.
Kimberly, the spriest one, had trotted off, only to find no Elsie!
No, not in any of the rooms used by the Peabodys. She had had
no luck at awakening the landlord either. So they were very glad
to see Mr. Storm and seek his advice. Should the police be called,
did he think?

Cliff had been very much upset. His fault. He'd forgotten. But
where could Elsie be? He had taken their word that she was not
in the house and borrowed a flashlight from Mrs. Moran in order
to search the yard.

He had done this slowly and thoroughly, while their three sil-
houettes watched from the windows. Then he had tried the door
to Sherry's sun porch and had come in through that room, astonishing all.

But that door had been nailed shut years ago! The Norns went
to inspect it. How could it be open?

Cliff had let drop (as if it slipped from thought to voice),
"Yeah. So much for all her lonely nights in there."

Time had been artfully used up and stretched in all this activity.

But at last, before conceding that the cops must be called,
Cliff had gone to check, one last time, with his own eyes. The
ladies had trailed him. But he had crossed the kitchen alone and
opened the door to Elsie's room. He had frozen. He had seemed

to listen. He had made "stay back" gestures. He had reached within and snatched up Sherry's short gray coat. He had carried it to the sitting room and thrown it over the back of a chair. "She's in her bed," he had said grimly.

Then he compressed his lips and said no more.

But what? But how? But where? But why?

At last, Cliff had said that he thought, since Elsie *was* safe in her own room now, Mrs. Reynard should be questioned before they told anybody anything at all. This seemed to him to be only fair. Elsie had been somewhere. (Cliff had been pleased to note that Elsie had seemed to be missing at least three times as long as, in truth, she had been gone. Dramatic time, he told himself complacently.) Perhaps, he had said, Mrs. Reynard could explain, since this was her coat, and there might be no need for too much turmoil.

But the old ladies had argued with him. Well, the fact was they had decreed that he must do otherwise. Mrs. Peabody's house, Mrs. Peabody's child, Mrs. Peabody's business. Mrs. Peabody must be told what was known, immediately. He had thanked them for enlightening him.

Now they believed that he had told Mrs. Peabody all about it. What was driving them mad was their suspicion that he (and now the landlady) knew something they did not know yet.

So Cliff had them exactly as he wanted them, avid to learn, and more than ready to believe, what and when and as he chose.

He predicted to himself that they were bound to question Sherry, in some fashion, even if he did not. Sherry must answer with the tale that she had waited in vain for the mysteriously promised arrival of her old friend. She still did not know the "niece's" phone number or surname. Nobody could check. She could not prove. And *that* tale was going to sound peculiar and unlikely.

Then, depending on his judgment of the ripeness of the atmosphere, he would decide.

On the whole, he fancied having this explosion come in the morning. The later the better, really, since there were going to be hysterics, which do not keep their highest pitch forever. He would prefer to have his characters in as much emotional turmoil as possible when he dumped the whole mess before Reynard and his lawyer, Murchison, and, by fulfilling his guarantee, would escape any reprisal for failure and keep the prize. Nor was it a matter of trusting Reynard to keep his word. Reynard would be helpless. He had conspired. He had commissioned this. So Cliff would go his merry way, immune. He really didn't care what happened after that.

But where the devil was Sherry? It was taking her a long time to catch on and come back. Well, she was broke, and bus connections were uncertain.

The Norns were playing their cards in soft pitter-patters. Mrs. Link burst forth. "You are looking so bothered, Mr. Storm. Elsie is safe, isn't she?"

"Oh." Cliff looked up from his musings. "I was just wondering if there's been some mistake. As I remember, the even flight numbers, on American, go from west to east. Well, I'm sure I must be wrong. I haven't seen a timetable for a while."

He jiggled one foot, flopping it on the ankle. Hold it, he said to himself. Don't overwrite now. That's good. But hold it.

He went over the scenes that were coming up. Mrs. Peabody would go up in flames or collapse, or both, in succession. Whatever she did, Mr. Peabody was bound to weep or curse, or both. They might reproach kind Mr. Storm. But no matter. Sherry would be attacked surely. If both the Peabodys fainted dead away, then he, Cliff, could always do the attacking. She would deny and deny and deny and wind up screaming. The Norns would be compelled to admit what they had "witnessed." And Cliff, in the midst, with a touch here and a touch there, would mold all these performances to suit himself.

Of course, Sherry might, in the end, get out of it on the sophisticated ground of reasonable doubt. But Cliff had no intention of letting reason take over for quite some time.

He wished Sherry would come back. He wanted to hear how her tale of a wild-goose chase would seem to an audience. She did have that air about her, what might be called an honest face. But he could fix that, too. And time it to be dimmed down when he chose for it to be dimmed down . . . when it would count the most against her.

He had a vision of the state to which he would have reduced her by the time of that hearing, and it came to him, with a little stab of resentment, that Edward Reynard, who had ordered this done, was going to believe every word of the canard.

Mrs. Moran said, "You have a very annoying habit of jingling your change, Mr. Storm."

"Oh, I'm sorry," he said with a start.

Mrs. Link said, "Girls!"

Mrs. Kimberly said, "Ah, here she comes!"

Cliff put both feet on the floor and bent forward. "Mrs. Reynard?" he said tensely.

"Here she comes," said Mrs. Moran. "Some man is driving her home."

And Cliff bit his teeth together so hard that they ached. *What man?* There could *be* no man! He hadn't turned a trace of any *man!*

He only just kept *himself* from going up in flames. He did it by remembering that his whole story might now very well fall apart, unless he could work this into his plot.

Damn her and whatever man!

Sherry came in alone, with her handkerchief to her face. She had been crying—and crying hard. Cliff thought he might have used her tears if she hadn't turned up in the company of a man. *What man?*

Something in himself, but not in his control, spoke up and said to her, through his hard jaws and nastily, "Did the niece's husband drive you home?"

"That was Michael," said Sherry, still muffled in the handkerchief. "Excuse me." She was hurrying across the sitting room toward her own door.

"Michael?" said Cliff. (Who the devil was Michael?)

"You know Michael," she said, taking the handkerchief down. "The Reynards' houseman."

She blinked a moment. She glanced at the Norns and said to them, "Excuse me. There was nobody at the airport. So I went to see my husband, and it's upset me."

Of all things, they said nothing. Cliff was also speechless. But Sherry had braced up.

"Okay. What now?" she said wearily. She turned her tear-swollen eyes to Cliff. "What was the trick? What did you cook up for me while I was gone?"

He stood there. He couldn't speak. She was supposed to think he was on her side now, as he remembered the script. She was supposed to forgive him.

Sherry, through those puffy lids, gave him a glance of blue lightning. She opened her purse and began to grope around inside it. "All right," she said. "Now hear this. I left International Airport in a taxicab at exactly eight twenty-five. The driver's name was Rudolph Mintz. I asked him the time, and I'm sure he'll remember me. He took me to the Reynards' house, and Michael just drove me home from there. Is that good enough for an alibi?"

"For God's sake!" Cliff said hoarsely. "What are you talking about? Who said you needed an alibi? For what?"

She turned on the Norns. "For what?" she demanded. "What's happened?"

"Elsie went somewhere," Mrs. Link said feebly.

"Well?" said Sherry.

"She wanted *you* to take her somewhere," Mrs. Kimberly said stiffly. "The door from *your* room to the yard was open."

"Elsie went somewhere," said Mrs. Moran, narrowing her eyes. "She had *your* coat."

"Where is Elsie now?" Sherry said.

"In her room," said Cliff. "We found her there finally."

"And you are all upset," said Sherry, "because you think Elsie stole my coat? Well, I see it there. Am I supposed to call the police, or sue somebody, or what?"

"No, no, no," groaned Cliff.

"The other door to my room, eh?" said Sherry. "I see. That's how somebody got in to steal my money and my ticket. And it wasn't Elsie. Was it you? Or was it the other man?"

"For God's sake!" Cliff's voice was about to rise. What was he doing? Denying and denying?

"Oh, you are such a baby!" said Sherry. "Such a damned baby! You and your silly games! You haven't the slightest idea what it's all about. You had some game on, when you wanted to drive me? Well, you won't drive me. I'm ashamed that you dragged me into playing at all." She took the piece of paper with the cab-driver's name on it. Fixing him with her scornful gaze, she began to tear it deliberately into tiny pieces. "Go ahead and play by yourself, why don't you?" she said. "I'm tired."

Cliff seemed to be able to hear the Norns hooting softly, although they were not making a sound. His face was reddening, and he could not help it. He said stiffly, "Ask the ladies if some very strange things didn't—"

"I'll tell you a strange thing," Sherry said coldly. "How come *you* knew that anybody's niece was involved? Or that she was supposed to have a husband? I didn't tell the ladies that."

He was caught. He had goofed there, and she knew it, and he knew it.

But Sherry was not looking triumphant. On the contrary she glanced down at the bits of torn paper in her hand with a grave and thoughtful expression. She opened her purse and tucked the bits carefully within it. "On second thought," she said (and now that blue gaze hit him again), "you did fool me with that fake phone call. So maybe I had better not throw away any advantages." She began to shake her head from side to side sadly. "You are not going to win," she said quietly. "I am not going to scream and howl, no matter what you do. I choose not to," she said haughtily. "And I am much too worn-out to run away to a hotel. I really can't be bothered. So good night, ladies." She snatched up her coat and went around the screen, moving gracefully.

Cliff was left standing there. The Norns were staring at him. Three owls, they were? They thought they were! They thought they were such damned wise old women, did they?

"It does seem," drawled Mrs. Link, "that whatever happened, Mrs. Reynard had nothing to do with it." Was she simpering?

Was Mrs. Kimberly about to giggle? Was Mrs. Moran going to draw in her breath in that snort of hers? Yes, she *was!*

Cliff Storm went off his head. "You believe her?" he snarled. "You take her word, just like that? How do you know who that man was? Nobody at the airport? Wouldn't let *me* drive her? What if she did take Elsie to a party? Because, if not, then why was Elsie saying, 'Sherry, Sherry,' over and over again? And why did Elsie say this?" He then repeated, in her own words, a thing that Elsie had said, not in her room, but earlier on; still, it would serve. The remark was all the more appalling for the authentically childish phrasing.

"Don't try to tell me," he said, as the three old faces winced before him, "that Elsie learned *that* from television!"

He clumped away. He went down the hall and up the stairs. Let them think that one over! The film, ten minutes of which he had run for Elsie Peabody, could never possibly be let loose on public television. (Cliff ought to know.) He had chosen the altar bit. Elsie's report of it was naive, but sufficiently horrifying. Oh, yes. And Sherry had put her own little neck in this noose when she had said so prettily, last Saturday night and also this very evening, that poor Elsie never went anywhere, never saw anything, never had any fun and that any experience was better than none. Well, Elsie had had an experience tonight, vicariously, as usual. But she'd lived a little, especially when *she* couldn't tell a motion picture from reality. So . . .

All of a sudden Cliff came to himself with a jolt. What! Had *he,* just now, and to no purpose except to slap the complacency off those silly old faces for his own satisfaction, had *he* touched off his bomb at a most unwise moment? And a bomb that was almost certainly a dud at that? Sherry had an alibi, and when she found the money and the group's name and address in her dresser drawer, she'd hoard the one and tear up the other. And that would be that. Cliff slammed his door shut.

The Norns sat in their window. Mrs. Link, with her forehead in her palm, had her fingers in her pompadour. Mrs. Kimberly had her head thrown back, and her dainty jowls had disappeared with the tension of her neck. Mrs. Moran, with her head bowed, held the deck of cards and was slipping them sideways, one behind the other. Mrs. Kimberly said with a choking effect, "Did Elsie say such a thing, or was he joshing us?"

"If she didn't say it," Mrs. Link said quietly, "it's almost as bad as if she did."

"We can't believe both of them," said Mrs. Moran. "*He* cooked up some trick. Or *she* cooked up an alibi."

"Strange," said Mrs. Link, "about that door. So secret, you know."

"Well, I always try to look on the bright side," Mrs. Moran said grimly. "If Sherry Reynard took Elsie off to any . . . well, we've got to have a word . . . call it *orgy* . . . was she trying to be kind?" Mrs. Moran dealt out the queen of hearts, slapping it, faceup, on the table.

"If Sherry Reynard *goes* to those . . . call them orgies," said Mrs. Kimberly, "it's no wonder there's a divorce."

"Now why would she do such a stupid thing at this point in her life," Mrs. Link said in her normal languid voice, "as to take *Elsie?*"

"He was good and mad," said Mrs. Moran. "Maybe he thought he'd get a kick out of shocking his elders." She found the knave of spades and set it down in opposition. "If so, he's not so much the knave as the joker. That means a fool. For there is nothing new under the sun," brooded Mrs. Moran.

"I *am* shocked," Mrs. Link said plaintively. "A fight is a fight, and a game is a game; but Elsie is not a football."

Sherry bolted the door to the passage. The room felt as if it had been invaded. There was a difference in the very air. She threw down her coat and inspected the outside door. It was locked now. On the floor she found a nailhead with a very short stem to it. She realized that the door must have been fixed to open sometime ago. So she had not been safe, even in this cell?

What was it to be safe? *Forget it,* she stormed to herself. Everything would be settled tomorrow. The world and time would *move.* She could come out of this paralysis. She tossed her purse on the dresser carelessly. Money didn't matter anymore.

Nor did Cliff Storm matter. Whatever he had been trying to . . . to stage, she thought (*stage,* that's it!), he hadn't succeeded. She wouldn't let herself be curious about the details. She was too furious with him already. It was hard to remember that he didn't matter. But she must. She couldn't afford to indulge her natural human impulse to scream and howl at him. Not now.

Upstairs Cliff kept rendezvous with his own dark thoughts. Damn and damn. How the devil had Sherry messed it up this time? How could she have been leaving the airport at such an early moment? How could she have got there so fast, and understood so soon, that the call was a hoax? What had got into her, to take notes of the time and the cabdriver's name?

And why to the Reynards? He couldn't call Reynard, at this hour, to find out what she had said or done there. (Or else he didn't want to know.) She was probably just stupid enough to be weakening on the divorce, to be looking for a reconciliation. All that guff! Mother love. What love? Why had she been bawling her head off? What for? He chewed a bitter cud.

He didn't know what was going to happen tomorrow. Elsie was going to say *something.* Mrs. Peabody would go into some kind of uproar. Because—damn—he *had* pulled it off. Beautiful! Beautiful! He'd had even the Norns where he wanted them. Everything. Everyone. Until the queen, herself, had slipped off again— out of turn and to a square not in his calculations.

All right, she was damned slippery. Or could it be that he had never had any purchase on Sherry Reynard?

Why not? What did *she* have to protect her? *Who was she anyhow?*

Sherry prepared for bed. She didn't expect to sleep, but at least she could lie down, and for the last time, in this bed. She had no fear of tomorrow. Ward understood himself. She knew that now. So what could Edward Reynard do about it? Nothing. Nothing.

And neither could Cliff Storm. No, forget him.

So, after tomorrow, all Sherry had to do was keep on living; this she would manage somehow. She got into bed, resolved to weep to her heart's content, and discovered that she could weep no more. She slept.

Upstairs Cliff Storm knocked himself out with warm whisky and dreamed of wine.

Chapter 18

WHEN CLIFF AWOKE, miserably hung over, he nevertheless found that his dreaming mind had turned up some questions. Why did he tend to believe Sherry, without checking? She could be pulling some kind of bluff to confuse him, to make him think his trap couldn't close.

Supposing that, after all, he took Elsie with him today. Let her mumble a sentence or two, then whisk her away? Would he not then have fulfilled his guarantee to Reynard? And if Sherry had countermoved, that wouldn't be Cliff's fault. Aw, come on, he chided himself. What do you expect, justice?

Wait a minute. Why not pass the buck? Let Reynard deny Sherry's alibi for last night. The cabdriver wouldn't count for much, if Reynard said she had never come to his house. He had the power to say so. Emily had no force; she'd go along. Cliff didn't feel Ward was a factor. Michael worked for wages, didn't he? Wait. There Cliff was, believing Sherry again.

And so would the lawyers and the judge or any unimpassioned mind. Okay, concede this in cold blood. So the thing for Cliff to do was to dim her down from that honest look, that convincing manner, or whatever it was she had. *Damn her eyes!*

His head winced as Joe Bianchi went clattering down the stairs.

But he took his usual measures, pulled himself together, and went down to breakfast.

See how the land lay. Improvise.

Joe passed him in the downstairs hall. "Domestic crisis, I guess," Joe said with a grin, and dashed away.

Cliff entered the dining room braced for the explosion. But the dining room was in sedate order. Only the Norns were there. Mrs. Kimberly sat in Mrs. Peabody's place, in charge of the coffeepot and the toaster. The pitcher of orange juice stood on the buffet beside the tray of small glasses. No Peabody was in sight, and no sound came from the kitchen.

"Good morning, ladies," said Cliff solemnly.

"Mr. Peabody wants to talk to you, Mr. Storm, at your earliest convenience," Mrs. Link said dutifully.

"Thank you, ma'am." Cliff poured himself some orange juice. "I don't know that I want to face anybody without a drop of breakfast," he said somberly. (Why should *they* believe Sherry?) Now he could hear her coming across the sitting room. So could the ladies, who began to give each other Looks. Cliff dropped the tiny sugar lump into the glass of orange juice he had just poured and turned and set it on the table at Sherry's place. He said, at the same time, gathering the Norns' attention, "I want to thank you ladies for being calm women of the world. You make me see that it is possible. Elsie got into Sherry's room the back way, and the poor thing fell asleep in there and had a dream."

"God forbid," said Mrs. Moran. To whichever of his sentences she so responded there was no telling.

Cliff poured his own glass of juice and remained standing as Sherry came in. "Good morning," he said to her, changing his voice to sound humble and placating.

Sherry simply nodded. She sat down. She was dressed in an especially neat and smart fashion in a frock of pale clear blue. Her hair was shining. Her face was just a little drawn, but she seemed serene. The Norns chorused good mornings, and Cliff sat down in his own place. Mrs. Kimberly began to wield the coffeepot.

A less hysterical scene was impossible to imagine.

"This is the day!" said Cliff suddenly. Sherry looked at him. He smiled and lifted his glass of juice, as if in a toast. "May the better man win," he said.

A ripple of response to open challenge went across her face. She lifted her glass to toast with him. Eyes locked, they drank. Cliff looked away first. Quietly, and almost as if she had sensed the triumph he needed to hide, Sherry put the glass down, still half full.

"Did you really see Ward last night?" he said, letting them all know that he didn't quite believe this. (Let her begin to affirm and insist.)

Sherry turned to Mrs. Link at her left. "I was reminded of you ladies last night," she said pleasantly. "Mrs. Reynard had a table of cards going. And all ladies, too. Of course," she said, and now she glanced at Cliff with open contempt, "it wasn't Hearts they were playing. I believe there is a game called Contract?"

Cliff swallowed his coffee too hot and excused himself. With the inside of his mouth burning, he went out to the kitchen. So Sherry had that alibi sewed up, and she knew it. There was no way to cast doubt upon it.

All right. Twist, then. Improvise. What about Saturday night, for which Sherry had no alibi now that Archer was gone, except the testimony of kind, troubled Mr. Storm? Aw, no, wouldn't work. Those infernal old creeps had come home from the show too early. Granted they had come upon Sherry and Elsie holding hands. But there was no black altar stone in the sun porch. No room for masked and capering figures. No blood-red light.

Still, confusion? That, alone, was something. And pretty soon Sherry would be feeling the effects. He had won a trick just now.

Sherry said to the Norns, "Where is Mrs. Peabody? I'm moving out, and I ought to say so."

"There seems to be some trouble," said Mrs. Kimberly. "Are you ready for your coffee, Mrs. Reynard? Shall I start your toast?"

Mrs. Kimberly intended to achieve crisp toast, and Sherry smiled at her. "Yes, please."

Mrs. Link said, "It would seem that somebody's put ideas in Elsie's head that needn't have got there. A good thing, I think, if you *can* prove where you were last night." Her eyes were bright and inquiring. Can you really? they seemed to say.

Sherry said stoically, "I thought it might be."

"You don't know what . . . well . . . what's implied?" Mrs. Link queried. "It's on the devilish side."

"No. I don't want to feel any more angry than I do now," said Sherry. "The whole miserable *battle* will be over by this afternoon."

"It's a fight for the child?" Mrs. Moran said quickly.

"Yes."

"Your husband wants the child?" said Mrs. Link.

"No. My father-in-law wants the child. For himself."

The ladies clicked their tongues.

"Now how does Mr. Storm get in on it?" said Mrs. Kimberly.

"I don't know," said Sherry.

"I guess you realize," Mrs. Moran said cozily, "that he ain't taking any regular treatments over at the hospital. Or if he is, he flies there on a broomstick."

But Sherry was staring at her half glass of orange juice. It seemed an uncanny color, orange.

She said dreamily, "It's nice of you to be interested. I'm in kind of a funny spot, though. I have to be careful. I mustn't get so mad that I start to scream. All I can do, I guess, is keep standing on my feet." She got to her feet.

She didn't want to talk anymore. She didn't want to hash things over. She felt a little ill at the moment. She had better go and pack her things. She smiled at the Norns and said so.

Mrs. Kimberly pursed her mouth, creating dimples. "We *are* a bunch of old snoops."

"She's right, she has to be careful," said Mrs. Link, sighing.

"She's *absolutely* right," said Mrs. Moran. "That's what's so annoying. How can we snoop, if she won't even talk?"

In the kitchen Mr. Peabody was alone and sober.

"I don't want to bother you, Mr. Storm, but I thought maybe you ought to know we just called the man at the school, and he seems to think he knows how we can get some help. So the wife and I are taking Elsie right over there, just as soon as they're dressed."

"What's wrong?" Cliff said softly.

"Well, we're not sure," said Mr. Peabody. "See, last night, when the wife looked in like she always does to see if Elsie's okay, Elsie began talking pretty wild." The landlord's red-rimmed eyes slithered away.

(*Last night!* Cliff felt shaken.)

"Well," said the landlord, "Elsie's never been, you know, quite up to snuff, but not crazy either. But now if she's getting . . . you know . . . delusions, I guess something has got to be done. Don't *you* worry about it, Mr. Storm."

"Well, I certainly," Cliff began in righteous indignation, "am worried about it, and I want to do whatever I can do."

The landlady came into the kitchen. She was dressed in her going-somewhere clothing. "No," she said with a withdrawn dignity, "Elsie is our problem. Did Harold tell you? This man seems to think there are ways to get help for her. There's such a thing as public assistance."

"I've been a lousy daddy to that girl," said Mr. Peabody, "but that don't mean I don't care what happens to her."

"Now wait a minute," said Cliff. "She . . . The fact is, and the ladies can tell you . . . Elsie may have been away from the house somewhere last night. And I'm afraid, when I finally found her in her room, she did say some odd things."

"I'm sorry if you heard any of that," Mrs. Peabody said coolly. Her eyes were sad. "I would rather, if you don't mind, Mr. Storm, not talk about it and not have it talked about in the house."

"So we won't bother you," said Mr. Peabody. "Maybe you'd kind of check and be sure the coffeepot is unplugged, when they're finished in the dining room?"

"You've been so kind," chimed Mrs. Peabody. "But we also—"

"If Mrs. Reynard had anything to do with this, last night or ever," Cliff said hotly, "certainly something ought to be done about *her*."

But the landlord drew up his shaking body. "It's Elsie who counts," he said. "And my wife was about to say, Mr. Storm, we think we won't be taking on another big old house to run. Thanks, just the same. My wife, she's had enough put on her. It's time I looked out for her and Elsie better than I done. It don't help much if I'm passed out cold all the time. I was so out of it, *last* night, I got scared." He had been scared sober.

"You do know," said Cliff, lowering his voice to the level that tempts the listener to listen hard, "that on Saturday night, when you were out and the three ladies had gone to the show—"

But Peabody was shaking his head voluntarily now. His eyes had a strange expression. "See," he said gently, "Elsie says *you* showed her some moving pictures, last night, on a little screen. People dancing and somebody tied down, like, and blood and— Well, it sounds crazy. Naturally, we're not going to take her word *you* was in on it. We wouldn't want to get all excited and start blaming you on the strength of some kind of delusion. Wouldn't be fair. Far as blame goes, I know I shouldn't have let things go the way I done. I'm the one always did realize there was dangerous things in the world maybe my wife don't even think of or ever heard of. It's our problem, Mr. Storm, like she says. But thanks for everything you tried to do for us."

"We'll manage somehow," said Mrs. Peabody. "Elsie could have been taught, better than I knew how to teach her, all along. I should have been thinking of her, and not so proud. And not blaming—"

Somebody said, "Sherry?"

Elsie had come out of her room dressed for the street. She was looking at Cliff; the face was sly, and he could have sworn that, for a moment, one of her eyes went off track. "Sherry?" she said again, as Cliff had thought she would. He'd whispered that name, many more times than twice. (Wishing the film had had better quality. Missing the throb and the sweat and the stink.)

"Come along, come along, Elsie," her mother said gently. "We're going now. Going now."

Mr. Peabody was turning to follow. Cliff said in his ear, "Listen, man, you mean to say you're going to let that pass? 'Sherry,' she said. You heard that name!"

"Well, but see"—the landlord's eyes were flickering—"she don't know it's anybody's name, no more. She thinks . . . well . . . She seems to think it's . . . the name of the game, I guess you could say." He sighed deeply. His eyes steadied. "But we're not going to believe a terrible thing like that unless, you know, we'd have to?" He sighed again; then he followed his family.

The three of them, going quietly, went out of the house by the back door, Elsie docile between her parents.

And Cliff thought: So the hell with them! If they don't have the *decency* to go into hysterics—

He then had a mild fit of silent hysterics himself.

In the sitting room the Norns stood in a close group. When he appeared, Mrs. Kimberly became their spokeswoman. "Mr. Storm," she demanded without preliminary, "is it true that Elsie said what you said she said?"

He looked into her bright eyes. "Oh, she did all right," he said with no force at all. "And more. But Mrs. Peabody," he added in the same discouraged way, "doesn't want it talked about."

"Where is Elsie now?" said Mrs. Link, stretching her neck with a certain restlessness.

"Oh, Elsie's off to see the wizard," he burst out bitterly. "It's only in her mind. Somebody will just analyze it until it goes away. By the way, I'm not leaving on Friday. I'm leaving *now*."

He went upstairs. And damn them, too, he thought.

"Now what?" Mrs. Moran said thoughtfully. "Did one of them win?"

The three of them settled slowly into their seats at the table. "If Elsie had a dream," Mrs. Kimberly said fretfully, "she sure had it at what could have been a bad time for Mrs. Reynard. How can you make a person dream? Hypnosis, do you think, girls?"

"I don't believe in hypnosis," said Mrs. Link, "but I don't believe in coincidence either. I can tell you that."

"Well," said Mrs. Moran, "they say you can't reason without facts. But that's wrong. You can have premises. Elsie certainly would have gone someplace where she could have seen or heard or had done to her . . . that sort of thing. She'd have gone, if somebody bothered to take her. But if it was Sherry Reynard—"

"Being kind?" murmured Mrs. Kimberly.

"Being stupid!" snapped Mrs. Moran. "One simple lie would have been just as good as all those monkeyshines. She could have said she was taking Elsie to the movies. Would have been safer, believe me." Then she added darkly, "But not safe enough either. And better a millstone."

"One of them is playing games," said Mrs. Kimberly. "Unless— Maybe he wants us to believe such a thing because *he* believes it. By the way, whose side are we on?"

Morosely Mrs. Moran was hunting through the cards. She dealt out the queen of hearts and the knave of spades again.

"Now, now," said Mrs. Kimberly, rapping smartly on the table to indicate the symbols. "That could be prejudice."

"How's about intuition?" said Mrs. Link. She put forth her blue-veined old hand, plucked out the king of diamonds, and slipped it behind the knave. "Edward Reynard?"

"Somehow or other," said Mrs. Moran, grinning and making her mustache saucy, "comes opinion. And to each her own, eh?"

Mrs. Link put her forefinger on the queen of hearts. "Loyal to our sex and to motherhood," she said grandly.

"Nonsense!" said Mrs. Moran. "You know you can't stand coincidences."

"All right," said Mrs. Kimberly, putting her forefinger on the queen, too. "I'm prejudiced. I can't stand people who try to fool me. With a deck of cards!"

"Oh, come on," said Mrs. Moran. "He did it, and you know it, and naturally you're going to think he might be trying to fool us. There ought to be such a thing as 'judice,'" she grumbled.

Then she put her forefinger with the rest.

"Just because," she said, looking sideways mischievously.

"Helpless old fools, that we are," said Mrs. Link, touching her hair and looking well satisfied. "I'm glad we know who we're rooting for at least."

Chapter 19

As SHERRY put her open suitcase on the bed and began to pack, the light began to change, slowly but continuously. The sun hadn't moved. But the whiteness was, nevertheless, blazing up into a superwhiteness that seemed very strange. She blinked and rubbed her eyes. She opened her middle dresser drawer, and looking down at her heaps of lingerie, she knew she had never seen such a sight in her life. She caught her breath.

In a few minutes she was very frightened. She snatched up her purse and rushed out of the room.

But as she went across toward the Norns, she couldn't help thinking what a lovely thing dust was. It rose in charming clouds as her feet fell. She kicked at it and made it swirl. She tried to wipe what she felt must be an idiotic smile off her face and said to the ladies, "I don't think I'd better stay here. I'm scared. Maybe I'll go over to the hospital. If my lawyer . . . His name is Allen Jordan . . . He said he'd call for me. Could you please . . . tell him . . ." She was gasping.

"Why are you scared?" Mrs. Moran said sternly.

"I feel as if I were going away from myself," gasped Sherry. "I don't like it. I *hate* it. It scares me!"

Mrs. Link sat up very straight and gave her friends a Look. "I wondered at the time," she said. "What was in that orange juice?"

"Oh, no," said Mrs. Kimberly. "I can't believe—"

"*Try*," said Mrs. Link, not languidly at all.

Sherry stared at her. Either that face was changing, or Sherry's vision had become in some way penetrating, as if she had microscopes for eyes. Mrs. Link's size was bland and heavy, but within there was something like a sharp-winged butterfly, darting and veering.

"Then God forgive that wicked man," said Mrs. Kimberly, "for whatever he's done to Elsie Peabody." Sherry looked at her and seemed to see a tight little soul, splitting and tearing between disgust and compassion.

"What did he do now?" Mrs. Moran said angrily. "That nasty brat? Chemical warfare, eh? Well, at least she only drank half of it."

Sherry looked at her and said, "So it can't last. So I *will* get over it. I'll *wear* it off. I'll *walk* it off. Oh, you are so beautiful!" she cried to Mrs. Moran's inner design, the mathematics of her, as noble and as wildly lovely as the veins in marble. "You all are," Sherry cried. "But then I knew that."

Her mind was racing. She couldn't talk fast enough.

"Oh, listen," she said, "I have a little boy."

She was seeing the world and time in one piece; she wanted to tell them. *I* never wanted to get out of it, she thought. "Oh, listen," she cried, "it rolls in time, doesn't it?" They should know, she thought. They've rolled through most of it. She was seeing something like a huge classroom, rows and rows, and all of it rolling on a kind of drum. "And you get into the first row," she said aloud, "when you're born, and somebody in the next row helps you on. And you keep moving, moving, into the next row and the next. And then you're in the back row, and after a while, you've got to graduate and die. But Ward—" Ward *wouldn't* understand that, she was thinking. Ward said that was vegetable, too low for the dignity of man. "He said my father was a farmer," she cried, "but he was a landscape gardener."

She knew she was beginning to leave things out. But she couldn't stop. "And everything else can be beautiful, or not," she cried, "but what are you *doing* here? It's a species!"

It doesn't matter which row you're in, she was thinking. It's only there, where you are, in time, that you're free. To mess it up or not. "I *never* wanted to get out of it," she said. "I *know* what row I'm in. Tell them . . . Because I'm getting mixed up. But the thing I know . . . I have a little boy . . . If I forget that . . . Oh, please . . ."

"This isn't your fault, dear," said Mrs. Kimberly, starting to rise.

"Of course, it isn't!" blazed Sherry. "But now it's what *I* do! I have to try to get myself back. Make it wear off. I don't want to flop and flap and just blow in the wind. Because that's the human difference! And I want my bones back! And you would, too. You would, too."

She danced away from them. She ran through the hall and out the front door.

"Girls," said Mrs. Moran, "if this is a game, I think we've just been dealt a hand."

"That devil," Mrs. Kimberly said somberly.

"Come on, girls," said Mrs. Link. "Three guardian angels should help the odds."

Cliff was standing at his window when he saw, through the gap between sign and tree, Sherry Reynard crossing the street. She was moving in a strange gait. She seemed to flutter along as skittishly as a blown leaf. She did not turn toward the hospital entrance, but the other way. Cliff put his nose to the upper pane and saw her turn into the park.

His brain turned over sluggishly. He wondered how the drug was making her feel. She hadn't wanted to know; she'd find out now. He wondered whether it was going to have some permanent effect on her. One dose? One-half a dose, in fact? The truth was, he didn't really know. Nor did he know, for sure, how long the drug might affect her, in the instance.

He fingered the other lump of sugar, still wrapped in foil in his pocket. Should he try? He was curious. No, no, stupid. A way to be nothing.

So now Sherry Reynard was *nothing?* His teeth hurt where he was clenching them.

Then he saw the Norns straggling, in some agitation, across the street on Sherry's tracks. First in line was Mrs. Kimberly, the youngest and the spriest. But Mrs. Moran was shuffling at an uncanny speed not far behind, and last marched Mrs. Link, the stoutest one, putting her large feet down heavily.

Cliff began to laugh. Line of old ducks straggling after one pretty duckling. He laughed until he cried.

"Listen, I have to try to reach the doctor," said the male nurse. "Listen, Mr. Reynard, I got to ask him if it's okay. I mean, I can't take the responsibility."

Ward, with one leg in his trousers, said, "I'm not waiting on him."

"Yes, but listen, it's not so smart. You haven't been out. You got to brace up to the hearing this afternoon. That's enough. You're not going to feel so good. I'm warning you."

"I gave up feeling good quite awhile back. So what's the difference?"

"Oh," cried Emily at the door. "Ward! What are you doing, dear?"

"Getting ready to go out," he said. "I'll take your car."

"Oh, no, no, dear. I'm sure I shouldn't let you. We'll all help you to the hearing later on. Where did you want to go now?"

"Sherry's in some kind of trouble," her son said. "I've got to help her. And I'll tell you something else. *She's* got to help *me.*"

"But, Ward, you have everything here. She's not a doctor, dear. I don't know what you mean." (But Emily knew.)

"If anybody is going to help me, it's going to be Sherry," Ward said stubbornly and rather childishly. "If Dad hadn't stuck his nose in last night, she would have promised me. I *know* she would."

"But what could she ever do, dear? It's a medical thing, and Daddy only wants you to have everything you need—"

"I'll take Sherry and give up a whole lot of 'everything,'" Ward said stormily. "I'll even give up Johnny. How's that? *You* take him. That's all right, because it may not be for long."

His eyes sat in a skull, suddenly.

"Oh, no, no, no, dear," Emily cried. "You must be good, and do exactly what the doctor says, and be quiet, and then, after today, you'll get better," she lied. "You'll get better. You mustn't be so upset!"

Emily could remember last night. If there was something—that she had never had—something wild and sweet and terrifyingly *not safe* in the world, she feared it. Oh, she trembled.

"Daddy won't like this," she said, as she used to say when Ward was three and a half years old.

"I don't *care* what Daddy likes," Ward said furiously. "You may as well shut up, Mama."

"Oh, Ward, how *can* you—"

"Look, I'm sorry," said the nurse, "but I won't let you—"

"Oh, yes, you will," shouted Ward. "You can shut up, but good." His father wasn't here. So he hit the man.

Emily screamed. Her scream was ladylike. The houseman was in the kitchen, kidding the cook. Neither of them heard her scream.

Cliff Storm had started to pack his suitcase. It had suddenly occurred to him that he was solitary here. He was the only living soul in the entire house. Well, not for long, he wouldn't be!

Unbidden to his mind came the thought: *New York might be better.*

Sherry was talking fast to herself, not loudly. Her mind ran circles around the words, going twice as fast. "Got to wear off," she was saying, trying to use words to hold things down. "Got to wear off. Going to wear off. Isn't going to last very long. Not forever. Why is it like 'forever' *now*? Somewhere else it isn't?

Well, then, I'll walk this off. The thing to do is keep moving. It must be good to walk. They always do it in the movies. Certainly it is good to walk, but that's a very peculiar thing to do, just the same. Look at all the people scooting around on two long legs? Isn't that ridiculous! And everybody has to do that. Kings and queens. Everybody goes around, putting one foot in front of the other foot, and balancing along, and that's pretty clever. I wonder how that was ever thought up."

She stood still to wonder about that and a dozen other marvels, and the Norns came swarming around her. "Now, dear," said Mrs. Kimberly, "we're going to watch out for you. You're not going to get into any trouble or danger."

Sherry beamed. "Oh," she said, "blue is so important!"

Her mind raced through all she knew about the spectrum and wavelengths and such matters, and she thought it was strange that color *meant* so much to the human race when it was only wavelengths, for pity's sake.

"Of course, so is green," she babbled. "Green is very, very important." Her face crumpled as if she would cry. "But I know that. Oh, stop, please! Let me be!" She went running across the lawn.

The three ladies gave each other Looks and picked up their feet. They went straggling after the running girl. The sparsely scattered denizens of the park, this early in the morning, turned to watch the sight of a girl in bright blue, sparkling over the grass, and Mrs. Moran, in her gray, grim of countenance, rapidly scuffing the turf in pursuit, followed by Mrs. Kimberly in her navy, atrot, and, in the rear, Mrs. Link in her rusty brown, trampling the innocent blades quite fiercely.

The male nurse, on the floor of Ward's room, had come to enough of his senses to know that his right leg was broken. It hurt like hell. So did his head, but he could hear the voices.

Emily was trying to stop her son at the top of the stairs. "But you are not well," she was wailing. "You can't go to Sherry, dear. You can't go. You don't even know where. You shouldn't drive."

"I *do* know. I *am* going. I *will* drive."

"But why, dear?"

"Because she sees me, and she's the only one who ever did. Can't you understand that?"

"No, no. The divorce!" Emily was thinking of how Edward had run off and got himself married to some showgirl when he was only eighteen years old, but fortunately his people had brought him to his senses.

"You have to come to your senses!" she cried shrilly. She teetered and grabbed for him with both arms. "You have to do the *right* thing now. You *have* to!" *She* had been the "right thing."

Ward said, "Mama, I have to do what I have to do, and there isn't much time. So for once and for all, will you get out of my way?"

He put his hands to her wrists to break her embrace. But Emily, who clung to the meaning of her own life, clung hard.

Sherry was standing at the edge of one of the ponds, taking account of water. If it should rain, could she bear it? She seemed entranced. Time was sometimes going so slowly. Then it would whizz again. Space was doing tricks as well.

Mrs. Kimberly said nervously, "I used to be quite a good swimmer, but not in a girdle."

"It's not deep," said Mrs. Moran, "is it?"

Mrs. Link, having no breath left, did not comment.

Sherry threw out both arms as if to embrace the sky. "All right," she said argumentatively, "I knew it was. So I wish . . . Oh, please . . . Well, I suppose not. I know there are laws. What is it? The blood? Yes, I suppose . . . Well . . ."

Her mind was racing over all she knew about the human bloodstream and how it carried substances here and there.

Mrs. Kimberly said, "Mrs. Reynard, dear? Sherry? Would you sit down on a bench, please, and talk to us?"

"Of course. Of course. Of course," said Sherry. "You never did fool me. It's the people in the back row who've been around!"

And they'll go winking over the edge of the drum, as it rolls, she thought, and I won't want them to die. And somebody has died already who shouldn't have lost his place, but I don't want to remember. I just got off, for a little while. Couldn't I? It's only time-out time. And no harm— "Yes, there is," she cried aloud. "Yes, there's harm." She seemed to herself to be wading, very slowly, struggling through green water, as she darted off again, racing up a slight slope. The ladies sighed and pursued.

At a red light a cop on a motorcycle pulled up opposite Ward. "What's the hurry, fella?"

"I have to get to the hospital," Ward said. He looked ghastly.

"You okay to drive?" said the cop.

"It's my wife," said Ward. "Before it's all over, I've got to see my wife. Oh, God, once more!"

The cop said, feeling heroic, "Which hospital?"

Ward told him.

"Follow me." The siren wound up to scream. Ward swung his mother's car into the wake of the noise.

Edward Reynard said to his secretary briskly, "I want to get all this cleaned up. I'll have to be out this afternoon. Important personal business."

In the kitchen of Reynard's house the houseman told the cook a dirty joke, and she was careful to be shocked, but also entertained, while upstairs the male nurse, in pain, was trying to drag himself to a telephone. It was slow and anguished going.

In the park, they sat in a row, the four of them on a bench, at the farthest side of the park away from the hospital. Sherry was singing softly to the sun. "*Au clair de la lune.*" The sound was good; it kept her entranced. It was so exquisitely both strange and familiar.

Mrs. Link was busy with her breathing. Mrs. Kimberly wore

her squirrel-cheeked smile, but Mrs. Moran was looking glum. "The one of us who can go the fastest," she pronounced, "ought to go get help from the hospital."

Mrs. Kimberly said, "The fastest one of us ought to be here to, you know, catch her."

"I'm the slowest," gasped Mrs. Link, "but I don't think I'd make it, girls. I don't seem to be as young as I used to be."

> *Ma chandelle est morte,*
> *Je n'ai plus de feu.*

Sherry changed tune. "I have a little boy named Johnny . . . Johnny. But I won't scare children. Don't scare children." She dropped the tune. "They'll be scared enough in their day. Because it sounds simple, but it's *very* complicated. It's not so easy to be simple. Oh, please . . ." She sobbed and surged forward. The fits came and went. Nothing was reliable.

"Sit still. Sit still," said Mrs. Moran. *"Pour l'amour de Dieu."*

"Ouvre-moi ta porte," sang Sherry, *"pour l'amour de Dieu.* Elsie just might have a very sweet voice. Maybe she hears more than she can manage. Oh, so do I! *Wear it off,* then! That's the only thing. You all sing, too?"

"Very well," said Mrs. Moran.

They sat on the bench in a row, and all (but Mrs. Link) began to sing.

Cliff heard the siren. He rose from where he had been sitting, with his packing abandoned. He looked out and saw the cycle swing into the emergency driveway and the car swoop drunkenly after it. When the driver, the only occupant, got out of the car, Cliff looked again and looked hard.

"What is it?" the young doctor said impatiently.

"Reynard," said Ward. "I want Sherry Reynard." His eyes rolled. He looked terrible.

"Is she a patient here?"

"No, no. You don't understand. Peabody."

This was going to take awhile to untangle. The doctor saw that at once. So did the cop. He shrugged and trundled off. So he'd done his duty, he hoped. Or else the guy was nuts.

Cliff went downstairs and phoned Edward Reynard.

Reynard said at once, "Be in Murchison's office at one o'clock, and bring what you've got. She's in a bad way, I can tell you that. I think she's regretting quite a few things already."

"Is that so?" Cliff said wonderingly.

"She put on quite a scene at the house last night. By the way, did you take her money?"

"That was more or less an accident," said Cliff. "Was she . . . after a reconciliation?"

"She won't get it," snapped Reynard. "Murchison says we've got to bring Ward, but he won't say much. We'll be honest about him."

You will? thought Cliff.

"You *have* got something?" Reynard was demanding.

"Oh, yes," said Cliff, "and I'll be there."

He hung up. What was the use of being honest?

He hadn't told the man that Ward was across the street now, no doubt looking for his wife. Cliff didn't doubt there would be a reconciliation. And that would tear it. So what was the use?

He went back upstairs to continue the packing he had barely begun. But first he looked out the window.

In the park, Sherry was running on the grass again.

"She goes like the wind," wheezed Mrs. Moran.

"Mrs. Link, dear?" panted Mrs. Kimberly.

"Oh, yes . . . I've had it . . . girls." Mrs. Link was heaving and billowing. "Better part of valor." She sat down.

"All right," croaked Mrs. Moran. "We'll all get our breath. Then, in a minute, we'll go for help. Whichever of us can make it."

The three of them sat down on a bench, in a row, in the sunshine. Mrs. Moran was mumbling, "For surely goodness and mercy—" She put her old claw over her eyes.

Sherry was talking to herself again. "Do I want to run? Do I have to run? I think there was a reason. Instinct? Who said that? Well, I'd rather run than walk. I really would. Walking seems so silly. So here I am running. Isn't that nice? And also pretty silly. I'm not running anywhere. That's because the only time is now. Whee! But I can remember when there *was* time, and it went. And you figured out, from now to then. And I remember that I liked it that way. Well, figure to do . . . what? I've lost something. No color, all color. No time, all time. Well, I never said it might not be some fun, not to be anything. But just everything. Which *isn't* anything, of course."

She began to laugh—the same thing as crying. The green of the grass was up to her knees. The blue of the sky was going to come down to her eyes, her chin. She saw spots of other colors. She threw up her right hand and closed the fingers into a fist. She had grasped something; she held it in her mind.

Cliff, from his window, saw Ward plunge recklessly into the street. A car braked violently, but Ward came on. He was aiming for this house. He was full of force, as if he proposed to tear his way into it with his bare hands.

Cliff turned away from the window, his mind making one more try. He was all alone here. Could he use this? Could he talk Ward into or out of something?

The doorbell began to ring. It shrieked through the emptiness. It hurt the ear. Cliff started out of his room, but a thought struck him. How did he know what Sherry might have told Ward last night about the activities of his old school chum, Cliff Storm? It could be that Ward had brooded on these things and was here to, complain. Cliff picked up, from his dresser, the scissors he had borrowed from Joe Bianchi. He wasn't going to have that kind of trouble, not he. A weapon was the thing. A threat would help. Didn't it always?

He went down the shining wooden way and opened the front door.

Ward Reynard looked at him with terrible eyes. Out of Ward's mouth came a strange, soft, rushing roar. Ward came surging into the hall. His rush carried him beyond Cliff, but then he swung around.

Cliff closed the door and said, "Oh, hi! Say, Ward!" in the old way.

But Ward was looking into the mouth of hell. He growled, and his right arm began to swing. Cliff was cornered against the door. Wait a minute! *He* wasn't going to get physically hurt. Hey! He held the scissors in an underhanded menacing fashion. "Hold it!" he cried. "I'm warning you!"

But Ward, beyond human warning, lunged.

So Cliff killed him.

Chapter 20

"Where is she now?" said Mrs. Moran.

"I can't see her," said Mrs. Kimberly, wrinkling her nose with the effort. "I think she went out the way we came."

"She went back to the house then?"

"That's probably what she did."

"Well," said Mrs. Moran, "that's the safest place for her, I suppose."

Mrs. Link said, in her normal voice, "Girls, I may be in the back row, but I don't think I'm graduating today."

They hooted and rocked, rejoicing just a little.

Cliff looked down at Ward's body where it lay, with neck and shoulders on the two bottom steps and the long legs sprawled and the blood flooding the shining wood of the hall floor where the pseudo-Oriental rug had been rumpled away.

God, how quick! How *quick* it was to kill a man! No particular thrill, either. Cliff felt heavy and cheated.

As he stared, there was a clicking. Through the slot in the front door came a cascade of letters and circulars and finally, plop—one magazine. Some of the morning mail fell into the puddle of blood.

Cliff backed away. He backed as far as the mirror. He caught a glimpse of his face. He didn't look like a murderer. He looked like a scared little kid. He looked away.

Then he looked at his right hand. It was clean. He could see no blood on it. So much for the damned spot, he thought coldly. He opened the small drawer of the semicircular table and took out a pair of scissors. They belonged to Mrs. Peabody. He had seen her use them as a paper cutter.

He felt his ears to be stretched and two feet long as he crept back to where his old school chum was lying in that blood, besprinkled with the mail.

Cliff's heart beat slowly and steadily. This was no kick. He'd better be ingenious. And hurry up about it, too. He tugged at the scissors that were deep into the body, under the rib cage. It took strength, but he had strength. He'd better have. He only just forbore to put one foot on the body as he drew out Joe's scissors, and then, with a hard swallow and a flame of resolution, he drove the landlady's scissors into the wound. He then smeared their handles. He thought of pulling that hand up, to make prints. That was the convention. But he couldn't. Hell with that.

He stepped carefully around the head and shoulders and went, slowly creaking, up the stairs. He thought that if he could pack and get out before anybody came, he'd be all right.

He took the surgical scissors into the bathroom. He vomited into the washbasin. Afterward he ran the water to clean it. He mopped it with a hand towel. Then he filled it with water and slipped the scissors in to soak. He threw the towel in, on top.

Don't forget science, he thought nervously. Miracles of science, don't forget!

He went into his room and took the merest sip from the whisky bottle. It wasn't going to set well. So he put it aside and began to pack frantically. His head was heavy and his wits confused. He straightened and tiptoed and closed the door of his room. He didn't know why.

He started back toward the bed but ended at the window. Pushing his nose against the glass, he looked as far as he could to the left, and he saw her. Sherry was there, at the park entrance.

She was talking to the balloon man. Cliff thought: She's a widow now. In bright blue, she's a widow.

He saw her give the man money, or he thought she did. The man gave things to her. They were talking. In a while she put something into her handbag and came prancing. God, she moved pretty! Should have been a dancer. Sherry was dancing across the street. She was coming here!

He didn't know what was going to happen. Everything was in pieces. He forced his brain.

Okay, okay, okay. So now he couldn't go out the front door. Why not? Because if she saw him coming out and she *then* stumbled into what was down there— Wait, wait. He never should have thought of going the front way. He could go the back way, through the kitchen door or through that door in her room. No, he couldn't. It was morning, broad day. Why would he lug a suitcase down the alley when his car was parked on the street in front of the house? And if he sneaked along the hedge to his car, that would be suspicious, too. Somebody would see. "I'm not thinking," he said aloud. "I'm leaving out something." In a moment it came to him what he was leaving out. Why must he bother with his suitcase? He could have been long gone. He must be crazy!

He heard something. *Ward?* His heart jumped. He opened the door of his room; he tiptoed to the top of the stairs.

The front door was ajar. It was open only as far as it could open before it was stopped against Ward's legs. The sound he could hear was strange. It was a kind of gurgling. Laughter? Sherry? Down there? *Laughing!*

He heard the sound begin to form disconnected phrases. "Rags . . . Well, then, that's because . . . And silence? Somebody said that . . . Now, try, try . . . And shut up! Oh!"

Cliff felt paralyzed. Then he knew she must be dialing the telephone. He could hear that whirring. He heard something else.

Mrs. Moran said, "The door's open." And then, very sharply, "What's this?"

He heard Mrs. Kimberly's short shrill scream.

Mrs. Moran said, "Be careful, girls. Something's happened here."

He heard Mrs. Link's heavy tread break and recover. "Who is that?" she said aloofly.

He heard Sherry say, trillingly, "That's my husband. But nobody answers the telephone."

Mrs. Moran said, "Did you put in a dime?"

Cliff pulled out of his paralysis. He would have heard Mrs. Kimberly scream. He must respond so as to seem . . . to seem— He started down the stairs, stopped at the landing, exclaimed, stared, did a take. He felt like a perfect ham, but he couldn't help it. The Norns, who turned up their old faces, their shocked old faces, did not seem critical of his performance.

So he came swiftly down to where Ward was lying and bent over him briefly. "That's Ward Reynard," he said. "The man's dead! What happened here?" His head kept on turning far enough so that he could look at Sherry.

She said, "There was five cents' tax. So now I've got four ones and two fifty-dollar bills. Now look at that! How intricate!"

"Mr. Storm," Mrs. Moran said with great dignity, "please call the police. Whatever has happened here, we're none of us as young as we used to be."

He had his role. Cliff closed the front door all the way. (That took care of his fingerprints.) He said, "We don't want the Peabodys walking in on this." He took strides to the phone, feeling in his pocket for change. Sherry had gone wandering off to the sitting room.

Cliff made the call briskly, asking for homicide, making his report as crisp as he could. He had to play it this way now. The man who knew nothing, had heard nothing, but naturally now took charge.

He turned (what he had no trouble making) a haunted face to the ladies. "I have a feeling . . . Something is wrong with her? Do any of you know who her lawyer is?"

All three of them were looking at him solemnly.

"Shall I try to ask her?" Mrs. Kimberly said in a moment.

Sherry was sprawled in a chair. "*Au clair de la lune,*" she was humming softly. On her knee she dandled a small rag doll.

"His name is Allen Jordan. She told us this morning. There is no need to lose our heads completely," said Mrs. Moran.

"She couldn't have done *that!*" Cliff lowered his voice. "You ladies were with her, weren't you?"

"Until we lost her," Mrs. Link said sadly.

"Call her lawyer," said Mrs. Kimberly. "She's not herself. That is not fair."

Cliff's head seemed to be clearing nicely. "I certainly will," he said. "Now the point is, none of us must touch anything. The best idea is to sit down and wait quietly for the authorities."

"We have also been to the movies," Mrs. Moran said rather explosively. "We know what to do. Call her lawyer."

The Norns all turned away although, in respect for death, not too abruptly. Solemnly they went into the sitting room.

Cliff found Allen Jordan's number in the book. "Your client, Sherry Reynard, may be in trouble, sir," he said to the man. "She's at Mrs. Peabody's rooming house. Nobody knows yet just what happened, but Ward Reynard is here, in the front hall, stabbed to death."

Jordan said, with a remarkable lack of loud or excited noise, that he would come at once. He knew where it was.

As Cliff hung up, a part of him couldn't help taking notes. Less hysteria in the world than he had imagined. *He* wasn't hysterical either. He felt keen and crafty now.

He had a role. He was the male, tough-minded, the one to do the hard, disagreeable, necessary things.

But one thing he didn't want to do.

He said as if to himself, although he knew the Norns were listening, "I ought to call his father. God! I don't want to do that!"

So he found Murchison's number.

"Mr. Murchison, that is Clifford Storm. I'm afraid I have some shocking news."

Murchison listened, got the address where Cliff was, said he would indeed inform Edward Reynard, and hung up, having gravely and quickly assimilated all the news and displayed no more verbal commotion than his colleague had.

Cliff turned toward the Norns. He had behaved well, he felt. Been very fair. They were standing in a cluster.

"Nothing to do but wait," he said softly.

Mrs. Kimberly trotted over to Sherry. "My dear," she said rather severely, "your husband is dead. You ought to sit up and pull down your skirt."

"Why?" said Sherry. "Why is that?"

"How could he get into the hall," Mrs. Moran said musingly, "unless somebody let him in?" She caught Cliff's eye. She was afraid, the old lady, but she was brave, too. "You were here, were you, Mr. Storm?"

"Yes, I was. Upstairs. Packing," he said. "My door was shut. I didn't hear a thing. That's hard to believe, I know."

"You were on his side?" said Mrs. Link.

"Yes, of course I was." Cliff sighed. He spread his fingers, showing his palms. "But I've lost. That's for sure. Not that it matters now." *Cui bono?* He could remember the phrase.

"If I am a widow," Sherry said in a loud clear voice, "I don't have to get a divorce, do I?"

Everyone was silent.

"That's good," she said. She was thinking: I never did really want a divorce. It was only that Ward couldn't have Johnny, and Johnny had to have somebody. Now there's only me, and there can't be any more fighting, and that's better for Johnny. This went through her mind in one flash, too fast to be spoken. What she said aloud was, "Oh, yes, this is much better."

Everyone was silent. *Cui bono?* Cliff thought.

The police came.

Chapter 21

THEY CAME in a swarm. The man in charge wore plain clothes. He had a cap of fine blond hair, combed sideways across the scalp and tufting into tiny curls along one side of his head like a miniature breaker. His face was heavy of feature and rather fleshy, but his eyes were shrewd and cold. He had a quiet voice; the other men were soon deployed on various duties.

Their leader announced himself to be Lieutenant of Detectives Clyde Palmer. He wanted to know who the victim was. Cliff told him.

"And who are you?"

Cliff told him. "I'm staying here temporarily. I have a room upstairs. I've known—knew—Ward Reynard ever since we were kids.

"He stayed here?"

"No, no."

"Come here to see you, did he?"

"I don't know. I doubt it. His wife also has a room here. There's a divorce pending."

"I see." The lieutenant saw a little too much or thought he did. "Friendly with his wife, are you?"

"Since we've been here. Before that I'd barely met her."

The lieutenant did not necessarily believe this. He divined at one glance which lady in the sitting room was Mrs. Ward Reynard.

"You his wife, ma'am?"

Sherry said brightly, "Oh, no, I'm his widow. Just in time, too." Her eyes were brilliant. She was thinking that the marriage had lasted till death did them part, and she would be glad to be able to say so. Because it was true.

Mrs. Moran said sternly, "Her lawyer is on his way."

"I see." The lieutenant turned. "Who found the body?"

"It must have been Mrs. Reynard," said Cliff. "I was in the house, upstairs. Didn't hear her come in or . . . anything happen. I can't understand—" His nervousness was only natural.

"Where were you?" (Cliff told him.) "Anybody else up there?"

"Not a soul," said Cliff. "And as far as I know, nobody down here, either." There he was, out on a limb. But candor had an appeal, didn't it? (*Cui bono?* he said to himself for comfort.)

More men came. One man began to take photographs, dozens of them. One newcomer, who seemed to be a doctor, took the lieutenant's attention. One man, his hand on a gun, went upstairs. Cliff could hear doors open and close in rapid succession above his head. The man came down very soon and went off through the dining room. Just checking, Cliff thought.

The hallway buzzed with activity. The Norns had seated themselves, Mrs. Moran and Mrs. Link on the loveseat, and Mrs. Kimberly in a chair at right angles to them. They had chosen a place of vantage and were watching and listening.

Sherry had begun to sing a lullaby, very softly, to the little rag doll.

Cliff stood against the wall near the mirror, pulling his middle in, not to be in the way. He didn't know what was going to happen next. He must watch and listen to everything these men were saying and doing; yet he could hear her singing voice, and it scratched on his nerves.

The policeman came out of the dining room and went into the women's wing. Cliff thought of the money and that secret name. But the man wasn't searching the dresser drawers evidently. He came back to the hall. "Nobody," he said to the lieutenant.

The hall seemed in confusion, but it was not. The scene reminded Cliff not of such a scene in a motion picture, but of the false face of confusion on the set when the scene was being made.

Allen Jordan arrived. He identified himself, was admitted, went directly to Sherry, took her hand, pulled her up from her sprawl in that chair, and shifted her to the sofa, farther into the sitting room, from which spot she could not see the activities in the hall or be seen from there. Jordan began to ask his client questions.

She said, with brilliant eyes, "I can't feel there's anybody *there*. On the *floor?* Like a rag doll . . . A rag . . ."

The lawyer saw the lieutenant approaching, and he hushed her. He wasn't sure what was the matter with her. She wasn't normal; he was sure of that.

"I am told," said Lieutenant Palmer, "that Mrs. Reynard may have discovered the body. I'd like to ask her."

"Did you, Sherry?" said Jordan. "Just answer that much."

"Well, you know," said Sherry, for whom time was billowing and folding in on itself and flying outward again, "he hurt Johnny. He threw poor little Johnny all the way across the kitchen. I couldn't do that. I couldn't do that." She brightened up. It was true. Sherry couldn't do that. Ever. So she smiled.

Jordan said, "I think you'll have to wait to question her, Lieutenant."

"So strange, I didn't *mind*," said Sherry.

"Be still," said Jordan.

"Because if things don't hurt you, then you must be nothing," she said, and thought: It's wearing off! I'm making sense. And smiled again.

"Shock?" said the lieutenant, locking gaze briefly with Jordan. Then he went to question the Norns.

"The facts are what you want," Mrs. Moran said briskly. "Our eyewitness accounts. Not hearsay. And not opinion."

The lieutenant agreed, with faint amusement, that this would do very well.

Well, they told him, one of them speaking at a time, but all of them nodding agreement, they had followed Mrs. Reynard to the park across the street, where they had been with her or watching her for quite some time. Since about a quarter of nine o'clock until—while they had been resting on a bench—she had left them.

Yes, she had gone in this direction. No, they had not been sure she had been going to the house. Nor could they tell him the time, the exact moment, when they had lost sight of her. The Norns were pressed to state what time they themselves had come into the house, but they could not say. Mrs. Reynard had been here, at that indeterminate time? She had. She had been on the phone or trying to be. Now the lieutenant heard how Cliff had come down (upon Mrs. Kimberly's scream), had looked at the body, closed the door, and made the phone calls.

"So Mrs. Reynard came in *before* these ladies?" the lieutenant was querying Cliff directly now. "But you didn't hear Mrs. Reynard scream?"

No, Cliff hadn't.

"Oh, I must have screamed!" Sherry said. "I screamed in my head. I screamed bloody mur—" Jordan put his hand over her mouth.

(I should have, she was thinking. But did I? I don't know whether I did or not. *Where was I?* Oh, what is happening? Ward is dead? Yes, but he *was* dead. Now I remember how I had to keep remembering that. But what is happening now? Is *this* now?)

She was frightened. She could tell that something bad had happened, was happening, might happen. She closed her eyes and tried to close her ears and kept on trying to sort out the tenses.

The lieutenant thought of something to ask the Norns. "Why did you follow Mrs. Reynard in the first place?"

"Because, *in our opinion*," said Mrs. Moran, grinning at him, "she had been drugged."

The lieutenant said, "*Been* drugged."

"Oh, we know who did that," said Mrs. Kimberly, "but we can't prove it."

"We didn't see it done," said Mrs. Link, "but we know, of course."

All three pursed their lips primly.

The lieutenant cast a glance at Sherry and changed the subject. "What time is the mail delivered here?"

Usually, close to ten o'clock, within slight variations, they told him. The lieutenant glanced at his watch and gave one of his men an instruction before he turned to Cliff again.

Cliff wished the old crones would keep quiet. Still, they couldn't prove, they hadn't seen, no matter what they said; they *did not know* that he had given Sherry any drug. Cliff resolved to volunteer no more than he absolutely had to. This was surely wise. He was stuck with his story that he had been alone in the house, but upstairs, when the deed was done. And had heard nothing. Ah, but he had found an ingenious explanation for that, while he had been standing so quietly here against the wall.

Sure enough, the lieutenant was interested in his erratic deafness.

"No, I did not," said Cliff, "hear any shouts or quarreling voices or thumps or crashes. But I did hear, perfectly, Mrs. Kimberly's scream when she came in. That's what brought me downstairs. It wasn't loud either."

"How do you explain that?"

"The only thing I can imagine," said Cliff, "is— Well, we are across from the hospital, as you see, and the emergency entrance is right straight over the way. We have sirens howling in here many times a day. If an ambulance was coming in when it happened, whatever did happen, I wouldn't have heard— I couldn't have heard even a gunshot."

"There was no gunshot," the lieutenant said. "Speaking of the weapon—" A man brought him a kind of tray on which the scissors were lying. Cliff scratched his throat nervously and stepped away.

"Recognize these scissors? From the house, are they?"

"I don't know," Cliff said.

But the Norns knew. Mrs. Peabody's scissors, they thought. Who was she? Mrs. Peabody was the landlady. Where was she? They didn't know, but Cliff had some idea. She and her husband had left the house early, and he believed that they had taken their daughter somewhere. Something to do with entering her in a school. A special school. The daughter was mentally retarded. The lieutenant wasn't interested in the Peabodys' daughter.

"Where are the landlady's scissors normally kept?"

The Norns said they were normally kept in the drawer in the table under the mirror.

"Were they there this morning?"

Nobody knew. The Norns had the impression that no scissors had been lying on the tabletop this morning. But that was, they said scrupulously, only their impression.

"Ward Reynard, the victim, had been in this house before, had he? Was familiar with it?"

Everyone thought not. No.

"Did *Mrs.* Reynard know where the scissors were kept?"

Jordan said, "Maybe you can ask her tomorrow. By the way, may I ask whether it could have been suicide?"

"Possible," the lieutenant admitted. "A terrible way to go about it, but not unknown."

"Hara-kari?" Cliff said, and got a hard glance that asked who had asked him.

"Now, how about that front door? Was it kept locked?" The lieutenant cast this question abroad.

"Oh, yes," they told him. The tenants all had keys.

"This man was not a tenant. Who let him in?"

Nobody knew. The Norns said that the door had been ajar when they had arrived.

Sherry said, making them all jump, "You never know what's going to be on the other side of a door. A door." She tasted the word.

"Please take my advice, Sherry," Jordan said tensely. "*Please* don't talk. Not now."

"But that's just it," she said. "I *don't* please to." His kind and worried face began to recede. It went away down a long tunnel, becoming even smaller. She said, "Oh, don't go." He put his arm around her, and she closed her eyes and pressed her face against his shoulder. (Don't, everybody in the world, leave me! she was thinking. Or how will I know if I'm real?)

An insistent voice in the hall announced the arrival of Sam Murchison. "I am an attorney. This is the boy's father, Mr. Edward Reynard."

Cliff glued himself even tighter to the wall. The house fell silent. Edward Reynard was shown his son's dead face. He nodded and turned away. Cliff strained to hear the quiet conference, during which Murchsion asked incisive questions and the lieutenant murmured the answers. Edward Reynard was listening with a face of stone.

Men were waiting to take the body now, and permission was given. Outside (Cliff noticed with shock) a crowd had gathered on the sidewalk. For the first time he clearly realized that Ward was *dead*. Well, he couldn't help that now, could he?

Murchison followed Edward Reynard closely as Ward's father moved into the sitting room. Reynard's face was parchment. Cliff shifted his weight and swayed forward from the wall. "I'm very sorry, sir." Reynard looked at him as if he had never seen him before.

"Where is she?" he said harshly.

Murchison said quickly, "Be quiet. I insist that you be quiet. Let me handle this." Reynard's lawyer approached Sherry's. (They're like the seconds in a duel, thought Cliff.) "I'd like to ask her just one question," Murchison purred, "about Emily Reynard?"

"Sorry," said Jordan. "I can't allow her to answer any questions."

But Sherry lifted her head and said, "I remember her!" (Hah, *he* can't control her either, Cliff thought to himself.) "And there *he* is," she cried, pointing at Reynard. "He's an enemy of mine. And there's another." She pointed at Cliff. "And he's *not* dying! Because I—"

Jordan managed to get his hand over her mouth again. He pulled her back deeper into the sofa. He said sadly, "You must be quiet."

Reynard said harshly, "That does it, doesn't it?"

Jordan said, "Does what? She is in such a state as to be absolutely not responsible—"

"I don't care what state she's in," said Reynard bitterly. "As I understood it, just now, the question is this." He was erect, the little man, and all bone. "When *she* came into this house, was Ward already dead? Or was he then alive? You tell me how *she* knows my wife is dead unless my son was alive to tell her so." Then he looked as if he would topple over.

"Sit down, sir," said Murchison. "Sit down." He said to the lieutenant, "This man has had about enough for one day. His son has been . . . well, for want of a better term, call it emotionally disturbed. This morning, when Emily Reynard tried to prevent him from leaving the house in search of his wife, Ward Reynard threw her down the stairs. There is no doubt what happened. His nurse, a man, was injured. His leg was broken. He could do nothing. But he heard the whole thing. The poor woman has passed away."

"He was homicidal?" said Jordan alertly. "*This* morning? And in search of his wife, you say? Might well have attacked his wife, then?"

SELF-DEFENSE. The words hung like a huge subtitle in Cliff's imagination. He could see the picture now. The sour taste of having lost, although *Edward Reynard* was going to win, came into his mouth. As neatly as if he had directed the sequence, Sherry was the prime suspect for the killing of her husband. If she was a killer, to any degree at all, and especially if she were to be judged insane, she couldn't keep the child. Yet even if Cliff could have or had arranged for *this* "important something" to enter the custody fight, how could he ever have proved it? Would the dead boy's father reward him if he had arranged for that death?

Cliff felt the fear rippling down his spine. What frightened him was, not that he had killed or that he might be exposed as having killed, but that he had momentarily forgotten what he had done. The thought of Elsie came to him. God, was *he, too,* unable to tell the difference between fiction and life?

Meanwhile, over the room had fallen the pall of the news of death upon death.

Murchison broke it. "May I ask," he said in his quiet, but crisp way, "whether the weapon, those scissors, were in or out of plain sight?"

PREMEDITATION. Cliff saw another title flash across his inner screen.

"Nobody knows so far," said the lieutenant. "Excuse me." He went into the hall to confer with a man who seemed to have returned from some mission. Murchison sat down beside Reynard. They were twenty feet away from the sofa where Sherry sat beside Allen Jordan. The Norns, between these lineups, sat like a jury. Their old eyes were busy on the new arrivals. The body, covered decently, had gone away. Chalk marks were on the hall floor for remembrance. More flash bulbs flared. A man was very gingerly and carefully picking up the blood-stained mail.

The lieutenant came back into the sitting room. He seemed to have decided to be informative. He said, "The mail was put through that slot almost exactly at ten o four. That time is going to stand up. It can be corroborated several times over. Now, it fell in such a way—excuse me—it's plain that it fell into the man's blood. There is a reasonable assumption, then, that the victim was already, if not dead, at least fatally wounded *before* ten o four. "You," he said to Cliff, "were here. Does the mailman ring?"

"No, no," said Cliff.

"You do not know at what moment Mrs. Reynard came in?"

"No, I don't," Cliff said. He didn't. He now knew that she had come in *after* ten o four, but he couldn't say so.

"And you ladies do not know at what time she entered this house?"

The Norns said, honestly, that they did not. Both lawyers had been listening intently. Sherry sat up, suddenly straight. "Hey, there won't *be* any hearing, will there?" she cried. "Oh, then it doesn't matter? I was trying to walk it off, but I couldn't . . . couldn't."

Murchison said, "What does she mean?"

Jordan had reached for her, but Sherry escaped his friendly hands. She sprang to her feet. "It was my enemy," she cried. "Oh, please give me *myself* back? I knew who I was. I used to know." Jordan was trying to restrain her. "The blood!" Sherry cried in despair. Her mind was on the stuff in her blood that her blood must be rid of.

Jordan succeeded in wrestling her back down to the sofa. Sherry began to sob. Sobbing and raving, thought Cliff, and pretty soon she will be denying. He looked at the wreckage across the room, feeling heavy and cheated. This was the hearing? But he had no control.

"She's mad," croaked Reynard. "Drugs. You see? *She* taught my son to take drugs. They had a child, there is an innocent child, a little boy."

"Don't worry," Murchison said soothingly, "John is safe, where he is."

"At the moment," Reynard said grimly. "But I want him moved. Get whatever it takes. A court order? *Anything.* I won't have her near him! Let me save something!"

He bent his head, at last, and pity blew in the room. Cliff could feel the consensus as it thickened here. Even the Norns were feeling it. Both young people mad. Both killers. The son kills his mother. The wife kills her husband. And they were mad, mad from drugs, their minds rotted and gone. No use to try to understand. It was just another tragedy. The only thing that could be done was to save the child, who was not mad yet.

Sherry had understood some of the words. "But I didn't go—" she was trying to say. "I told the balloon—" Jordan muzzled her. How could he know when she was lucid and when she was not? Sherry wept, because she couldn't blame him.

He said, "I'd like to get her to a doctor. Can't you see she's suffering?" He sounded angry.

"Not quite yet," the lieutenant said gently. "We have doctors."

What did he mean? Cliff wondered. The doctor who had examined Ward's wound was gone. Did he mean police doctors?
Then he *is* going to arrest her?

Cliff felt his heart lurch. But she'll get off, he told himself. On
some kind of plea. Insanity. Self-defense. Come on, they don't gas
girls just for killing a husband or two. Happens every day. They
may put her in some loony bin. For a while. Just for a while.

And when they set her free again— Free?

Sherry had managed to stop crying. She was holding the rag
doll to her cheek. She swayed and closed her eyes.

It was better with her eyes closed, because everything was
fantastic then, and familiar pieces of the world didn't jump in
and out so. And Ward was dead, and she was all alone? No,
wait . . . There was surely . . . Why, she'd thought of it a moment ago. Ago? "Everything *isn't* everything," she murmured.
This made a kind of sense to her. She didn't want to feel one with
the universe. The whole point was to feel some limiting distinc-
tion, the difference that made you *something*. She could almost
grasp it. Almost . . . Sherry began to croon to the rag doll: "Lullaby and good night—"

Jordan sighed and sat back to wait. Everyone knew what was
going to happen in a little while, whenever the lieutenant was
ready.

Mrs. Kimberly had her mouth pursed. A tear rolled down her
cheek, but she kept silent. Mrs. Link was jabbing hairpins into
her scalp. Mrs. Moran was looking straight ahead of her with nar-
rowed eyes. "An enemy hath done this," she murmured.

Cliff Storm thought: If this wasn't over soon, if somebody
didn't do something that would stop the sound of her singing, if
somebody didn't soon break this up, he might go right off his
head. He felt like screaming!

Chapter 22

THEN CLIFF'S HEART leaped, stabbed by a shaft of primitive terror. The front door had opened. Something *white* was standing there!

It was only Joe Bianchi, in his white coat. Suddenly there he was, arguing that he lived here; he knew nothing about any crime; he wanted to come in.

When he was let in, he came swinging into the sitting room, took one look at Sherry, and said in a loud voice, "What's the matter with her? What's she had? I'm a doctor. This kid is high. You can't question her in this condition. She doesn't have control."

"I'm her lawyer," Jordan said warmly. "That's what I've been telling them, Doctor."

"Well, you were darned right," Joe said angrily.

"Hi, doll?" said Sherry, opening her anguished eyes. "Are you a doll?"

Joe said, "Don't listen to her. Listen to me, whoever's in charge here. I'll tell you something. This kid would no more do that to herself! I don't believe it." He stood, on widespread feet, and gave an opinion.

Mrs. Moran was on it like a fox. "I believe," she said, "that Mr. Storm gave her something in her orange juice this morning. *I believe* it, I say."

"Why would he do that?" said the lieutenant, neither believing nor disbelieving. He'd been harboring some reservations about this Storm and the nutty little blond chick.

"Because he's her enemy," said Mrs. Moran.

"Certainly, he's her enemy," said Mrs. Link.

"Oh, yes, indeed," said Mrs. Kimberly.

They fastened owl looks on the lieutenant. Call us mad? they challenged.

"That's a funny word—" began the lieutenant.

"Good English word," snapped Mrs. Moran. "Look it up, why don't you? Enemy: one who wishes to do her harm."

(No, I don't, really, thought Cliff with shock. No, no. Myself good, that was all.) "No, no," he said aloud.

Joe said, "Ask him what he's doing in this dump, why don't you? See if he tells *you* he thinks he's a dying man."

Mrs. Moran said, to the lieutenant's stunned-looking face, "You've been thinking they were lovers? Forget it!"

"Edward Reynard's behind it," said Mrs. Kimberly.

"Oh, certainly," said Mrs. Link. "*He's* only the puppet of Edward Reynard."

Murchison, who was looking drawn around the eyes, said silkily, "Be a little careful, ladies."

All three Norns looked at him, anticipating delight.

"Are we," said Mrs. Kimberly, "going to get to make statements?"

"Going to get to be witnesses?" said Mrs. Link, patting her hair.

"Going to be sued?" said Mrs. Moran, grinning at Murchison in her gargoyle fashion.

But now there arose, in the hall, Mrs. Peabody's wails and Mr. Peabody's bluster, and the lieutenant, not without relief, went to them. Murchison began to whisper to Reynard, but his client didn't seem to hear him. Cliff was plastered against the wall, pinned there by the needle-sharp glances of the Norns. He couldn't understand what he'd ever done to them. Why were they against him?

Suddenly here came Mr. Peabody, rolling through the crowd. He said to Cliff in a hard voice, "So you did take my girl someplace, and you did show her some damned filthy moving pictures. Well, you made one big mistake, mister. I told you she wasn't crazy."

"Mr. Reynard?" Murchison said in soft alarm.

The landlord turned his red eyes. "Reynard?" he barked. "What about that house?"

Reynard roused and said coldly, "What house? I don't know you or what you're talking about." He put his hand over his eyes.

Mrs. Peabody came, in a tripping run, to her husband's side and clung to him for support. "You lied to us, Mr. Storm," she said, her eyes flashing weirdly. "You are a cruel and wicked man. Get out! Get out!"

"Not yet," said the lieutenant, who had come up behind her. "There's an investigation going on here. Sit down, please."

Murchison said, "That's right. Whatever this may be about, aren't we wandering?"

"Oh, I don't know," drawled Allen Jordan.

It was Edward Reynard who lost patience and burst all restraint. "My son's been killed!" he shouted. "*Did she do it?* Because if she did it, then she did it!"

Sherry sat up. "That's right," she cried. "That's absolutely right!" She had opened her eyes. She stared at him. Reynard stared back.

"Did you do it, Sherry?" he said in a choking voice.

"Don't answer," said Jordan.

"No, no," said Sherry. "But I wish"—her voice began to shake— "I wish this damned stuff would get out of my blood. I can't think in time."

She was thinking of time, that rolled from past to present to future—time that you put behind you, full of deeds, and used for doing what would look forward. She had almost had it back. Almost. She held the rag doll to her cheek again and closed her eyes. Time and place trembled and shook. "Oh, Ward," she mourned.

"Nothing that she says is admissible," Jordan said stiffly. "So may I request, again, permission to take her over to the hospital?"

"I'm afraid—" the lieutenant began.

Sherry was making a terrible effort to get time to behave as time should. "Oh, yes, the hospital," she said brightly. "Oh, yes, Johnny will be wondering." There was silence briefly. Reynard, who had been standing, now sat down, still staring at her. Sherry looked around at all of them. "That's my little boy," she said, explaining. And she had not forgotten. Not forgotten. She remembered who she was. So she smiled. "I have a child, you see."

Reynard said wearily, "Oh, no, she doesn't."

Mrs. Kimberly said with a snap, "Oh, yes, she does."

Reynard turned a blind face toward the Norns. "Ask Storm," he said. "She's not fit. Cliff, you had better tell them." He gestured. His hand moved command.

Oh, no, I won't, thought Cliff. I'm not your puppet, old man. He leaned forward from the wall. "Where did you get that doll, Sherry?" he called to her in a loud voice.

She looked at him now, full blue, full gaze. "If you'd only just hated me, like Mr. Reynard does—"

He understood her in a flash. He wanted to tell her so. But she closed her eyes; she was gone again. The Norns, however, were *not* gone. They were on to the meaning of the little rag doll like diving birds.

Mrs. Moran was the quickest. "From the balloon man!" she cried.

"In the park," cried Mrs. Kimberly, nimble to be second.

"This morning," pronounced Mrs. Link.

Jordan was on to it now. "You bought that doll *this* morning, in the park, *before* you crossed the street to come here? Tell me, Sherry. Tell me, now. Remember, carefully."

Sherry opened her eyes and nodded her head. "Yes, I did," she said quietly. "And then I saw the mailman, and so I crossed, because you know I was expecting money in the mail."

"Check that!" barked Mrs. Moran.

"You can find him," shrilled Mrs. Kimberly. "Look for the balloons!"

"He may know," boomed Mrs. Link, "and settle the whole thing. Hurry up!"

The lieutenant sent them an exasperated look before he sent a man to check.

In a moment Edward Reynard got up as if he were very brittle. Murchison sprang to his side but did not prevent him from crossing the twenty feet to where she sat.

He said, "Sherry?" She looked up at him with that X-ray vision. "Did Ward do it himself?"

"I thought so," she said earnestly. "I thought he knew it was dangerous, but he chose, you see, to keep on taking that stuff. Should I have been his mother?"

"Did you see him use those scissors?" Reynard was suffering.

"What?" Time slammed in. It hit her. She rocked. "Oh, no," she said. "I unlocked the door, and there he was, but not he—only the rags he left behind." Her eyes widened. "Oh, Mr. Reynard," she said as if her heart were breaking, "it was just like killing *you*, wasn't it? Oh, did you say Emily, too? Oh, poor Ward! Oh, Ward . . . He couldn't live . . . He couldn't live that over." She raised both hands, letting the doll tumble away. She clapped one hand and then the other, over her mouth, and squeezed her eyelids down. Sparks flew in an inner twilight.

Reynard seemed to crumple. "She's right. My son could not have been in his own control," he said to the lieutenant, "when he threw his mother down the stairs. He must have come to himself here, and realized—and killed himself." He looked at Sherry. "As you see," he said painfully, "she is not herself right now. I wouldn't pay too much attention. She doesn't want to be like that. Neither would I." He lifted his head high on the end of his very straight back. "I'll go now. I don't believe I am required to stay? I'll wait outside. You might," he said to Murchison, "explain about the estate. I don't mind waiting alone."

Edward Reynard walked past Cliff Storm without a look or a

word or any admission on his part that Cliff existed. He went through the hall and out of the house. And left behind a thrumming silence.

Murchison started to break it, but now the lieutenant's man returned with the toy man.

Before an attentive audience the man answered the questions. Why, sure. He remembered the time perfectly. He had only just come on the job. He had walked from the bus stop, as he always did according to his schedule. He knew the time. Absolutely! He'd stopped at the park entrance to blow up his balloons. He had this little gadget. The girl had come running—sure, she was the one—just as he was starting his day. That was at two past ten. He'd swear, certainly. She had bought the doll, sure. She'd asked him if he'd take a message to the hospital for her little boy, so it was kind of like doing a favor for a favor. She'd said she didn't really ever want a rag doll or to be one. He had thought she was high on something. She had said to him, "Is that the mailman?"

He had looked and agreed that it was. Oh, yes, going up the steps to *this* house. He remembered perfectly. Thereafter, he had made change, giving her four ones for her five. She'd had the nickel tax. They'd kidded a little bit more. She'd said his balloons were beautiful. Color, she'd said, was a strange thing. Why was it beautiful? she'd asked him. Oh, no, she could not have crossed the street and reached this house until ten past ten, at the earliest. The toy man was positive of all this.

"Now you saw the mailman come here, while she was there with you?" the lieutenant insisted.

Certainly did. Certainly did.

(Cliff's mind went twisting along with the lieutenant's. So she couldn't have got here and picked up the mail and then, *after* the killing, thrown it down to make herself an alibi. Cliff recognized an ingenious mind. And why would I, he read it further, fix her an alibi, when I'm her enemy?)

But he just had! Of course, it was the truth.

Sherry was calling across the room to the man from the park. "What did you do with the balloons? Oh, please?"

"I cut them loose," the man said, "one by one."

And Sherry cried, "How *dear* of you! Oh, lovely!" At once she began to cry. Because Ward was dead, and still the world was not as ugly as it ought to be.

But the Norns, wreathed in smiles and wrinkles, were clapping their hands softly. The lieutenant deployed someone to take the toy man's statement, "if he wouldn't mind going with the officer?" Allen Jordan said to Joe, "Doctor, do you think something can be given her? To counteract the effects of this whatever drug?"

"Try Dr. Jeffers," said Joe. "He ought to be over in the lab." He turned and glared at Cliff. "And if you know what she got or how much, for God's sake, say so."

But Cliff could only shake his head and sag against the wall. He didn't know. He didn't understand. He had just saved her, hadn't he, and very cleverly? Didn't she know that? Hadn't anybody noticed? What was so damned *dear*, for God's sake, about cutting a bunch of toy balloons loose to the sky? Was this worthy of tears? No, he never had, and he never would, understand her.

The lieutenant was now willing to let Jordan take Sherry to a doctor. Jordan said that she wouldn't leave town. He was going to take care of her.

Murchison said, "Just a minute, Mrs. Reynard. Jordan? To continue. Mrs. Reynard—Emily, that is—leaves rather a large bequest to her grandson. Mrs. Sherry Reynard, as his guardian, will be able to use it for his welfare in any way she likes. Now Emily Reynard, who had large holdings in her own name, you see, also left a considerable amount of property to her son, Ward. Whether Sherry Reynard can touch that estate, since Ward was a matricide and ought not, under most circumstances, to inherit by virtue of his crime, I cannot say. All that will have to be wrung out in a court of law."

"May be quite a hassle, counselor," Jordan said amiably.

"I daresay," Murchison said courteously. "Good day, everyone."

Edward Reynard was waiting in the car. Murchison said nothing, got in to drive. They had gone a few blocks when Reynard said, "I married a nice girl. But God help her, poor Emily—" He stopped speaking. He did not weep.

So Murchison said, "You'll see your grandson, surely, from time to time. I don't think his mother would be so cruel."

"I doubt I'll see the boy much," said Reynard. "I've been alone in the world, you know, since I was eighteen years old."

Then he pulled himself erect and clamped into pattern. "You realize," he said, "that if *I* had been at home this morning, none of this would have happened?"

"Perhaps not," Murchison said softly. But he thought: Doesn't he know the spot he's on if he hired this fantastic idiot, Storm? Did they really believe that the everyday world can't tell what's real from what isn't? Or is it just that *they* can't? Now, what is "mad"? And what is "sane"?

Sherry was working her eye muscles, fighting to be rid of the spells of strange vision. She was able to think how stupid she had been. Edward Reynard had never seen Sherry Coleman Reynard as herself at all. He loved-and-hated somebody else. It must be so. He had got his place confused, or his time, had had Sherry in the wrong row or himself in Ward's. But hated-and-loved someone who had hurt him, or whom he had hurt. Poor, human, little old man! She wished she had realized— All that was past.

Jordan brought her a check. "This was in a letter," he told her. The lieutenant had to keep the envelope, with other pieces of mail, for evidence, but Jordan and he had agreed he should not keep the money.

"Jessie N. Holmes," the check was signed, in lovely loops. "Pay to the order of Sherry Reynard, Five hundred and no one-hundredths dollars."

"Well, I *knew*," said Sherry, "the whole world couldn't possibly be against me." Her brain was slowing down surely. No. All of a sudden she knew that her brain always had gone as fast as this, but she hadn't been so mercilessly aware of it.

"Can you fetch your things?" said Jordan. "I'd like to get you out of here."

"I think so," she said.

She went to her room. It was as coldly white as ever, but the light was not now superwhite. It was a white that the ordinary human eye could almost manage. So grief would come to an ordinary heart that must learn to live over it.

She took her possessions out of the dresser drawers. Money? Yes. Yes. Well, here it was then. She threw a scrap of paper into the wastebasket. It wasn't hers.

Sherry had *been* in mourning for a week and a half already. She could almost cast her mind ahead and know how it was going to be to have lived over it. (Ah, time was settling to its old familiar ways.) Well, it wasn't going to be so darned great, she knew that. But the worst thing you could do, when somebody died, was to try and pretend that he hadn't mattered very much anyway. But he had! Ward had! He had been very important. Johnny has to know that, thought Sherry. Gently she packed the rag doll.

Meanwhile, Jordan was saying to the people in the sitting room, "I take it there's been some attempts to discredit Mrs. Reynard? To hurt her reputation? I will say"—and he must have been very angry to be willing to say such a thing—"that whoever thinks to profit from any such behavior may find he's damned wrong. Excuse me, ladies."

"Damned," Mrs. Moran said comfortably, "is a very good English word. Quite Biblical."

Cliff Storm felt only numb, and only gazed numbly.

When Sherry came out of her room, lugging the two suitcases and her gray coat, Jordan took them. "Fine. Now you are getting out of here. You're all right. You're rich," he added foolishly.

She didn't take it amiss. She thought she ought to say good-bye.

She looked at the Peabodys. She saw the pain in the landlord's head. She saw the resolution. "Will you tell Elsie good-bye?" she asked.

"She'll be okay," said Mr. Peabody. "She don't understand too much, you know. She's kind of protected, the doctor says."

Sherry wasn't following him, but she knew he meant to be re-assuring. So she said, "I'm glad."

Mrs. Peabody spoke up, having the grace to say, "Mrs. Reynard, I'm sorry for not making you more . . . more comfortable."

Sherry could see the welling up of a certain peace in the land-lady's odd eyes. Mrs. Peabody was off the defensive. She was going to be defended.

"It would have been nice," said Sherry, "if we all could have done better. But the time's gone, now, and it didn't happen. So good-bye."

Joe said, "Go see Dr. Jeffers. He knows as much about this junk as anybody. Good luck, doll. I'll be seeing you."

"Maybe." Sherry smiled at him. She liked him very much. "Ah, well, who knows?" she said gently. "But I don't think so."

Joe grinned, ducked his head in acceptance, and went along the hall, threading through the men from the police department who still milled there. He climbed, like a monkey, the shining stairs.

So Sherry said to the Norns while this lovely clarity was hold-ing. "Oh, *dear* ladies! *Cum laude? Cum laude?*" She was delighted to have remembered something she'd said to them a long time ago.

All three of them understood at once. Mrs. Link kissed Sherry's cheek and patted the spot she had kissed with the flats of her fingers. Then, making the old floor creak, she marched in maj-esty to her seat at the card table. Mrs. Kimberly took Sherry's temples by the flats of both hands, to bend Sherry's higher head and kiss her on the forehead. She then nipped herself briskly to her chair. Mrs. Moran shuffled up, held out her right hand, and wrung Sherry's in a hard grasp. Then she shuffled off, without a word.

The three of them settled down and peered about them, unwilling to miss whatever might happen next, while they were still around.

Allen Jordan, who had fallen madly in love with the Norns, began to bid them a fond farewell.

Cliff Storm was waiting for his turn, with his wits churning helplessly. So she was free, and the thing was over, and the assumption was going to be suicide, and he— But here she came.

The mists were coming down on Sherry now. Or the stuff was rising up again. She said, "I can't see you. I'm not sure there's anybody there." She was holding out her right hand as if she were groping for him.

Cliff couldn't speak. He took her hand. It felt lively. It had bones. But she couldn't see him. Although she wished to, and he wished she could. *Just once more!*

Jordan came up behind her; Cliff let go, turned away, and started after Joe. He heard the lieutenant calling, "Storm? I'll be up in a second."

Cliff said listlessly, "Yeah. Sure," and trudged up the stairs, feeling lonely and bewildered, heavy and cheated, and lost, though he did not know from what.

Jordan, carrying her bags, shepherded Sherry out of the house and to his car, into which he put the luggage. "Come along. We'll go over to the hospital. Find that doctor. See what he can do."

"I'm not so sure," said Sherry, walking in a mist all shot with violet and blue, but with her tongue more or less belonging to her in the moment, "that I want any more drugs. Well, if I had a nice stable, well-understood germ . . . I would rather . . . and I don't know why . . . I would just rather take my luck and see what I can do with it. Could I dare go see Johnny?"

"We'll see," he said gently.

"You must not hurt children," she declaimed. "You must not stunt them, or scare them, or stop their growing. And that's just because you mustn't. That would do in the species, *that*

would. I don't know why, but you mustn't *do* that. My father
was a gardener. I'm not terribly smart, Mr. Jordan . . ."

"You're fine," he said.

"No, I'm not," said Sherry, "but maybe things will begin to get
better, as time goes on."

Cliff, looking out his window, saw them cross, Sherry moving
with a wild grace. When she had vanished into the huge building over there, he sat down on his bed, shoving his suitcase aside.
He didn't know what was going to happen next. He had been
kicked around somehow. Someday? he tried to think. But he
didn't seem to be able to plot ahead.

He had left his door open, so he soon found out what was
going to happen. Joe Bianchi came out of the bathroom, glanced
in at him, said nothing. But Cliff heard his young feet clattering
down the stairs. Something, perhaps the purpose in that clatter,
made him tiptoe to listen.

Joe was talking to the lieutenant. "You haven't been upstairs
yet? Well, maybe you better go, fast. There's a pair of surgical
scissors that belong to me. They're up there, soaking in the washbasin. This guy, Storm, *he* borrowed them a couple of days ago.
So?"

Cliff turned and tiptoed back. He looked out the window, but
she was gone. She was gone. He lay down on his bed and turned
his cheek weakly to the pillow. *Self-defense*, he thought feebly.
But he didn't feel that such a plea was going to help him much.
Not really.